HIT PARADE OF TEARS

HIT PARADE OF TEARS

Stories

Izumi Suzuki

Translated by Sam Bett, David Boyd,
Helen O'Horan, and Daniel Joseph

VERSO
London • New York

First published by Verso 2023
The stories here appeared originally in Japanese in *Keiyaku: Suzuki Izumi Sf Zenshū*
(Covenant: The Complete Science Fiction of Izumi Suzuki), by Suzuki Izumi
Collection copyright © 2014 by Suzuki Azusa
Originally published in Japan by BUNYU-SHA Inc.
English translation rights arranged with BUNYU-SHA Inc. through the Sakai Agency
Translation of "My Guy" and "Trial Witch" © Sam Bett 2023
Translation of "Full of Malice" and "Hey, It's a Love Psychedelic!" © David Boyd 2023
Translation of "Hit Parade of Tears," "I'll Never Forget," and
"Memory of Water" © Helen O'Horan 2023
Translation of "After Everything," "The Covenant," "Softly, as in a Morning Sunrise," and
"The Walker" © Daniel Joseph 2023

1 3 5 7 9 10 8 6 4 2

Verso
UK: 6 Meard Street, London W1F 0EG
US: 388 Atlantic Avenue, Brooklyn, NY 11217
versobooks.com

Verso is the imprint of New Left Books

ISBN-13: 978-1-83976-849-1
ISBN-13: 978-1-83976-019-8 (US EBK)
ISBN-13: 978-1-83976-018-1 (UK EBK)

British Library Cataloguing in Publication Data
A catalogue record for this book is available from the British Library

Library of Congress Cataloging-in-Publication Data

Names: Suzuki, Izumi, 1949–1986, author. | Bett, Sam, 1986– translator. |
 Boyd, David (David G.), translator. | O'Horan, Helen, translator. |
 Joseph, Daniel (Translator), translator.
Title: Hit parade of tears : stories / Izumi Suzuki ; translated by Sam
 Bett, David Boyd, Helen O'Horan, and Daniel Joseph.
Other titles: Keiyaku. English
Description: London ; New York : Verso, 2023. | Originally published in
 Japanese under title Keiyaku: Suzuki Izumi Sf Zenshū (Covenant: The
 Complete Science Fiction of Suzuki Izumi).
Identifiers: LCCN 2022054487 (print) | LCCN 2022054488 (ebook) | ISBN
 9781839768491 (paperback) | ISBN 9781839760198 (US ebk) | ISBN
 9781839760181 (UK ebk)
Subjects: LCSH: Suzuki, Izumi, 1949–1986—Translations into English. |
 LCGFT: Science fiction. | Fantasy fiction. | Short stories.
Classification: LCC PL861.U9265 K4513 2023 (print) | LCC PL861.U9265
 (ebook) | DDC 895.63/5—dc23/eng/20221221
LC record available at https://lccn.loc.gov/2022054487
LC ebook record available at https://lccn.loc.gov/2022054488

Typeset in Electra by Hewer Text UK Ltd, Edinburgh
Printed and bound by CPI Group (UK) Ltd, Croydon CR0 4YY

CONTENTS

My Guy   1
Trial Witch   25
Full of Malice   47
Hey, It's a Love Psychedelic!   53
After Everything   113
The Covenant   117
The Walker   157
Softly, as in a Morning Sunrise   163
Memory of Water   191
I'll Never Forget   219
Hit Parade of Tears   255

MY GUY

The first time I saw him, he was in a phone booth near Shibuya Station, but I never would have found him if that creep hadn't been chasing me.

This was years ago. I was way prettier and cuter than I am now (obviously!) and had a bad-girl image that made sense for my age. I wanted every man on Earth to stop and look at me. It was an all-consuming task. I was no girl next door, I'll give you that, but it's a lot of work to walk around in five-inch heels, tripled-up eyelashes, and a miniskirt with a deep slit in the front. My friends called me "The Blondster," because of my bleached hair. In one lap around the station, I could expect to get hit on by at least seven different men. The record for one lap was fourteen.

"Hey, want to grab a cup of tea?"

I say hit on, but these guys were wimps. (They assumed I was easy, as if any old pickup line would do.) All I wanted was to capture their attention. And maybe revel in a mixture of contempt and anger while I was at it. If I was going to say anything, it would've been: "Look, guys, I'm not that kind of girl, so why don't you just stand there, have a think, and come up with a better line?"

Instead, I'd turn up my nose, strut my stuff, and keep on moving.

That day, though, things went differently than usual.

This guy was pushy, a real creeper. He wouldn't stop following me. "Hey, come on, babe, let's grab a drink. Just give me thirty minutes," he said, sounding all carefree, as if he could have kept it up all night. His eyes were dead, like they were made of glass.

I tried speeding up, or running, or going into a café, but he followed me and showed no sign of discouragement. Running past the Toei Theater, I swerved toward a phone booth. I was going to call the cops. By that point I was really freaking out.

But somebody was already inside. I hadn't noticed him because he was sitting on the floor, like a vagrant slumped on the Bowery. When I opened the door, he looked at me like I was an intruder. Lunar eyes staring through the darkness.

"Um, excuse me?" I said, in a voice that sounded hysterically shrill. "Sorry, but I'd like to make a call."

No answer.

With the awe of a young child bumping up against the world for the first time, he blinked his mineral-white eyes at me, this random girl (remember, I was a girl at the time) who had thrown open the door.

"Get out of here, will you? Or help me scare that creep away!"

I was yelling now, I'd lost it. I stormed off, disregarding my absurdly high heels as I ran into the night. It'd have been different if I'd been in sweatpants, but dressed like that, I was out of breath in no time and had to stop to rest under a footbridge. My heels were honestly about to snap.

When I turned around, the creep was gone.

But in his place, the guy from the phone booth was standing inches from my face, the way people sneak up on you in a horror movie. I shrieked.

The guy just stood there quietly, with this sort of puzzled look on his face.

"Are you okay?" he asked me in a dopey voice.

"Yeah . . . you just scared me, that's all," I answered timidly, then looked him up and down.

He was a weirdo alright.

First off, he could have been any age between fifteen and forty. Gangly like a schoolboy but slow like an old man. His complexion was atrocious, but not waxen, like a corpse, so much as tinged with green. His hair was a strange vegetable color, like a moldy log, a little grungy. He wore a baggy T-shirt and a pair of pants that were too long for him, so that the legs bunched up over his shoes.

He looked like he had stepped out of a community theater. His face and posture made him look half-Japanese, though it was unclear where the other half of him was from. I studied his features, wondering for a second if he wasn't wearing eye shadow, but I guess his eyes just looked that way.

"Can you make it home alone?" he asked me, sounding honestly concerned. "What I mean is, when I saw you, I asked myself: can she make it in this world alone? Can

3

she survive in this life on her lonesome? Sorry if that sounds crazy. But it crossed my mind."

This guy sounded as crazy as he looked. I just stood there, unsure of what to say.

"I'll walk you home," he said, and rested a hand on my shoulder. His touch felt safe enough. I wasn't sensing any ulterior motive.

Since I was out of options, no choice left, I started walking. The weird guy walked beside me. I observed him shamelessly, watching his every move.

Under the right circumstances, he could have passed for normal. But there was something odd about him. Something was off for sure, but it wasn't something you could easily pinpoint.

He stuffed his hands into his pockets and some scraps of paper dropped in the street. Or so I thought, until I realized they were crumpled 10,000-yen bills.

I stopped dead.

"Who are you, the secret child of an oil baron?"

I'd meant for it to sound sarcastic. I saw right through this guy's game. Whether or not he was loaded was beside the point. He had done it on purpose.

"No, not me."

"No? Then go pick up that money. Don't be crass."

"Oh . . . that was an accident. I forgot I even had it. Didn't mean to drop it like that."

I was beginning to think that he really was a moron. It didn't matter, though. He was behaving himself, for the time being. If he made a move, I could decide how to respond in the moment.

We made it to the intersection of Meiji and Omotesando.

"Here's good," I said, giving him a little wave. "I'm fine going the rest of the way alone. Thanks!"

Leaving him standing at the traffic signal, I crossed at the corner by Hakkakutei, the yakiniku place. No way was I letting this guy know where I lived.

In those days, I had a ton of female friends and being around girls felt easiest. They weren't scary like men (except for the lesbians). We sympathized with one another. I could open my heart and be myself. I was basically a child, so the friendly company of schoolgirls suited me.

I had a few male friends, too. Guys I'd known for years. Brothers, basically. It was nice. Boys have an outlandish way of looking at things that I found invigorating. Since I was in it for the fresh ideas, I only added a guy to my list of friends if he was really smart. I welcomed gay boys too, for their unique point of view, getting so close to some of them that we were practically sisters. If I wanted someone to talk to, or to join me for a walk, I had no shortage of options.

It had been about six months since I'd broken up with the last boy I would call a boyfriend. I was so young that I'd missed the warning signs, overestimating him. Oh well.

Almost every man who met me fell for me.

Back then, it was safe to assume that all men, as a rule, found me attractive. Most women can relate to that. So long as youth is on your side and your looks haven't spoiled, you'll get more attention than you know what to do with. It lasts until you're twenty-four or so. You don't even have to be exceptionally charming. And if you dress up, or do anything to make yourself stand out, they'll come in droves.

I always tried to be sweet and kind, and I was in a good mood more often than not. But I had no interest whatever in sleeping with a man, and could not even imagine the disgustingness of sharing an apartment with one. For years, I blocked off the innermost reaches of my heart as a place where only I could go, not letting anyone peek in. But not because I couldn't bear to open up. It was because I was convinced that nobody would ever understand me.

I was a people-pleaser, outwardly bubbly. Sure, sometimes I'd raise hell. But I felt permanently sad, because I knew I was so weak inside. I wasn't looking to get married, but sometimes I liked thinking about it.

There were times I would start crying for no reason in the middle of the night, all alone in my room. "NOBODY UNDERSTANDS ME." I guess I'd never really been in love, or even learned what was involved in "liking" someone. This could be why I always seemed to wind up in relationships defined by mutual distaste and an inability to walk away. What I craved most was a partner who could be naked in front of me, completely vulnerable. The no-holds-barred romance of a married couple. I had read *Who's Afraid of Virginia Woolf?* a dozen times.

I shut the door, kicked off the instruments of torture my high heels had become, and pulled my clothes off as I walked to the bed. I was too tired to choose a record, so I set the needle on the single that was on the player without even looking at the label.

It was "Johnny Guitar" by Peggy Lee. I realized that the lyrics were kind of sexual. *Hey, Johnny, play that guitar, play it again.* Like she was wanting him to play with her. So hot.

6

I was smoking a cigarette, half-naked on the bed, and thought it would be nice to have some tea. But when I rubbed the butt into the ashtray and glanced up, I froze in place. The man from the phone booth was leaning in the doorway.

My mouth opened and closed, goldfish style, but he just looked at me and said, "I'd love to hear that song again."

I did as I was told and put the needle back to the beginning. The sentimental melody drifted from the speaker.

"How'd you get in here, anyway?" I finally asked him. I'd locked the door from the inside. The window was closed, and I hadn't seen the curtains move. I was sure of it, as I'd been lying down facing the window.

"How else?" He shut the door behind him.

"But it was locked . . . Don't tell me you can walk through walls."

"Oh no, I'd never do that . . . For one thing, it's not polite."

"It's a lot more impolite to walk into someone's apartment unannounced!"

Losing my head, I failed to spot the deeper meaning of his choice of words.

"Thing is, I have nowhere to go . . . My first task is to construct a base . . . But tonight, I have no place to stay."

"What a shame."

He must have snuck in like a prowler, using a hairpin to pick the lock.

"I guess you don't believe me, do you."

His voice was almost too quiet to hear.

"Of course not. Go on, get out of here. Out!"

"But I don't have anywhere to go. Not right now."

He dropped the large leather bag he had been carrying on the floor. It could have been a camera case, but it was the wrong shape. Maybe it contained a musical instrument? It must have been an instrument of some kind.

"LOOK, THIS IS MY APARTMENT!"

"Sure."

"Alright, just sit down over there."

I did my best to sound sore about it, but he smiled like he was genuinely pleased. It was the first time I'd seen him adopt anything resembling a facial expression.

Trying to act normal, I picked up the newspaper and opened it to the Breaking News page, where a headline stood out: "Flying Saucers Make Another Splash." I decided to read it out loud.

"Let me see," he said. I handed him the paper. He got out of his chair and came over to the bed, plopping himself down like it was his.

I can be slow on the uptake about this kind of thing, but finally I reached for my pajamas and put them on. I wasn't uptight about being seen with no clothes on, but I'd been so thrown by this whole business that I'd forgotten I was sitting there half-naked.

He read the story with intense concentration, like he had never seen a newspaper before.

"Sounds like they touched down in the woods of Kanagawa," I said, comfortable enough at that point to be talking to myself. "They left a big round burn mark in the middle of the mountain. It would have been much easier to land it on the beach. Were they trying to be discreet, or what?

Anyhow, the paper's probably just cashing in on the fad for UFOs and ancient history."

His eyes followed the newsprint slowly and carefully.

"It's gotta be a fake, right?" I asked him. "Just a hoax."

The record stopped on its own.

"Japanese is pretty tough," he said, dead serious.

"Hahaha."

I laughed at this dumb joke, playing along.

"Besides, this article is wrong."

"Sure it is."

He refolded the pages, working his way slowly through the paper.

"What's your name?" I asked, crossing my legs in provocative fashion.

"Kenji Sawada."

"Huh? Like the singer?"

I glanced at the newspaper and saw that he had reached the Arts and Entertainment section. Gossip about what "Julie" (as Sawada's fans called him) had been up to lately.

"I see."

I was beginning to like this guy. He had an odd ability to reel a person in (women specifically). I tried imagining that smile he had given me. It positively sparkled. He was sort of gross, all things considered, but who could resist a smile like that?

Also . . . I'm not sure how to put this, but his body gave off this bizarre aura, like an electrical charge, but it was all around me, like a smell. *That's strange*, I thought to myself. Pretty soon I was imagining him holding me. Though it couldn't literally have been his body odor, a sensual, dizzying smell had filled the room.

By the time Kenji Sawada got in bed with me, I was ready to let him do whatever he wanted. But he didn't do anything. He just lay there facing up, supine and immobile, like a meditating monk.

So I picked up an issue of *An An*, listened to some Sachiko Nishida, drank a cup of tea, smoked a cigarette, faked my way through a few calisthenics, changed from my usual sleep-wear into something more scandalous, puffed some powder on my face, buffed my nails and then chewed them, which did wonders for my manicure, and let out an elaborate yawn, pretending to be sleepy, before I finally lay down and closed my eyes.

Twenty minutes later, unable to bear it any longer, I opened them.

"Are you a homo?"

"Homo? As in homogenous?"

His arms had been folded behind his head, but all at once they shot out to either side, like the limbs of an automaton. His fingertips swept through my hair.

"Ah, sorry."

This was not something to apologize for. He sat up, looked through the leather bag I mentioned earlier, and got to fiddling with something for a while. Was he typing on a keyboard? Assembling some sort of communications device?

It wasn't long before I actually fell asleep.

And so I fell in love, just like that.

He would disappear for three whole days, or while away the day in bed, or come knocking on my window in the middle of the night—spending most of the time he was over messing with his instruments or with his nose buried in some thick volume of philosophy.

"Hold me," I told him. And he did. He held me all night long. Sometimes patting my hair or stroking my back. From the glimpses I stole while he was changing into fresh clothes, he had all the right equipment, though it was kinda hard to see. But things never escalated to the point of having sex.

"What's wrong?" I asked him. Thinking: *Maybe it's so small that he can't get it up enough for it to work*, but obviously I couldn't say a thing like that out loud. His private parts were almost nonexistent, like what you might find on a premature baby.

"I like you," he said, his face the picture of sincerity.

"Ohh!" I cried histrionically, striking a pose fit for Juliet.

"Don't believe me, huh. Well, if you want to know the truth, this planet's not my home."

"Oh, is that so?" I breathed, like a bad actor.

"I came here on a mission. Half of my comrades died in an emergency landing. I need to carry out the task that was assigned to me. Although, at this point, I wish I didn't have to."

"And why is that?" I asked him absentmindedly.

"Don't you get it? What else could it be? Because I love you."

"Thanks so much."

"One of my tasks on this planet is to conduct a survey. I need to gather all kinds of information, history and politics, stuff like that, but what we want to find out above all is how the people who live here think about things. What makes them tick. The workings of their hearts."

"Sounds like quite an undertaking."

"Sure, taken as a whole. What's baffled me the most so far is that each person on this planet has a slightly different way of handling their feelings and moods, a different spirit, if you will. Nothing like the planet I come from. Back home, everyone's the same. It's in the best interest of the population. Those who need to die, they die. They're fine with that. We have no wars. It's all because we take this special medicine. A marvel of research. It has no side effects. The meds update our genes. Wipe out our baser instincts. Barbaric impulses simply evaporate."

"What about murder . . . Isn't that barbaric?"

There was a note of hostility in my voice.

"It isn't murder. When I say need to die, I mean they want to die . . . at least they think they do," he muttered, looking oddly solemn.

"All the same, we still have to contend with mutations that don't respond to medicine. Once you reach a certain age, they put you through a whole set of tests. Every now and then a guy pops out of the woodwork who can't control his love of gambling, booze, money, or sex, just like you people here. We send those cases to the camps."

So, he was crazy after all.

"Most importantly, what you call romance is pretty uncommon where I'm from. My whole life, I'd never experienced romance of any kind. But then I landed on your planet and met you. Back home, everyone starts making love, so to speak, once they reach adulthood, except only with the partner that the government assigns them. Then they spend the rest of their lives as a happy couple who never fight. But that isn't what you'd call 'love' now, is it . . . I had a partner assigned to me, like all the rest. She's patiently awaiting my return. We were planning to get married soon. Since the marriage institution benefits the state directly, they make it fairly painless."

This guy must have escaped from a mental asylum. Some wackjobs think they're living in a science-fiction world.

"We use words like love and romance all the time," I said, "but the real thing is uncommon on this planet, too. That's how the women's magazines stay in business. Every issue dangles some new strategy for finding love, or making someone love you, but it's so . . . utilitarian. Too pragmatic for my taste."

"Yeah . . . but that's not the point. They're only holding back their primitive urges and emotions, like the people on my planet. I can't do that anymore. Guess I'm just a mutant, who somehow made it through the tests. I never would have thought."

"Quit messing around."

Running low on patience, I grabbed my cigarettes. It occurred to me that this guy didn't smoke. He barely even slept . . . I wondered if . . .

"I get it now. You think I'm a fool, don't you?"

"That isn't true," I said, only I wasn't sure I meant it. With most men, I'm able to *pretend* that I'm in love. It's a fun game. But this time it was different. Something about that electrical charge of his . . .

"I'm not convinced you actually have feelings," he said. "*Moods*, maybe, but not emotions. And yet, I mean, all girls feel things to some extent, right?"

"So, I take it you've been surveying other women?"

"Sure."

"Good for you."

"But like I told you, I've grown sick of it. My other task while here . . ."

"How, exactly, do you survey these girls?"

I was sneering.

"How? I treat them the same way I'm treating you."

"And they all fall for it?"

Quit wasting my time, asshole!

"Guess so. But man, your jealousy is really something, huh? Sometimes I'll be holding some girl in her bed, and I'll get hit with this colossal headache. It won't let up all night. Meanwhile, you're lying awake, smoking. Now and then a sigh, maybe a drink."

"How did you know?" I blurted.

I never should have said it. Shoulda kept it to myself. I hadn't been to class in forever, opting instead to spend my days in anguished pining. I'd stopped showing up for work, too. And for what? This scumbag?

"Because I understand you."

He smiled. It was that glorious smile, with the capacity to make anything right.

Scowling, I paced the room, holding a smoke between my fingers. The carpet was pocked with burn marks.

"I'm abandoning my mission. But that means my life is on the line. I'm ready, though. That's why I want you to understand me, too, to see me, where I'm coming from."

"I don't care! Fuck off!"

I pounced on him. His easygoing demeanor and smug self-confidence made my stomach turn. Who did he think

14

he was? Talking like he understood it all. Like the guru of some new religious sect. I gave his hair a tug. Really yanked it. But then he clamped his hands around my wrists.

"You son of a bitch! Cheat! Murderer!"

"I'm not a murderer. And I haven't cheated anyone."

"Pervert!"

I squirmed, grabbing for his hair.

"I'm not a pervert either."

"You phony! Go to hell!"

"I'm not, though."

"You tricked me, liar, didn't you, didn't you . . ."

Losing track of what I was so mad about, I felt myself deflate, and then I started crying.

He carried me over to the bed and held me tight, the way he always did.

"What's wrong with me? Why am I crying?"

Once I had calmed down a bit, I grinned, feeling embarrassed.

"It's fine. There's nothing wrong with you at all."

His voice was deadly serious. Like the voice of the divine.

One day, I came home and found him sitting on the floor with a man I'd never seen before. They were silent, staring at each other.

I sat on a corner of the bed and hugged my knees, watching the pair of them.

"Sorry," my guy said to me, "but would you mind waiting outside? Come back in two hours."

His voice was different. Not his usual soft tone, but a pained whisper, like he was struggling to contain his emotions.

"No way," I said loudly.

"Why not?" His voice trembled.

"BECAUSE THIS IS MY APARTMENT."

In this light, his eyes looked brown. He gave me a long look. Did he think I was stupid?

"Understood."

It was said with an air of finality.

The unidentified man was bigger than my guy. Despite the mild weather, he was wearing a knit hat pulled down over his eyes, along with a coat and a disposable face mask.

"It's so cold in here. I'm freezing. Young lady, I know you probably think I look like a buffoon, but I've caught a nasty chill. This virus is hard to shake, I tell you what."

The big man was trying to be chummy.

"Aren't you overdoing it a bit?" I snapped. "That coat makes you look like you're hiding some kind of weapon."

"Oh, no . . . hardly."

The big man raised his eyebrows and hacked through a few coughs.

My guy's lips quivered. I could barely hear his voice. The big man grumbled and waved his hands in a gesture of displeasure, then blurted out something I couldn't understand.

For a moment, they were quiet.

"That's enough!"

My guy jumped to his feet. The big man threw his arms up, opening his eyes wide, and fell flat on his back.

"I was hoping not to use this thing," my guy said, struggling to catch his breath. "But I reckon I'm a murderer after all."

He was holding what looked like a pistol. His voice was strained and raspy. I was speechless, at a loss to comprehend what had occurred between them.

"What just happened?" I finally asked. "What did you do?"

"I killed him."

He put away the gun.

"What? Why?"

"He came over to check up on me. Claimed it was a random investigation. So I told him what was on my mind. That I wanted to stay here, and live with someone from this planet, meaning you. That I was planning to give up my post. He wasn't a bad fellow. Granted, he was surprised at first, but he did his best to see my side of things. That didn't count for much, though, after I told him he couldn't make me change my mind."

"So you . . . killed him?"

"Did you think I was lying this whole time?"

I still wasn't convinced he was an alien, but I'd never seen anybody shoot someone like that before. I could have sprung off the bed like a grasshopper. And yet my mind was weirdly calm. I'd started to believe him. Ever since the night he held me in his arms and let me cry.

"Anyway," I said, "now we've got this to deal with."

"Yeah. I'm pretty tired, too."

"I can drive us, if we rent a car. We'll stuff it in the trunk and drop it off somewhere."

"No, that's no good."

"Why? You'd rather have a corpse in the apartment?"

"Do you have a blanket or something?"

"Yeah."

I pulled a fluffy blanket and a musty futon from the closet. "Make him a spot."

I spread the bedding on the floor. Then me and my guy picked the big man up. He wasn't as heavy as I'd expected. But dead bodies are awkward, a downright pain to move, so it was difficult to lift him.

"I'd rather you don't see what happens next. Go wait outside. Come back in fifteen minutes."

I closed the door behind me. My legs were shaking, so my high heels made a racket. Only now was the enormity of what had happened sinking in.

I walked over to the café, shaking so much I bumped into the chairs. I put the wrong end of a smoke between my lips. I spilled the coffee they brought me and dropped my spoon on the floor. I even walked out without paying, and when they called me back, I forgot to take the change.

The automatic café door slid open. My guy stepped inside. "We're going."

I walked out behind him.

"The blanket got a bit dirty. It really stinks in there, you know. I left the windows closed. We probably shouldn't go back. Not until the smell lets up."

"What happened to, uh, *him*."

"He's gone. Chemically processed without a trace."

He took my hand and hailed a taxi.

"Where are we going?"

"A hotel."

Up in our room, he tore my clothes off, chomped on my neck, and squeezed my breasts.

18

"Hey! Stop that."

"Sorry. I don't know how people do it here. I'm a little frazzled . . . What's the right way, then?"

"Just do what you usually do."

I fit perfectly into his arms. My fears were gone.

"Is this how people on your planet make babies?" I asked.

"Lots do, yeah. Maybe half. Your planet has been researching how to make test tube babies, too, I gather?"

"You mean, when you sneak off to spend the night with all those other girls . . . I can't believe this. Spreading your seed far and wide like that."

My guy said nothing.

His arms squeezed me tighter as his fingers slowed, combing through my hair.

I love you.

His feelings slipped into my heart.

What did you just say?

I answered him in kind, conveying what I felt, but not aloud. I had no idea that I could do this.

Surprised? Looks like I finally got through. Without even realizing, you've been telling me all kinds of things this way. For a person from this planet, your emotional reflexes are very strong. But every time I tried to show you how I felt, you shut me out. Hiding in your shell. At last you've dropped your guard.

You talk like this with all the other girls?

No, this is special.

I wrapped both hands around his neck. My feelings were so intense it made my muscles twitch. Crazy as it sounds, it was like our hearts were intertwined.

Then it was over.

"How was it for you?" he asked me out loud.

I giggled. "What do we do now?"

"I have to get away. The others won't take kindly to this."

"I'll go with you."

"I'd like that, but no guarantees."

"Why not?"

"The ship we used to travel here is in rough shape. I'll do what I can to fix it up and get out of here, fast. If it isn't blowing sparks, I'll let you come along."

"We're leaving Earth?"

"That's right."

"I want to go—I really do, but hearing myself say that makes me feel like, I dunno, we've lost our minds."

"We've jumped off of the short bus, that's for sure."

He laughed, like he was innocent of everything.

"I'm going with you. No matter what. I don't care if the ship can barely fly."

"No way. I'm pretty sure that I'd survive, but I doubt you could withstand the journey."

What have I got to lose by dying?

I screamed it from the bottom of my heart. From my heart into his.

But this time, he shut me out.

"No, we can't have that."

"Why not?"

"I'll make it back . . . Two years from now. I promise. The safest thing for you to do is wait, since . . ."

"Oh, I get it now." I clasped my hands around his neck. "I'm going to be a mother?"

"That's right."

"How can you be sure?"

"I heard your heart go click."

We burst out laughing, sprawled on the bed of that hourly hotel.

The magazines ran an odd story about a marriage scammer. This guy told girls he came from outer space, so that they lost touch with reality. For some reason they all believed him. And once they did, he ripped them off. He felt insecure about his manhood, so he took it out on women. But now he's under lock and key in a mental hospital.

Reiko and I were chatting about it on the phone.

"It'd have been one thing if he had some irresistible technique," she said. "How come everybody fell for it?"

"He must have been a charmer," I said, rather irresponsibly.

"Sure, I guess. Women are suckers for that. If it was me, though, trust me, I would've seen right through him."

Reiko sounded pleased with herself. I looked long and hard at the photo in the magazine. Part of me saw a resemblance, part of me didn't. It was too blurry to tell.

"It says he was a mix of French, Vietnamese, and Japanese," she said, practically singing the words. "I bet he's dead handsome in the flesh. I'm into kooky guys like that. The way they pin you down, acting like some kind of wild animal . . . Though I think it said this guy was impotent?"

"So he can't get anybody pregnant, huh?"

I asked her this because I had my own suspicions.

"Come on, you doofus. You're not in grade school anymore. Impotent or not, no one can get you pregnant just by kissing you. Not even schoolkids believe that nowadays. It's wild. They grow up quicker every year."

And then a UFO made headlines again. A mysterious explosion had been heard in the same mountain pass in Kanagawa. Scholars, armchair and otherwise, along with maniacs and people who had nothing else to do, flocked to the crash site.

He was gone. My guy had died.

I knew he wasn't coming back. My guy was gone for good, leaving me with nothing but sweet memories and a child. To this day I still believe he came from outer space.

Our son is already in kindergarten. His IQ is so high it's scary, over 200. His teachers and everyone who meets him say the same thing: "This kid's a genius."

Not that I care about any of that . . . There's just one thing bothering me.

I'm not concerned he'll get picked on, or that he'll turn out bad, with no father figure in his life. We struggle to make ends meet, but we get by. I'm not looking to get married. I don't need another man.

But sometimes, when loneliness threatens to drag me under, those memories are the one thing that keeps me going. I almost never cry these days.

The thing that bothers me is this: my young son started acting like a full-grown man way too early. I'm not talking about playing doctor. If there's a girl he likes, he'll walk right up to her and hold her in his arms. "It's a bit much, sometimes," his teachers tell me. "I guess he's starved for love. Single parenting will do that."

What am I supposed to do if one of these little girls shows up to kindergarten with a big belly? I can't just look the other way, on the premise that no four-year-old can ovulate. Not when my guy had gotten me pregnant with that ingenious method of his.

Besides, I hear my son picks a new girlfriend every other week.

What will I do if he gets all the girls at kindergarten pregnant? Would you believe me if I told you that this keeps me up at night?

TRIAL WITCH

My husband came home late again. By this point he's probably pickled his liver. It'd be one thing if I could've called it a night from the moment he went out, but he always woke me up later, in the middle of a sweet dream, calling out for "Water" and "Leftovers" as if those were my names. Though I don't like to admit it, I always crawled out of my futon and headed over to the kitchen.

I hasten to add, though, that he wasn't actually addressing me. He was talking to the kitchen. But since my husband wasn't a magician, no tall glass of water jumped into his hand, and no bowl of green tea over rice waddled over to him, huffing and puffing.

That night, I sat up with my elbows on the tea table, the evening paper spread before me. First I read the ads, especially the ones for the tabloids, my thrifty way of picking up some juicy celebrity gossip without making an additional purchase. Then maybe I'd read a couple of columns. If there was an article about a gory robbery or something, I'd read that too. I rarely spent time with the front-page news.

Just as I was folding up the paper, I heard the most incredible noise. *Was that a bomb?* I asked myself, as cloying smoke spiraled through the room.

It made me sneeze.

Behind the haze, someone else was feeling the same effects.

"*Achoo!* Gah, that's awful . . . *Achoo!* Well, that one was a dud . . . Duped again . . . Thirty percent off sounded like a good deal at the time, but this is ridiculous . . . *Achoo!*"

I said loudly: "Excuse me?" Then sneezed two or three times.

The yellow smoke cleared, to reveal a man standing with what looked like a black coverlet wrapped around him.

"Well then, how's that for an introduction . . . *Achoo!* Sorry, but might I borrow a tissue?"

"Why don't you just use that wacky cloak of yours. Who are you, anyway? Barging in here in the middle of the night. Watch out or I'll scream," I warned him, quite loudly already.

"I'm afraid this is the only time of day that I can manage. I have a number of side businesses to attend to, you see."

His voice was hoarse. The voice of a much older man. His wrinkled face switched between passion and austerity from one second to the next, like a ham actor begging to be pelted with tomatoes.

"Who are you?"

I wasn't the least bit scared. I figured he was lost and suffering from mental problems, though I couldn't think of any reasonable explanation for his abrupt appearance.

"You really don't know? Hmm . . . Could it be the acoustics? Or is my costume to blame?"

He stroked his chin, lost in thought.

"I'll need to ask you to leave."

"Well then, in that case, let's give it another try. This time I'll use some trumpets, for a proper fanfare. Or would you prefer a crash of thunder and lightning?"

"I'm not joking."

"Of course not. Neither am I. For I come on important business. I would never show up in so cramped and stuffy a place as this without an excellent reason."

"You have no business with me."

"Right you are. But I suspect you're not too keen on letting good luck slip through your fingers, either. Am I right? You see, my dear, you have been chosen."

The man cleared his throat emphatically. Then, from the shadows of his cloak, he produced what appeared to be a scroll.

"Technically this ought to be sheepskin, but lately prices have been soaring. I gave pigskin a shot for a while, but this is normal washi, what they use on paper doors. Anyway."

The man pulled out a pair of pince-nez spectacles and set them on his nose.

"Let's see, your occupation—none? I suppose that makes you a housewife. And your age—twenty-six, I see . . ."

"What difference does that make?" I exclaimed.

"Simply wishing to confirm," he said with a placating look. "My dear, please don't think for a second that I doubted you. This is strictly a formality, you understand, the first order of business. We'll be done in a second. Now, the other members of your household are your husband and . . . anyone else?"

The man muttered something as he completed the form.

"Seriously, who are you?" I demanded again.

"I'm a messenger. Were you not expecting me?"

He sounded a little hurt.

"Who sent you?"

"Who sent me? Why, none other than the League of Witches! Which is a fancy name for just three people. All of whom are well advanced in years. Each of them in their dotage and somewhat oblivious, I'm afraid. No surprise there, what with so few young people interested in traditional witchcraft nowadays . . ."

"Sounds like a joke to me."

"Oh my, you're very quick to judge. Remember just a minute ago, when I materialized in a puff of majesty? I would hate to think you still don't believe me . . . but we mustn't waste our time with nonsense. I'll give it to you straight. You've been selected to be a trial witch."

"I don't recall applying," I told him, in a tone that made my skepticism clear.

"Of course not, you were randomly selected."

"In that case, I respectfully decline."

"I'm afraid that's out of the question. This is your fate. You may as well accept it. For I will now invest you with a nominal amount of magical power. Mind you, I am unable to guarantee what kind of power you will receive. You may rest assured that the witches made a wise selection. If you practice hard enough, you can expect to be promoted in the future. And if it doesn't work out, we'll strip you of your powers as appropriate. Now, read this over."

He handed me the scroll, which I unfurled, but the writing made no sense.

"I can't read this."

"You have a lot to learn," he said, with a pompous flourish of his cloak.

"Can you read it?" I asked him.

"Sure I can, bits and pieces."

"Why is it written in red ink, though?"

"Technically we should be using lamb's blood, or the blood of a cat found prowling in the cemetery around three in the morning. But desperate times call for desperate measures, so red ink it is. Besides, the witches have been squeamish of late when it comes to animal cruelty."

"Take this b-back, I don't want it."

I was so discombobulated that I found myself stuttering.

"In that case, would you mind very much if I used it for a tissue? To be quite honest, that thing isn't worth the paper it's printed on."

"Spare me."

"Very good, so when you wish to summon me, just draw a circle on the floor with chalk and sprinkle bay leaves all around. This isn't strictly necessary, but you don't want any pesky devils showing up instead. The chalk and leaves are my signature design. Think of it as a direct telephone line to me . . . However, I do sometimes wish I'd thought of something more complex. Like burying the head of a kitten in the middle of a crossroads on a moonless night. Which sounds splendid, but these days it's concrete here and concrete there, everywhere you go. But alas, I digress. Now, if you'll excuse me."

The chatty messenger disappeared into another cloud of sticky, yellow smoke.

Next thing I knew, my cheek was smooshed into the tea table. What the heck? Was that whole thing a dream? It felt so incredibly real.

When I sat up, I saw a white cylindrical object by my knee. The scroll of paper! What on earth was going on?

For a minute, I sat there in a daze.

It sounded like my husband was home.

I could tell because of how the barking of the neighbor's dog came through the window. It was past two in the morning. Most people on the block worked normal hours. My dolt of a husband was the only one who would come home so late.

I opened the door and waited. He staggered down the hall and stepped inside.

"Hey, wifey, long time no see," he said, pretending to be in a chipper mood.

"Where've you been all night?"

I set the kettle on the gas range. Last time he came home drunk, he said, "Where's my tea" and slapped me in the face. He could have at least started with, "I want some tea." Otherwise, how was I supposed to know? I could hardly have been blamed for getting angry. But he just groaned and climbed into bed in all his clothes.

"No need to get your panties in a bunch . . . Come on, let's play nice, huh?"

My husband shed his suit jacket and tossed it in the corner. I fetched a hanger and hung it up. He pulled off his cotton polo easily enough, but had some trouble with his pants, so he dragged them and his underwear off in one go.

I handed him pajamas and fresh underwear, then folded up the clothes he had removed.

He hadn't answered my question.

"Where have you been?"

"Shibuya, then. Aoyama. Drank some local sake," he said, like it was no big deal.

"Just bars? You sure you didn't stop off somewhere and cozy up in someone else's bed?"

"Of course not."

As he pulled up his pajama bottoms, he looked off into space.

"Ah, right. Then how do you explain this lipstick stain?"

"That, uh . . . that must have happened on the ride home."

"So you rode the train without any pants on? The lipstick is on your underwear."

"Mohhh . . ."

My husband let out a mooing sound.

"Seeing as you love women so much, I wish you'd just turn into one. Then you could fondle your own butt and stare at your own—"

Before I'd finished speaking, my husband (or rather his body) transformed into something else entirely. As if another person had taken his place.

At first it was unclear exactly what had changed and how.

"Hey!"

Squirming and fidgeting, he did his best to assess his new figure.

Next thing he tore off his pajamas. What do you know, my husband really had become a woman. Several inches shorter than before, smaller overall in stature. There was no more stubble on his face, which had acquired a new roundness. Same haircut, though.

"Hey, what's going on? Hey!" he (I'll stick with "he" for now) squealed, in a peculiar high-pitched voice.

"Wow, look at you."

"How did you do this? Huh? How?"

Right. A minute earlier, I'd wished that he would turn into a woman . . .

Was this the doing of my magic powers? It seemed the man in the cloak had been telling the truth after all.

"Come on, do something, will you?"

My former husband stood up, utterly flummoxed. He needed me to intervene, but what was I supposed to do?

I wiggled my fingers, doing my best to cast a spell.

"Go back, go back."

My husband changed again, this time into a primate, or something like one. He must have taken my command too literally and "gone back" in the evolutionary sense. He was a female primate, by the way. Growling loudly, he charged at me, enraged at what I'd done.

"I didn't mean to. Stop! You're scaring me."

"Gimme a break."

"You may look like a monkey, but you talk the same as ever."

"Quick, turn me back!"

The primate let out a fearsome bellow, as if thirsting for blood.

"This is a bummer for me too, you know."

"Don't make me repeat myself . . ."

"Alright, alright. Okay, go back to your original form. But don't go back, like, a million years."

Shit. This time he turned into a baby girl, covered in thick fur. The paleolithic infant wailed relentlessly. I lifted the screaming kettle from the stove and made some tea. After all, this was as good a time as any to think things over.

"Dis keddo watts some chea!"

The grumpy child flailed its legs, staging a hissy fit.

"Don't tell me you can still talk."

"Coss I can."

"Your pronunciation could use a bit of work . . ."

"Jon't chease me."

I strolled over to the tea table and took a seat, then cut myself a slice of takuan. Delicious.

"You think I'm enjoying this? Last thing I want is to accidentally turn you into a T-Rex or something. I'm not lifting a finger now—hey, want some of this?"

"I jon't like it."

The baby was red in the face.

"No?"

I had another bite of takuan, drank some tea, and pondered the situation for a while.

"How does it feel to be a girl?"

"Jisgushting."

"But I thought these disgusting girls were what you lived for?"

"Jis and jat are two jifferent chings."

"Okay, fine. Now you're a boy."

I twiddled my fingers again. Ever so faintly, I could feel the magic do its work. After a few adjustments, my husband transformed into a baby boy. Though just as hairy as before.

"Now you're thirty-nine."

The caveboy grew long legs and stood up, but his back was pathetically bent.

"What's this? You're an old man. Last thing I need."

"Backed in, duh wife expecting see was at foot it is now."

I could barely understand him. Most of his teeth had fallen out.

"You look like you're about to die."

"Dance to weight. Do sun thing."

"Okay, jump ahead ten million years."

"Do eddy it! Chew man beans hub on lean bin a row fur chew many un years. Chairs no jelling what Cayenne d'Monster R2-N2. Bee sighs, en an azure aid many un years, chew man beans zar lye glee to go it stinked!"

The prehistoric geezer lowered himself, exhausted, to a cushion on the floor.

"Okay, then jump ahead two million years."

My husband turned into a slender man with rosy skin and purple eyes. This time his hair was brown.

"Oops, a bit too far. What now?"

"Since when have you been able to do this?" he asked me in a steely, strident voice.

"Ever since the . . . the messenger came by. The messenger, of course! I'll call him up. It's all his fault."

I had no chalk to draw a circle with. It was a shame to spoil the carpet, but I found a tube of lipstick that was sort of on the whiter side and drew an awkward ring. Then I sprinkled a whole bag of the bay leaves that I used in stews and curries on the floor. Sitting in the middle of the circle, I called on the messenger to return.

"Come back, come back!"

The future man was aghast at what he saw.

A cloud of blue smoke and a nasty sneeze betokened the arrival of the messenger.

"*Achoo! Achoo!* What's this stuff on the floor? I thought I told you to use chalk. *Ahh-choo!*"

The black cloak trembled as he spoke.

"Well, I don't have any."

"Just forget *it-choo!* Heavens, it's hot in here."

"It's the same as earlier."

"I was just at the North Pole . . . Did you want something?"

"If I didn't, I wouldn't have called you. Explain this."

"Huh?"

The messenger looked at the purple-eyed man.

"Is he a friend of yours?" he asked.

"He's my husband. Or used to be. But look what he's turned into now."

"My, what a specimen. As elegant a figure as ever I have seen."

"Don't mess around with me."

"Hardly. I would never mess around. Are you asking for advice?"

"Tell me how to switch him back to normal."

"Sadly, that won't be possible."

The messenger's eyes betrayed a hint of mischief.

"But it's your bosses, the three witches, that gave me these, uh, magical powers."

"It's magick, if you please . . . spelled with a k."

The messenger chortled like a clucking hen.

"Whatever, I don't care, just do something!"

"Not for free. By rights, this is something you should frankly be doing on your own."

The messenger flashed me a cheeky grin.

"What do you want, then?"

"Now that you mention it . . . this cloak of mine is starting to fray."

"I happen to have a black cloak I can spare. Made using hundreds of pieces of cloth. Long enough to reach your toes."

"Sounds like it's only good for winter."

"So what? It'll be getting cold soon."

"But my next trip is to the African savanna. I'd much prefer a silk number, maybe something with a crimson lining . . ."

"Fine," I sniffed, pursing my lips.

"Splendid, it's a deal. I'll expect it by next week."

"Let's make it the week after. You can have the winter cloak as well."

"Hmm . . . alright, it's settled. I can see it now. With these additions to my wardrobe, I'll be quite the dandy. Where were we . . . Ah, yes, I'll now teach you the magick word required to turn your husband back to normal."

The messenger leaned forward and whispered something in my ear.

"Kinda odd that I didn't need a magick word to change him into something else . . ."

"Changing something back is much harder to do, my dear. Take whiskey and cola, for example. Imagine how hard it would be to separate the liquor from the soda."

36

This silly logic cut no ice with me.

"If you say the magick word, you'll break the spell. It's that simple. On which note, I bid you good day. Don't forget, you owe me two cloaks."

Again the smoke churned through the air, disappearing with the messenger.

"Who the hell was he?" asked the future man, incredulous.

"Doesn't matter. Don't worry. Let's just try it."

I said the magick word. My husband changed back to normal. Though I won't pretend that he was happy. He put on his pajamas without so much as a thank-you.

"Don't blame me. I was in my trial period."

"You could've used your magic powers to make me a stack of money. Then I wouldn't have to go to work tomorrow."

I turned toward the bare floor and said: "Stack of money, go!" but nothing happened.

"There's no going back," I said. "Not really."

My husband set a box of matches on the tea table.

"Try turning that matchbox into a hunk of gold."

Nothing happened. I tried turning the matches into flowers or fruit, too, but it was no use.

"See, your powers are gone. If you ever had them."

"I can't believe it. What happened?"

I scratched my head, bemused.

"Who cares. I'm going to sleep."

My husband climbed into bed.

The next morning, I was convinced it'd all been a dream. I thought about saying, "Now be caviar" as I placed the breakfast pickles on the table, but didn't bother.

Once my husband was out of the house, though, I decided I would give it one more try. He had left for work at nine, his usual disappointing self, nothing prehistoric or futuristic about him. He worked for a music production company, where they had flexible hours.

I gazed into the fishbowl at our goldfish and said: "Turn into a tadpole." To my astonishment, it was a success, for the most part.

So, it only worked if something was alive . . . I tried transforming the cup of parsley growing on the windowsill, but no luck there; I guess it didn't work on plants. Regardless, I was having a great time experimenting.

Out in the street, I changed cats into dogs and dogs into cats. None of them knew what hit them. The cats, especially, must have been at a loss, unsure of how to go on living, now that they were dogs.

I stepped onto the train, but it was packed.

Between there and the next station, I turned all the passengers into homunculi, on average just over an inch tall. This gave me all the space that I could wish for. But the homunculi reacted badly. They were up in arms.

"You're getting sleepy, very sleepy. You have amnesia. None of this ever happened."

This time, the spell worked perfectly. The train fell quiet. I lay down on the bench. From outside, it must have looked as if the car were empty. We had pulled into the station, so I said the magick word. The passengers turned back to normal. Though they all looked pretty groggy.

This was great. Imagine doing it somewhere on vacation. So fun . . . I got off the train and went into a café. A waitress was leaning against the counter, looking bored. There were only a few customers. She yawned and watched a different waitress bring me a glass of water.

"Now you're a lion," I whispered, eyeing the bored waitress.

Boy, was everyone surprised! Most of all the waitress who had become a lion. She looked around the room, standing with her forepaws propped up on the counter.

I covered my face with both hands and laughed. Then I turned her back into a person.

Did the magick only work on others?

Out on the sidewalk, I tried it on myself.

"You're a bird, you're a bird," I told myself repeatedly, but no such luck. By then I was tuckered out, so I decided to head home.

Waiting at a traffic light, I spotted my husband across the road. With another woman. He's incredibly nearsighted, so I don't think he noticed me. They hailed a taxi and drove off.

It seemed like the news my girlfriend had given me over the phone the week before was true.

"The girl must live in Ikebukuro. Does he regularly stay out all night?"

"Yeah. All the time."

This was nothing new. By then I didn't care. In fact, I did my best to wipe it from my mind.

"The other day I saw them having breakfast at the café. Eating hot dogs. Total morning-after vibe. They were all over each other. Fact is your husband's awful cute, not gonna lie."

I'd never caught him red-handed before. With my friend's voice echoing in my ears, I walked the rest of the way home.

That night, I got a phone call.

"Hey. It's me."

I knew where this was going.

"Hi," I said, hitting myself in the ribs with a tight fist. "What's the matter?"

"What's the matter? I'm your husband, calling home."

"Oh, of course, dear."

I recited the words like they were scripted.

"What's wrong, had a bad day?"

He was trying to butter me up.

"I guess I'm not feeling too hot, now that you ask."

"Read tonight's paper?"

"Not yet."

I put a bit more oomph into my fist.

"There's a rather strange article, about a mass hallucination. Apparently a waitress at a café in Shinjuku suddenly transformed into a lion. Though some people say it was a tiger."

"Oh yeah?"

"Everyone's convinced, her especially."

"Did they call someone from the zoo, or what?"

"That's the thing, everyone was so shocked they didn't think of it. According to eyewitnesses, she changed back about twenty minutes later. After that, they called the police or the hospital, you know."

Twenty minutes? No way. I changed her back in thirty seconds, tops.

"If it was summer, I might chalk it up to heat stroke—but it's not."

He was obviously making the connection with last night.

"I know what you're thinking. But it wasn't me. You saw me yesterday, trying with the matches. I can't do it anymore."

"Oh, so it wasn't a dream, after all . . ."

"Where are you right now, anyway?"

"I was about to say. I'm stuck here late tonight. We're compiling this pamphlet for a music festival."

"You are, huh? Then put Yamashita on the phone. Isn't he next to you?"

"Nah, it's just me. But I'm not at the office."

"Where are you?"

"You know . . . Setagaya."

"Are you, now?"

I giggled into the receiver.

"Don't you trust me?"

He sounded uneasy.

"I saw you two today. Out and about."

"Saw what?"

"You got into a taxi with some woman. Today. Or tonight, I should say. Closer to five."

"That, uh, that was a work thing . . ."

"It's fine. Because now you're a bull. A big black bull."

I hung up the phone.

Then I switched on the TV and lit a smoke. About ten minutes later, the phone rang again.

"Excuse me, this is Nani Nani Design Studios calling."

It was a woman's voice. I didn't recognize her.

"Can I help you?"

"Can you? I sure hope so. What have you done? My work . . ."

"Work? You're a piece of work, you know that? Fess up, or he'll be stuck like that for good."

41

There were whispers on the other end. The sounds of them conferring. The woman and the bull.

My husband, who as far as I knew was still a bull, roared into the receiver.

"Hurry up and undo this! Now!"

"No way. You two can figure it out yourselves."

"I'll kill you for this."

"You say that, but how're you going to get out of there? You may as well enjoy your love nest. That's what you wanted, right? You've finally gotten rid of me."

"I wish you could've chosen something else. Anything, really . . . We're having a hard time being in the same room."

"I bet you are."

"Come on, switch me back."

"Come home first."

"Look, it's like you said, okay? I can't get out of here!"

"Then stay there. Fine by me."

"Maybe I will!"

He hung up.

I grabbed my wallet and walked over to the bar around the corner, where I had three whiskey and waters. This put me in a good mood. I came home to find a nervous-looking woman standing at the door. In fact, it was the very woman I had seen with my husband on the street.

"I need you to come back with me," she burst out.

"Hey, how's he holding up?"

"I was so scared, I couldn't stay! We're talking about a full-grown bull here. If he's there for one more day, I don't know what I'll do . . . Come on, let's go."

"It'll be fine, calm down. Let's get a drink."

42

"This is no time for a drink. We have to go."

She seized me by the arm and hustled me into a taxi.

"Nice digs you got here," I said, looking around the lobby of her building. We took the elevator to the sixth floor.

She was so scared she handed me the key. I opened the door to find a black bull sitting in the middle of a loft apartment.

"Come on, hurry up. Or you'll regret it."

The bull stuck out his peach-colored tongue, as if to intimidate me.

"I doubt I'll regret any of this. Now be a good boy and transform," I said, before whispering something more specific: "Into a T-Rex."

My former husband's muscles jiggled and distended. He broke the chandelier.

The girlfriend let out a frightful shriek and disappeared.

"Hey, where's she going? Your sweetheart ran away."

"Don't be cute. Who wouldn't run away from a T-Rex? This is a disaster. We gotta get outta here."

"How?"

"By making me small, how else."

"Shrink-a-dinky-doo. Now you're little."

My former husband turned into a two-inch-tall dinosaur. Just as I dropped him in my handbag, I heard three or four people running over from the elevator.

"What now?"

Stuck in the bag, my mini dino of a husband caterwauled.

"Alright, now be Superman."

~

43

That's how the pair of us escaped. Flying, obviously. But we were spotted by a ufologist (or hobbyist), which caused a certain hullabaloo. People thought it was the second coming of George Reeves.

You're probably wondering what happened next. Well, I'm happy to report we're still together. Except my poor husband is stuck hanging in the chifforobe. After I turned him back into a bull, he got furious with me and roared, "I'm going to spill the beans," and we couldn't have that, could we.

At the top of my lungs, I shouted: "Now you're a living, breathing piece of jerky!"

In an instant, he was as rigid as a dried and salted aramaki salmon.

Believe me, I planned to turn him back eventually. Once he'd cooled off. But then, no matter how many times I said the magick word, my husband wouldn't change. He just hung there in the chifforobe, with a dazed look on his face.

So I summoned the messenger. And what do you think he said?

"Your magick powers have expired."

"Well, can't the witches turn him back for me?"

"I'm afraid that's not the way it works. A magick spell can only be undone by the person who cast it."

I asked if there was any hope at all. He reflected for a moment.

"The spell will break once all three witches die. Which should be soonish. They're getting up there . . ."

"How soon?"

"Let's say twenty years."

That's how I wound up living with a mute paddle of salmon for a husband. At first I thought of turning myself in to the police, but no one had been killed or injured, and there's nothing in the law books saying it's illegal to cast spells.

The only thing that bugs me is that lately, one of my smoked husband's legs has gotten all stretched out and ribbony, on account of hanging there so long. It's not like I can cut it off. But it just keeps getting longer, I mean it's really in the way, so every time I close the chifforobe, I have to kick it shut.

FULL OF MALICE

There we were, me and my mom, standing in front of the black entrance to the massive white building. Staring into a gaping, indecent void. My brother had never come home. He'd been taken away—a long, long time ago. He was live at the time, and anybody could have told you he was a halfwit.

"Your brother's in a bright, clean place now, a facility where they can take good care of him." That was how my mom put it. The mentally ill and physically deformed are all happy there—they have to be. They're forced to smile at all times.

"C'mon. Let's go find him. I mean, what if something happened to him? He's never called, never written. I know he can't actually write, but he used to draw pictures of monsters all the time. If this facility's so great, then why aren't they sending us his drawings?"

My mom didn't seem to share my misgivings.

"Your brother's happy now . . . He's *beyond happy*" (something I'd never heard her say about anybody before).

Anyway, I insisted on dragging my middle-aged mother to this place, against her will, so she could help me find my brother.

Summoning the courage to walk through that door was no small feat; it looked like it led straight into nothingness. What if there was some empty universe waiting for us on the other side?

"How long are you gonna stand here?" I tried to get my mom to move. "Let's go!" Even though we'd come all this way, she seemed unwilling to enter. Then, the moment before I set foot inside, my mom ran for it. As I crossed an invisible threshold and stepped into another dimension, I saw my corpulent mother make a mad dash in the other direction. What a weird sight it was. She didn't even look human. More like some object in motion that definitely shouldn't be able to move. As the galumphing figure vanished from view, I let out a long sigh.

The facility was nothing like it had appeared from the outside. It was bright, quiet, spacious. I was in a modern lobby inside a modern hospital.

Looking around, I couldn't tell the patients from the orderlies. Everybody who walked by was wearing the same expression, the same mask of a smile, their heads turning slowly like automata . . . But those faces. Plastered with a happiness that would never fade away—a freakish, menacing happiness.

I tried to find the front desk, but had no luck.

A young man was walking down the too-bright corridor, so I went up to him.

"Sorry, I'm here to see a patient. Can you tell me which way to go?"

"I'm a patient here myself," he answered cheerfully. He was, of course, grinning away.

"I wasn't asking about you . . . I'm looking for a little boy. He's around five . . ."

Hold up. He was five last time I saw him, but that was ages ago. I don't even think it was this century.

"I'm twenty-two and my wife's pregnant with our third child now. This place is heaven! You know what they do here? They let us live together as families—as an experiment. When I was eighteen, the Director chose my wife for me. We're the same age, and—"

"I'm not asking about—"

"The doctors recorded every little detail of our lives together. They still do. Anyway, my wife got pregnant before long. The first time around, we figured we'd try an abortion. They say bell-bottoms and abortions are all the rage on the outside! Gotta keep up with the times, right?"

Now my curiosity was piqued. I decided to listen, then ask a few strategic questions to sniff out my brother's whereabouts.

". . . But the next month, my wife's period didn't come. She's a real angel! We're following the Director's orders, devoting ourselves completely to the task of procreation. Of course, we watch our fair share of television, too. We've even got a brand-new color set . . ."

"So why are you here? What's wrong with you?"

"Wrong with me? That's a good one! If anything, I'm too normal. I was smiling all the time even before I got here. That's why they put me in this place, but it's honestly the best thing that could have happened to me. Otherwise, I wouldn't have met my wife, the love of my life!"

The man was still going, an ad for himself on an infinite loop, so I just left him standing there. It was obvious I wasn't going to get any information out of this guy.

I kept walking down the long corridor until I entered a large sunroom. People were relaxing on sofas, nothing but smiles on their faces. There was no art decorating the beautiful walls—only some strange specimen.

It was him. My little brother, still five years old. Encased in glass, his belly ripped open. I let out a seemingly endless scream and fainted like a damsel in some classical painting.

When I came to, I was strapped to a bed. I felt weird, like some part of me was missing. Like I'd lost every memory I'd ever had.

"How are you feeling?" a kindly, handsome doctor asked me, chuckling softly. Dammit. Are these guys gonna kill me? I mean, after what they did to my brother . . .

But the doctor undid the straps.

"Now that you've come here," he said in a gentle voice, "why not stay with us? You can do whatever you want . . . You can enjoy true freedom."

I still had that funny, empty feeling, so I looked in the mirror. The top half of my head was gone! They'd sliced straight through my skull like a watermelon. Under a transparent plastic cap, I could see the remaining half of my brain.

"We took the liberty of removing your vitriol—your malice. We do the same for everybody here. That's why they're all so happy, and why they can handle true freedom. You'll be fitted for a wig, just like the others."

50

I am deeply twisted. There's no denying that. They gave me my own room and told me that I was free to leave—but I didn't. I holed up in my room and thought about how I was going to get even. They're gonna pay. They're all gonna pay. I've gotta hit 'em where it hurts. Even though they'd supposedly removed my malice, the only thing I could think about was exacting my revenge.

Among the older patients was a guy named KENJI MIYAZAWA. He was loved and respected by all. People were always going to his room to listen to him speak.

I hid my face under a ton of makeup and headed over to KENJI MIYAZAWA's room. He was enjoying a leisurely meal, expatiating on "what it means to be human," and everybody in the room seemed to be having a blast.

Impatiently, I waited for them to leave. My plan was to seduce our dear Saint KENJI MIYAZAWA—to drag him into wickedness, to sully his good name. As I watched, the old man would occasionally lose his train of thought and stare off into space in an effort to remember what he was talking about, then break into a broad smile.

Everybody else was eating, too, taking their sweet time. It didn't look like they were ever going to finish. They were just getting fatter and fatter before my eyes. Meanwhile, I was getting skinnier and skinnier and skinnier.

"Found you! So this is where you've been hiding!"

The handsome doctor came into the room and grabbed me.

"What a shame! It looks like the malice has spread through your entire head. We're going to have to get rid of it and give you a bionic brain. But you can choose your own face!

Any one you want. Who's in fashion these days? Catherine Deneuve? Jeana Matsuo? Name it and it's yours!"

Now I sit in the sunroom all day, staring up at my little brother's laparotomized remains. Time's stopped moving. I've been forced into a blissful marriage for the benefit of science, with nothing to do now but wait for old age to take me.

I never even think about leaving this place anymore. Now that all my malice is gone.

HEY, IT'S A LOVE PSYCHEDELIC!

1

Reico crossed her legs in her all-time favorite cotton pants and looked out the window.

A band of dull gray light cut across the sliver of sky she could see. The sky itself was an unreal shade of violet, about to dissolve into black. The digits on the clock were glowing yellow. Yesterday had been unbearably beautiful—and today was exactly the same.

"It's so beautiful I wish time would just stop." That's what Reico said to Michiko on the phone.

Michiko's halfhearted reply: "Yeah, that's what they're saying on TV . . . Nice and dry."

Reico was ready to wax rhapsodic, to lose herself in the beauty of the day, but she was cut short by the working woman on the other end of the line: "But damn, it's hot . . . I'm sweating so bad I've gotta use a special foundation. You can only get this stuff at the best department stores. Cost me four thousand yen."

Just like Michiko to rain on Reico's parade. But Reico shook it off, countering with: "Oh, I hear you . . . I'm using three different colors of pressed powder . . . Set me back thirty-eight hundred a pop, too." Then she gave it a little thought. Maybe it was pretty normal to see the world that way: products over poetry—at least for a self-styled "classic beauty" like Michiko. The light of the sun and the song of the wind meant nothing to her. She couldn't see it, couldn't hear it.

Michiko . . . What an embarrassing name. "Mi" for beauty, "chi" for intelligence. If it were me, I'd change my name. Maybe not legally, but still . . . She's carrying around a good thirty pounds of excess fat—that's why she's so hot, Reico thinks, but doesn't say anything. When Michiko steers the conversation in the direction of Momoe Yamaguchi, her favorite pop star, Reico finds a way to slink off the phone. For a time, Michiko was convinced she was Momoe. She'd spent a good three months walking Reico through how she—meaning Momoe—had ended up choosing Tomokazu Miura as her husband.

People talk about taste like you've got it or you don't—but it's actually a lot more complicated than that.

Reico turned to look around the café.

A hangout for trendy chicks. And look at them. That hair. All of them with the same big curls swooping away from the face. The same shimmery blue eyeshadow, a solid stripe maybe half an inch wide. Half of them in polos and the other half in T-shirts, but both camps falling squarely within Hamatora fashion. By Reico's count, three of them are carrying tennis rackets. Like they're hot shit.

Suddenly, Reico felt like she couldn't breathe. She felt nauseous. Being exposed to this many girls at once, Reico was filled with something like terror. All she could do was shake her head. (These days, even the boys are scary. Every damn kid strutting down Koen-dori has a daypack slung over one shoulder.)

Reico leaned in to sip her tomato juice straight from the glass, then reached for a cigarette to calm her nerves.

Of course, the destructive power of packs of girls was nothing new. Six or seven years back, they all had shaggy mullets. Maybe three years before that, they all went for straight hair, parted right down the middle like ghosts. Back then, Reico had her hair shaved down to around three-quarters of an inch. Dyed slime green.

The Jaguars came on: "I Want to See You Again." 1967. Focus on the song, Reico told herself. You're waiting for your man.

Just then, she heard something inside her head click. Like the snap of a circuit switching. Then a voice. "You're a wicked one, aren't you?" And a noise—like bee wings—for about three seconds.

Then silence.

Reico glanced over at the next table. Just a couple of girls, nothing doing. Weird . . .

Masahiko came in wearing a bright-yellow Hawaiian shirt like it was no big deal, and sat down without a word. Reico wanted to tell him about whatever it was she'd just heard, but when she saw Masahiko's face, her expression froze.

"What's up?" Masahiko asked with an easy smile.

"I dunno. I just felt like maybe you were, um . . . somebody else."

"Huh."

"Like you were somebody I know, but different . . . As if some creature from outer space had taken control of your body or something . . . Like you had a different personality. I get that kind of feeling sometimes. That ever happen to you?"

"I dunno, maybe," Masahiko said, going along with it.

When the waiter came over, Masahiko ordered the fruit parfait—one of the girlier options on the menu.

"Hey, this place is pretty packed," he said, looking around.

"Too Matchy for me," Reico said with a sly smile.

"Mmm . . . Thank Matchy it's Friday."

"Don't you hate sharing a name with that guy?"

"Matchy? I've been in the music world a lot longer than him."

"Yup, ever since the good old GS days."

"Right, back in my gas station days . . . Ha. Life was a real gas back then—in the groovy days of Group Sounds."

All smiles, Reico bounced up and down in her seat.

"Hey, you're back. I thought I lost you for a second there. You looked kinda out of it when I came in. It was your birthday yesterday, right? I didn't buy you anything—but I made this."

Masahiko pulled a tape out of his shirt pocket and handed it to her.

She looked at the handwritten track listing, reading every title on the insert.

"'Too Much Love' by the Dynamites . . . 'I Remember' by the Bunnys . . . Wow, these songs are amazing! Where'd you get 'em? I didn't know you had any of these records."

Reico was overcome by a sudden surge of excitement, but tried to keep it under control.

She looked up from the tape. Masahiko was looking back at her, smiling, relaxed.

"I just moved into a new place, a bigger one. You know me—it's been one six-mat room after another for a whole decade. But that's all in the past now. Anyway, I went to my folks' house to pick up my old albums. I found some real trashy singles, too . . . You wouldn't believe it," he said with a laugh. "So I put together a bunch of tracks I thought were up your alley."

"Yeah, this is great! 'Amy My Amy' by the Voltage! Ugh, I love the throttled vocals on that one. Like he's trying to sound like Shoken from the Tempters."

"Half the bands back then were trying to do something like that, weren't they? They thought chicks would dig it."

"Hey, the Davys! 'A Love Psychedelic'!"

"Yeah, I've been really into the psychedelic stuff lately. It didn't click for me back then. It's on the tape, but I was listening to 'Monday Morning, Three O'Clock' by the Cups for the first time in years . . ."

"What a song . . . A Louise Louis Kabe original."

"That track's steeped in the San Francisco sound, but way more cheery. I really need to dive deeper into what they were doing in those days . . ."

"Geez, you're livin' in the past! But hey, retro's all the rage these days."

"Ha! You're one to talk!"

"Anyway, how's the new single doing?" Reico asked, finally calming down. After a blank of a couple of years, Masahiko was recording again.

"I'll tell you this—it's got no shot at cracking the top one-hundred," he said with refreshing indifference. Reico held back a smile.

"So, you quit that job of yours yet?"

Masahiko had been playing piano and singing at some lounge where girls hang out. That's where Reico met him (half a year back).

Sitting at a see-through piano, Masahiko played all the golden hits in his wheelhouse: "Mojo Workin'," "Spoonful," "Shotgun" . . . Sometimes he'd mix things up and go with "The 59th Street Bridge Song" or "The Weight" . . . Even "Black Is Black" (which the other Matchy covered with the Tanokin Trio—never doubt the genius of Johnny Kitagawa).

"Nobody ever listens to what I play," Masahiko said. "Sometimes I even throw in some new songs (in heinous arrangements dripping with cosmic despair). All the girls are too busy scarfing down whatever they're eating: natto spaghetti, Mediterranean seafood salad, West Coast–style frozen yogurt . . ."

Masahiko's all-over-the-place setlist—a perfect fit for the venue.

"I'm free until tomorrow night." In other words, he'd quit. "Got somewhere you wanna go?"

"Anywhere we can listen to this tape," Reico said. Zero hesitation.

"You like it that much?"

"Oh, it's the greatest," Reico said. Then, with a theatrical touch: "And so are you."

"I bet you say that to all the boys." Masahiko laughed as he signaled the waiter with his eyebrows. "Come over to my place? You still haven't seen my new digs."

Reico took off the red-and-black men's button-down she'd been wearing as a jacket. She stuffed the shirt into her bag, threw the whole thing over her shoulder, then stood up, ready to hit the road.

While he waited for change at the register, Masahiko turned to Reico and told her his new place was over by the west exit. "It's a bit of a walk from here. You up for it?"

— So far, so good, said a voice . . . Warps in the timeline are common enough.
— But those are minor differences. After all, timestreams tend to reconverge. If you let things go on this way, though, we're going to end up in a rogue present, and they'll have to cut it off. Once that happens, there'll be hell to pay.
— Not to worry. I'll stop it before it gets that far.
— I dunno, buddy. I wouldn't mess around with the Timekeepers.
— C'mon, it's just a little harmless fun. Everybody's doing it.
— Sure. You keep telling yourself that. It's a Class-A offense. A big-time crime . . .
— Against what? Humanity?

No response. Just crickets.

~

It was a beautiful evening out. Reico and Masahiko stayed above ground, looking up at the buildings as they walked.

"Nice pants," Masahiko said, swinging his arms.

"Right? You can't find normal pants anywhere these days. They're all shorts, capris, pegged pants . . . I got these off a boy, a long, long time ago. Yokosuka Mambo style. Six inches at the ankle."

"Yeah, a good pair of pants is hard to come by. Boutiques kill me. Even the cheap spots around Nakano almost never have anything I like. Hey, check out these pockets. See how easy it is for me to get my hands in there? I swear, patch pockets are pure evil . . . And it's like drainpipes don't even exist anymore. Best you can hope for is a straight cut. Nine, maybe ten inches at the bottom."

"A style that straddles the line between in and out . . . That's all I want. Marchin' to the beat of my own drum—like Beat Takeshi. Know what I mean?"

"If you can't beat 'em, right?"

"I make most of my own clothes these days. Too bad it costs more than buying the trendy junk off the rack. There's always second-hand, but I usually come up short in those places."

"Darn. So you can't dress up in vintage and go hang around all the used record shops in Suidobashi like everybody else."

"Ha. I know this guy, a keyboardist for a fusion band, and he's always asking people if stuff makes them feel good. One time I was telling him how a friend of mine was upset over some stupid thing I did, and he was just like, 'But did it feel good?' I kinda feel like borrowing that."

"Just go on what feels good?"

"Uh-huh!"

"The pleasure principle's fine and all . . . But your idea of pleasure is somethin' else. 'It's so gross, I love it' . . . 'It makes me sick, I gotta have it.'" Masahiko broke into a smile.

"Hey, I hate what I love and I love what I hate. Like 'Bride of Samba.' You know when the guys in the back start singing, 'Here, there, and everywhere'? When they sound like a bunch of zombies? So insanely lame it drives me crazy."

"Ha, Hiromi Go's got you covered."

As they sauntered down the street, Masahiko gave Reico a little elbow, his eyes fixed on the girl walking ahead of them. She was wearing the kind of shorts that all the girls were wearing, but her legs were unbelievably stumpy—not an inch over two feet. And that wasn't all. Her butt was gigantic, way out of proportion with the rest of her body.

Reico watched silently until the girl turned the corner. As soon as she was out of sight, Reico let out a loud sigh.

"That girl was totally normal . . . She didn't have criminally bad taste or anything. She just didn't have the body to pull off that outfit."

Masahiko looked like he was on the verge of cracking up.

"But what was with that floral pochette? And her hair! Was she going for Seiko Matsuda or what?"

"Ha. With a face like that?" Masahiko turned to look at Reico. "Hey, what's wrong?"

"I dunno . . . Why do I always have to judge other girls like that? I was thinking, you know . . . I should stop . . ."

Reico did her utmost to put on a serious face.

"For what, a full minute?"

"Well, you know . . ."

"Hey, you hungry? The place over at Lotteria does a mean American bento. Or we could eat at my place. It'll be quicker if I make something at home . . ."

"You don't mind?"

"Nope."

"Cool, home it is."

The two of them headed through the passageway to the west exit.

"Hey, is that record shop still closed?"

"You mean the one on the other side of the bridge? On the first floor? I haven't been there in a while, but yeah, I'm pretty sure . . ."

A few spaced-out students were handing out flyers in front of the department store. Every time they locked on to a passerby, they'd come to life and lean in at an aggressive angle. After a successful hand-off, they'd drift back into their default catatonic state.

After dodging the first two, Reico figured they were in the clear—when a third student stepped in their way and handed her a brightly colored piece of paper. Masahiko wasn't a target, apparently, so it had to be an ad for a beauty salon or something . . . Without reading it, Reico stuffed the thing into a pocket of her polyvinyl tote, which was always overflowing with junk like that by the time she got home.

"It's kinda far," Masahiko said again. "That cool?"

"How far are we talking?"

"On the other side of the KDD Building. What's that place called again? Bunka Fashion College? Right around there. On the opposite side."

"Nishi-Shinjuku?"

"Yeah, it's not Okubo."

"Hey, were you born in Tokyo?"

"Unfortunately . . ."

"It'd be a whole lot cooler to be from Honmoku, huh?"

"I was born in Azabu. My dad used to work in Akasaka."

"At the radio station?"

"You guessed it. What about you?"

"Yokosuka. The world of Nikkatsu movies. I had a class-mate whose mom ran one of those bars for foreigners."

"Far out."

They stopped at the store so Masahiko could pick up some groceries. As Reico watched him grabbing green beans and potatoes, she heard that same click in her head . . .

And then Masahiko was standing in front of her, a full bag in his arms.

"You feeling okay?" He peered into her face.

"Uh, maybe . . . I was just . . ."

"You looked a little spacey."

"Yeah."

"I thought I felt something for a second there—like there was some kind of spooky energy right behind me. When I turned around, I saw you standing there with this totally blank look on your face."

Masahiko was always picking up on stuff like that.

"Wanna take a breather at the coffee shop over there?"

"Nah, it's no biggie."

"You sure?"

"Yeah, I'm fine . . . I just lost track of time or something. Like I'd been standing here for a million years . . ."

"That can happen when you're feeling drained . . . You sure you're alright?" He seemed genuinely concerned.

"Yeah, fine."

Maybe it was all in her head. Déjà vu or something like that.

"Can you walk?"

Reico was starting to feel herself again. She smiled and nodded reassuringly.

"We're going to go over this bridge, but you go up first. We'll switch when we get to the other side. That way I can catch you if you fall."

Reico did what Masahiko said.

She'd had a similar feeling when she was waiting for him at the café.

It was like she was seeing everything around her for the first time . . . But not like seeing the world in a new light. And not like the whole world had come alive 'cause she was in love, either. Definitely not. This was a whole lot weirder than that. Like . . . she'd been thrown into some world— some time—that wasn't her own.

She started to tremble.

I hope Masahiko doesn't notice, Reico thought to herself as she tried to control the shaking.

As they climbed the steps, Masahiko put a hand on her shoulder. He leaned in close to her ear and said something, but Reico missed it. No, she heard the words. She just didn't know what they meant. It had to be the noise. But she nodded—automatically. Happens all the time. The body reacts before the brain. But her brain usually caught up (at some point).

Masahiko pulled his hand back.

They walked across the bridge.

All of a sudden, the sky went dark. Night doesn't come on gradually, at a consistent speed. It holds itself back as long as it can, and then, as if to say, "Fuck it, I'm outta here," it free-falls into darkness. Another beautiful day was coming to an end.

Reico made her way over the bridge, still feeling woozy. Something's going on with time, she thought. Everything's just . . . off. In the past, she'd had a few (not too many) experiences when she felt time was moving at a different speed for her—different from everybody else. But this wasn't like that, not at all.

It was like all time—the time surrounding the buildings, the bridge, the two of them—was distorting in the same way.

When they made it to the stairs on the other side, Masahiko quickly got in front of her.

Reico laughed. It wasn't like her to think about stuff like time. Dwelling on the metaphysical wasn't really her style. Other people didn't see her as "deep," either. Even if time flips around, even if Masahiko flips out, what's that got to do with me? *I'm me, the me I've always been* . . . The words popped into her head. And just like that, she managed to regain her typical swagger. Her mood changed. Unbelievable—all she had to do was decide to change her emotional state. Like switching out one cassette for another. Easy breezy.

"Hey," Masahiko turned to look at her when his feet landed on the sidewalk. "We're almost there."

"Nice place," Reico said when they got there, looking up at the building.

"A step up, for sure," Masahiko said as he pushed the glass door open. "After hopping from one dump to the next for years."

As she listened to the elevator making its descent, Reico chuckled for no real reason. The clean, bright box opened and they got in. Masahiko cradled the bag with his left arm and pressed the button for the eleventh floor with his other hand.

"So, got any openings for new ladies in your life?"

Reico couldn't just stand there in silence, staring at the numbers glowing over the door.

"Why?"

"Oh, just wondering . . ."

"Wait, are you thinking of that friend of yours?"

"Yup. She's a real catch."

"Yeah, I bet. I caught plenty of her that one time . . . Her, though? Why's it gotta be *that one*?"

The two of them talked about Michiko like she was more product than person.

"Because *that one* is exactly what you need, trust me."

The elevator stopped.

"Oh, it's this way."

"You've never known anybody like her. She'll blow your mind, I'm telling you. It'll be a real ride."

"Yeah, I knew that as soon as I took one look at her."

"So you're the superficial type, huh?" Reico asked, though she knew the answer. Damn, I'm such a bitch.

"Hey," Masahiko said. "Rotten on the outside, rotten on the inside. It's a time-tested truth."

"She's not like that, though. With her, it's all about the

stuff on the inside. Brain, heart, that kind of thing. She's got this unshakable confidence in herself."

"Whoa. Good for her."

When they got to Masahiko's door, he reached for his keys.

"She's always like, 'Guys are so stupid . . . They judge me for the way I look and can't see how amazing I truly am . . .'"

"Sometimes when you're not getting any help from the outside world, self-affirmation's the only way to go."

Masahiko went in first, then put the bag down in the kitchen.

"So what? You're turned off 'cause there's a yawning gap between the way she sees herself and the way everybody else does?"

Reico popped the snaps on her shoes, then stepped out of them. No slippers in sight, so she headed on in.

"Sure am. But you actually like it when people around you are like that. The bigger the gap, the better."

"Those are the fun ones."

"Yeah, for you."

Masahiko walked over to the fridge, got out some mugi-cha, and passed Reico a glass. Not even a second later, it was frosted with condensation.

"Hey, switch the cooler on."

She got up on the sofa and did as he asked.

"This one's new, right?"

Even in his six-mat days, Masahiko had had an air conditioner. He couldn't stand the noise, so he had to keep his windows shut all the time—even in the middle of summer.

That's how it is for a musician. Can't live too close to train tracks or on a busy street.

"My old one's still in good shape, so I thought about bringing it with me, but this place already had its own unit built in."

In a corner of the room, there was a normal-looking grand piano in a normal piano color. It wasn't even pink or white.

"You hungry?" Masahiko asked as he brought over some watermelon slices on a rectangular tray.

"No rush," Reico said back. "Take a load off."

Masahiko grabbed a cushion and sat on the floor. Reico did the same. On the low table was a ripped-open bag of mixed nuts and a bottle of vodka.

"That reminds me," Reico said, waving her hand in the air. "That friend of mine? She's a big-time drinker. Drinks every night."

"Out?"

"In . . . Most of the time. She's pretty stingy, and there's no guy on earth who'd be willing to cough up enough money to cover her tab. She drinks in front of the TV, before going to bed. She cracks me up sometimes. 'I feel like I'm turning into an alcoholic. I'm well on my way . . .' I swear, she's always bellyaching about how her liver's gonna be the death of her."

"Sounds like she's proud of it, though!"

"Totally! The other day, I said, 'Hey, I think you're drinking below your weight,' and she said, 'Yeah right, these days I'm putting away a whole bottle every night . . .'"

"No way."

"Oh, she just meant a bottle of beer . . . You know those kinda big ones?"

Masahiko heaved a drawn-out sigh, then said, "Sheesh, gimme a break."

"What can I say? That's the kind of girl she is—all the way down."

"All the way down . . ."

"She's single now. Just got dumped by the first man in her life. You should hear the way she brags about not being a virgin, too. She's twenty-eight. Perfect for you, right?"

"Yeah, perfect . . ."

"Oh, and the guy she was with . . . You know that cannibal guy in Paris? The one who killed that Dutch girl? Her man was the same height as that guy, only heavier. A lot uglier, too. The guy's only twenty-five, but he's pretty much bald already. God, I felt so tall when we were walking around Shinjuku together. I had heels on, so he only came up to around here."

Reico was laughing as she held a hand up to her shoulder.

"You've always looked pretty tall to me."

"But yeah, I felt like I was walking a pet or something. Remember Oliver the Humanzee? The so-called missing link? Like that, but way, way uglier. I started to wonder if I should stop by the kennel to get him a collar . . ."

"Damn, Reico!"

"What?"

"Nothing . . . So you think I'd make a good replacement for that dude?"

"Oh, ha. It's nothing personal. I'm asking every guy I know. 'Hey, wanna go out with my friend?' Finding her a new man is pretty much all I live for these days. But listen, she's got some really outstanding qualities! For one thing, she never lies. She's an open book!"

Reico leaned in and slapped Masahiko on the knee. "She's a regular Isshin Tasuke. Results mean nothing. Process means even less. All that matters is heart. She's totally committed to commitment!"

Masahiko groaned.

"She's got no flair, but she's consistent. Keeps her nose to the grindstone, completely incapable of cutting corners . . ."

"And she's super slow, right? So you're pretty much saying she's not the brightest bulb . . ."

"She's not exactly observant, I guess. She hates taking risks and *everything* goes over her head. But why should that matter any when she's got a heart of gold?"

"She seemed real thick to me. And not just because of how big she is."

Masahiko drank some mugicha.

"But wait, what if she was the opposite type? Brazen! Moody! A liar, quick to give up!"

Masahiko burst out laughing. Reico kept going: "Happy-go-lucky, irresponsible, unfeeling! Crafty and calculating!"

Reico gave Masahiko's knee another slap.

"Hey, sign me up. I can't handle all that emotion. Sympathy and compassion wear me out. Meanwhile, she's all drunk on her own saintliness, right?"

"Yup, that's her. All sixty-five kilos of her."

"Hey, those types are pretty rare these days . . . Dark, damp, nineteenth-century personalities."

It was getting late.

Masahiko went into the kitchen.

Reico reached for the TV and pulled the knob. Alice came on. Wait—didn't they break up? She sat right up and lost herself in the screen.

The band was playing "Crazed Fruit." Every time Reico saw Shinji Tanimura sing, it made her think about Hoichi the Earless, strumming his biwa among the Heike graves with all the moaning spirits gathered around, will-o'-the-wisps burning like great balls of fire. That was how much heart Tanimura put into his music—playing his acoustic guitar like he was trying to break the thing.

How the kid ended up rotten to the core. That's what the song's about.

Of course, in the end, the times take the blame. When we first meet the kid, he's tossing a half-eaten apple into the pitch-black heart of the city. (You never see kids walking around with apples, not these days . . . Maybe a burger . . .) But it's got to be an apple! It's gotta be! If you threw a burger down some dark alley, a dog would probably jump out and chase after you . . . Besides, guys like Yūsuke Kawazu and Tamio Kawachi wouldn't be caught dead eating a burger. Too easy, too breezy—too greasy.

Then the boy makes a phone call—with the same hand he used to throw away his knife! I bet it was a switchblade . . . A flick knife. Nothing else would cut it. Same goes for the phone. Rotary or bust.

Next, the boy remembers his mom calling his name the day he ran away. Yeah—you can't just waltz out of the house with your Walkman on full blast! If you can't hear your mom over the music, how the hell are you supposed to be racked with guilt later on?

"Wow, this show's insane!" Reico barked into the kitchen.

"Yeah, I can hear it. *Alice in TV Land*, right?"

"*Alice in TV Land*? How long's this been on?"

"A couple of months, maybe. Ratings are through the roof . . ."

Reico couldn't believe she'd been missing out on a show this funny. But she'd never been that into TV anyway. So wait—how did Masahiko know about it?

The band started playing "Espionage."

This one's about Golgo 13. (Even if somebody told Reico it wasn't, she wasn't about to back down!) I mean, who else would pray to the night sky, pistol clutched to his chest, gratuitous red roses showering down as he vanishes into the distance?

So powerful! So vulgar! So sublime! So incredible!

Reico was laughing so hard she fell over. She rolled around, pointing at the screen as she shrieked: "This is amazing! It's amazing!" She could barely see through her own tears.

Tonight's guest act was a real throwback . . . The Tanokin Trio. Toshihiko Tahara, Yoshio Nomura, and Masahiko Kondo—aka Matchy.

They were singing "After School," the B-side from Toshi's first single, "New York City Nights."

When Reico first heard this track, she had to wonder if it was okay to put out a record like this. The three of them shouting cheerfully over the melody. It was too much.

"We won't burn our youth for your stupid tests!" Yeah, no shit. I mean, is there literally anywhere on this planet where kids happily waste their youth taking tests?

At this point, Reico had to throw in the towel. Uncle. I give up. She bowed to the TV screen, forehead to the floor.

Time for a commercial break. She took a breath. Long and deep. God, that was wild . . .

"Good stuff, right?" Masahiko came out holding a pot, grinning away.

"I dunno, that was a lot to take in at once . . . Pretty extreme. I'm still feeling it."

"I can't believe you didn't know about it . . . Everybody loves that show."

Reico pushed in the knob and the screen went black.

"I kept things simple. Oh, you don't have to . . ."

Reico was getting up for plates.

"You don't know where anything is, do you? Yeah, over there . . . Those are fine. And a couple of the big glasses, too."

Reico went to the fridge, grabbed two rolls and a stick of margarine, and came back to the living room. Masahiko filled their bowls with soup, then they dug in. Trout and cheese baked in foil with tomatoes, green beans, sliced onion, and bell pepper.

"I make this one all the time. It's quick, and clean-up's a breeze."

"I'm gonna put it on, okay?"

Reico slipped Masahiko's tape into the machine and "My Love, My Love" by the Youngers came on. Listen to that guy. Almost no breath in his voice. So pure—he really knew how to sing.

"Geez, GS kills me."

"Same here. Everybody's got a weakness, right? Hey, what about that friend of yours?"

"Steaming hot rice straight from the cooker . . . Nabeyaki udon . . ."

"Right."

"Oh, and booze and TV and cutesy comics. But yeah, the biggest one's gotta be other people's sex lives. She's always going, 'Something's up with those two . . .' 'That guy's crazy for me.' Of course it's all in her mind—at least when it's about her. When it comes to other people's business, she's abnormally obsessive . . . After all, it's all she's got."

"Hmmm."

"Nothing but Love" by the Taxman came on. As soon as the guitar got started, Alice's vice-like grip on Reico's mind finally started to loosen.

"Hey, you were eighteen ten years back, right? What were you up to in those days?" Masahiko asked lightly. Around that time, he was probably just hanging out. (That was right after his band split up.)

Up to?

Reico tried to think.

Up to?

A vision floated into her mind. The stage at the Golden Cup. Honmoku's suburban sprawl. But Reico wasn't even sure she'd been there. Maybe she just wished she had. Memories are always kind of made up, right?

"I don't know . . ."

Reico put her half-eaten roll back on the plate.

"You don't know?" Masahiko repeated back gently, as if singing.

"I don't know. I can't remember anything! Where I was, what I was doing . . . Hey, I think something's wrong with me. You know how people always say, 'I don't have a past'? Well, I'm not just saying it . . . I literally can't remember anything!"

Reico moved around the table, closer to Masahiko.

"What the hell's going on? What's going on with me?"

Masahiko looked down at her with gentle eyes.

"What if I have amnesia or something? I really can't remember who I was." Reico was desperate.

"Okay." Masahiko was deep in thought. "So who are you now?"

She couldn't answer that one, either.

"Can you remember your job? Your family?"

Reico just shook her head.

"When you wake up tomorrow, it'll come back. Where you live and what you need to do. All that stuff. You freaked yourself out trying to remember your past. That's all."

"How can you be so calm about it?" Reico muttered weakly.

"Hey, it's pretty common these days. Some psychologist just wrote a book about it. There are tons of people out there experiencing the world like they're fictional characters, living out their lives with no backstory until somebody—a voice or another character—comes along to fill in the blanks."

"First I've heard of it."

This can't be . . . This can't be my time . . .

"Hey, there's a first time for everything," Masahiko said. "Anyway, eat up . . . You came over to listen to the music, right?"

Reico let his arm go. She was hoping he'd give her a hug, maybe stroke her hair, but it didn't look like that was about to happen. Even though he always did when she was feeling down (unless that was just some bogus memory, too . . .).

Maybe it really wasn't a big deal. Otherwise Masahiko wouldn't just leave her hanging. (At least she hoped he wouldn't . . .)

Reico gave a heavy nod, reached listlessly for her roll, then took a bite.

"Come on, cheer up." Masahiko smiled at her.

"I'll give it a shot."

"What's going on? You seem a little out there."

"No, I'm over it."

"Yeah?"

"Yeah," Reico said back—clearly and forcefully. After all, Masahiko said it happens all the time.

"Hey, I love this song. Check it out."

The B-side from "Goin' Home" by the Dynamites. So much better than the A-side. (Probably because it's studio musicians on the record.) A rhythm and blues track, and they aren't even screaming.

"Up to my neck in love . . ." The lyrics made Reico yelp with delight. "A stupid line from these lips of mine you long for . . ." Oh, yeah. That ego. A boy who's used to getting everything he wants. He pushes away the hordes of groupies and makes it sound like he's the one going through hell, even though it's the girl who's in tears.

"Only You." "The Girl for Me." In those days, all the bands kept their acts clean, pandering to the prudish tastes of teenage girls. (*Those days* are so clear. Down to the tiniest detail. And maybe that means . . . Maybe there isn't anything to agonize over, even if I can't remember my own past . . .)

The Dynamites were pretty wild for a GS band. And when the Jaguars came out with their first album in '67, they were just as explosive. I mean, that was the oppressive age of Kazuo Funaki . . . "Stick to mood music" and all that. Still, it was the Jaguars who first brought the fuzz pedal to Japan.

The track was "Dancing Lonely Night." As soon as Okitsu started to play, the engineer jumped in and shouted, "The amp's busted!" (It was the kind of fuzz you hear at the start of "Satisfaction" by the Stones. The sound coming from Keith's guitar . . . Yeah, I have no idea where I was ten years ago, but I can still remember "Satisfaction" getting used in some car commercial on TV a couple of years back.)

GS is a far cry from rock—a far cry from music, really. That goes for most of the bands in the scene. (Reico likes to act like it's the good old days, like the Golden Cups are still in their heyday . . . But the Cups were always pretty dark, weren't they? I mean, just listen to the lyrics on "If I Could Live Again.")

Group Sounds never made any sense, at least not musically. There was even that one band whose frontman washed up on the feel-good shores of the Mahina Stars. Talk about the zenith of meaninglessness. Like how the Ox would play a medley of literal lullabies at their shows? (God, Reico loved all that crap with a burning passion.)

That's why the Roosters and the Mods today are a cut below GS . . . 'Cause there's actually some kind of musicality to what they're doing.

"These lyrics are the best." Reico smiled at Masahiko. She was in heaven—just drinking in the tape, Masahiko, and the view of the city from his window.

Just then, something caught her eye. "Hey, did you see that?"

A bunch of spots appeared in the distance. Light-brown dots that coalesced in a corner of the night sky.

"Huh?" Masahiko lowered his head to look outside.

"What's that light? Wait, is that—"

Translucent yellow orbs were pouring into the Triangle Building—into the hollow space in the middle. (The building was shaped like a sushi roll with nothing on the inside.)

"It's salmon roe," Masahiko said like it was no big deal.

"Salmon . . . roe?"

"Yeah, you know . . . Goes on a hot bowl of rice? You eat it?"

"I know what salmon roe is. But what's it doing in the sky? And why is each egg like ten feet across?!"

"I mean, what can I say?"

High in the sky, Reico saw what could only have been a giant pair of chopsticks, which proceeded to press the giant salmon eggs into the empty space in the middle of the building.

"I have no idea how it happened, but I'm pretty sure we're hallucinating!"

"Maybe, maybe not . . ."

Then the top third of the Triangle Building—packed full of salmon eggs—suddenly broke off, rose into the sky and disappeared.

"What the fuck is going on?"

"Somebody's eating norimaki," Masahiko said calmly.

"But, but—"

"Hey, this kind of thing happens all the time. The other day I saw the Metropolitan Police Department start to vibrate, then vanish into thin air."

"First I've heard of it!" Reico screamed.

"You really gotta pay more attention if you're gonna keep up with the times, Reico . . ." Masahiko looked at her. "I mean, you don't wanna get left behind, do you?"

"Um, is there anything there now? Where the MPD building used to be?"

"Nope. Pretty sure it's just an empty lot. But, you know, Japan's lucky enough to have the greatest police force in the world, and they were quick to regroup, so we've got nothing to worry about."

Masahiko seemed completely uninterested in watching the sushi getting eaten in the sky. He reached out for Reico's neck. "You can't peel your eyes off that thing, can you?"

"Well, I'm in shock, yeah . . . How am I supposed to look away?"

"Cool, cool . . . Whatever floats your boat."

Through the space between Masahiko's skinny arms, Reico could see that the Triangle Building was now completely gone. The sound of the first synthesizer ever recorded in Japan filled the room.

— It's too late. We're going to have to cut it, said the Timekeeper.

— We can't graft it onto another timeline?

— I'm afraid it's out of our hands now.

— Those bastards . . . They've really crossed the line this time!

— You can say that again. Everybody's rattled. I just hope it hasn't spilled into the past connected to this time system.

— The present can have that kind of influence over the past?

— It's certainly possible. Because the future's the same as the past—in that they aren't the present.

— Because the past is *no longer* and the future is *not yet*?

— Exactly. People are always living right where they are, constantly in the present.

— Well, we'd better go back then, to make sure the past hasn't been affected.

— Okay, let's start off ten years back.

— Yessir.

2

The couple Reyco met while she was walking around the city didn't live far from her apartment.

"Make yourself at home," said the guy in the mesh shirt. It had a golden rose on the front. "My girlfriend's a designer. She made this for me."

"Cool," Reyco said as she flopped down on the sofa.

The guy went into the kitchen for tea and biscuits. The girl in the crazy dress had to be taking a shower.

After the guy put on a record, he came back and sat on a round stool, then waited for the song to come on.

"Somebody to Love" by Jefferson Airplane.

"What year was this? Sixty-seven?" Reyco asked as she dipped a hand into her mirror-stuffed bag to find something to smoke.

"It's a real oldie. The Japanese title was 'Only You.'"

"Yeah, I know. The Mops did a cover—with Katsu Hoshi on vocals. It's mind-meltingly good, too. He just leaves Hiromitsu in the dust."

"Man, that was ages ago."

From the depths of her bag, Reyco fished out a crushed pack of Mild Sevens. Weird. These weren't supposed to exist yet. Reyco used to smoke Seven Stars—before Mild Sevens. But wait, if Mild Sevens weren't a thing yet, then why did she know about them?

Whatever. Stuff like this happens all the time.

No need to dwell on it—classic Reyco.

The guy was drumming along with the song, tapping his knees to the beat. What a maroon. When the psychedelic guitar started to fade out, he got up to pick out another single. Just go with an LP, dude. That way you won't have to keep getting up every two minutes. Anyway, he put another song on, then came back to his stool. These had to be his favorite tracks, time-tested crowd-pleasers. Cassettes weren't a thing yet. They were out there, but they hadn't made it big. Most people were using reel-to-reel. But if a guy like this doesn't have a tape deck, Reyco thought, he's gotta be in a band—and they've gotta be garbage.

"No one wants to listen to rock these days," he said during the Zombies' "Time of the Season." "And it's a damn shame."

"Yeah . . ."

Reyco didn't care, but she played along, just for the hell of it.

"It doesn't look like real rock music is ever going to take off in Japan . . ."

The guy sounded like a rock critic from one of those magazines they had *back then*.

"Why are we even trying?"

Reyco looked at him. Hey, don't blame rock. The problem's how you look, she thought. The guy was neck-deep in London kitsch—skinny as a twig, too. But you've got to be pretty skinny to pull off frilly shirts and polka-dot ties. If he's wearing a shirt showing this much skin, he's gotta have confidence in his body, too . . . And that long face. Geez. Talk about a hard sell.

"Folk, folk, folk. That's all they want. The people in this country are a lost cause."

"Uh-huh." Reyco was bored already, but she threw the guy a bone just the same.

"I was late to the party. Missed the GS days. I coulda been a star, though, if I'd gotten into music a little earlier."

The hot air coming out of this mouth-breather.

He put on "She's Not There," "I've Got a Mind to Give Up Living," "You Really Got Me," "Love Potion No. 9."

The girl with the crazy dress came out in a muumuu, drying her hair with a towel.

Reyco got up and walked over to the hi-fi to check out their records. Most of them were imports. *Back then*, all the guys in bands were hooked on British and American stuff.

"Whoa! Green Grass!"

Reyco grabbed the blue-tinged album from the collection. This group was one of the first in Japan to play rhythm and blues.

"What's that doing there?" the girl asked, still toweling her hair. "I thought we threw that one out."

"What? It's just one record . . ."

Reyco took the album back to the sofa. On the cover, all the guys in the band were standing in a row, wearing what looked like black robes, each his own animal in a rock 'n' roll menagerie: The Pig, The Bear . . . and Joel the Giraffe, sporting his round eyeglasses. Above the photo, the album name was written in English: BLUES MIND. I kid you not.

"Man, they were cool. Really popular in Yokohama." The guy stretched for no apparent reason.

"Yeah, the guys from the Grass were always rollin' in tail," the girl added indifferently.

Meanwhile, her boyfriend was getting more and more excited. "The singer was the only guy in the band who was a hundred percent Japanese. They had an American when they first started, but he had to quit the band to go back to Hawaii. Visa issues. The lead guitarist's from Hong Kong, and even Okinawa's a foreign country . . . Then there's Joel. Half French-American . . ."

"A G.I. baby?" Reyco had to rain on his parade.

"Dunno . . . His dad's a dentist, though, and he lives in some gigantic mansion with an iron gate out front."

"Hey, madhouses have iron gates, too," the girl said teasingly. "You could always find Joel at one or the other . . ."

"The drummer was a real spud boy, and the schoolgirls out in the country ate him up, even though he didn't look like much and could barely keep a beat. But Joel was something else, worlds away from normal."

"His eyes are wild," Reyco said, staring at the sleeve.

"Yeah, he's a real devil, isn't he? I can't stop staring at him either."

"He's missing a few marbles, though, that's for sure . . ."

The girl started rolling an ordinary cigarette with her French cigarette roller. Guess she really wanted to look like somebody who gets high.

"From all the glue . . . He used to make it look like he was drinking cokes and stuff, but he was really huffing glue. He kept it in the bottom of the can." Now the guy was positively giddy. They obviously knew Joel, but wouldn't come out and say it. Yeah, they wanted Reyco to know—but were taking their sweet time getting there.

"It got really bad for a while," the girl said. "I'd go backstage, and he'd just grab my boob. Then he'd be like, 'C'mon, let's go to the bathroom.' He was always on something, so he was in a kinda weird state, sexually . . ."

Reyco listened, one hand stretched along the back of the sofa, a Mild Seven in the other.

(But seriously, what's the deal with these cigarettes?)

"You know . . ." the guy said, finally geared up for the big reveal. "She used to be Joel's woman."

Cue the sting! The dum-dum-dum of the timpani!

"It didn't last long," she said with a casual wave of the hand. "He's the forgetful type . . ."

"Wild, huh? For the longest time, I wanted to be just like him. I'd watch him do his thing on stage. He never looked at the audience when he was playing. He'd have his bass down on his hip, like this, staring at god knows what . . . And all you ever saw were the whites of his eyes!"

I guess it's a really big deal. To have some kind of connection with a star. No matter what shape that takes.

"Whatcha think?" the girl asked Reyco. "Visually."

Reyco took another good look at the image on the album.

"I like the shape of his shoulders. Nice and square. I guess I'm not a fan of sloped shoulders or bulky ones. He's got a pretty long neck, too."

"What about his face?"

Geez, she won't quit.

"He's got a round face, and he's really skinny, too . . . Not bad."

"Think you'd wanna get to know him?" the girl asked, leaning in.

"Sure," Reyco said back.

"'Course you would," the girl said as she slowly moved away. "Boys this gorgeous are hard to come by."

The guy was staring off into space. What an actor. Slowly, he turned to look at the girl and said, "You've still got his number, right?"

"Well, yeah. It's no big deal, though . . ."

What's no big deal?

"You should give it to her . . ."

"Hmmm . . ." The girl acts like she's thinking it over. "Okay. But only 'cause it's her."

'Cause it's me? What the hell's that supposed to mean? We only met tonight.

"Uh, where'd I put it?" The girl dug into her bag and pulled out a notebook. Without missing a beat, the guy grabbed a pen and a sheet of paper and set them down in front of Reyco.

"Okay," the girl said. "It's oh-four-five . . ." Reyco wrote the number down.

"Why not call him right now? He's been playing at Mama Ringo in Kyoto, but he should be back in town now."

From what Reyco *remembers*, she calls him up. It's a little after nine-thirty.

Reyco dialed the number. And he really did pick up. The guy and the girl watched her, unable to contain themselves.

"I want to see you," Reyco said coolly into the receiver. The guy threw his hands up like an overexcited mime.

"Have we met before?" Joel asked in a low voice.

"Nope. Never."

"Cool . . . So you wanna come over?"

"Right now?" Reyco asked.

"Yeah. Where are you?"

"Yoyogi-Uehara."

"Okay. I'm in Ishikawachō, close to the station. Meet me at the bus stop in Hongocho at eleven, alright? Later."

She heard a click.

The others' excitement had spread to Reyco. She was almost trembling.

"You did it!" the guy shouted. "Right out the gate!"

Something isn't right here—but whatever. Reyco was a little fuzzy on what happened *back then*.

"Get over there and make us proud," said the girl, her own groupie days behind her. Now it was Reyco's turn. "Take a quick shower and do your makeup. I've got this pearly foundation you can use . . ."

Reyco decided to go along with it. To let the girl put her hair up, wrap it in a towel.

As Reyco adjusted the heat in the shower, she vaguely wondered what the future held for her. Eighteen. Stranded between high school and college. Am I gonna squeak into some third-tier school and end up working in an office? Or am I gonna answer phones at some record company? Pretty sure it'll be one or the other.

I know my own future. I know where I'll be in ten years. I've got this interference in my head from the future—and it's really throwing me for a loop. Gotta get my feet back on the ground.

Reyco washed her toes. They were beyond dirty from walking around all day. She was about to see Joel. The real Joel. But not at the bus stop . . .

She left the bathroom, did her makeup, and used the girl's perfume.

"Hey, look at you . . . Yeah, girl!"

And then, with the former groupie's blessing, Reyco went on her way.

— Did we miss the cut? asked the Timekeeper.
— No, it's her. She's especially receptive. Everybody else is doing fine.
— In that case, let's let it go on a little longer.
— This present's going to need a different future. We'll have to find a good match . . .

— Any future would be better than that hellscape . . .

— Okay, here goes nothing. I'll try to keep it natural.

Lightning, they announced over the loudspeaker—the Tōkaidō line was delayed an hour and forty minutes. Reyco called Joel from Ishikawachō when she finally got there.

"I was waiting at the bus stop. You didn't show, so I came back," Joel said, totally unfazed. "I'll be right there."

"Thanks."

Reyco dug deep into her memory: When I was eighteen, I wasn't a groupie or anything . . . I didn't know a thing about music. I was just a kid who wanted to have a little fun.

There was Joel. Tall and thin. He had to be almost six feet tall, 125 pounds. (He was twenty-two at the time.)

He had a giant paper bag in his arms.

"What's in there?"

"In here? Just some stuff I had washed, and some stuff to eat. You called me at my mom's house. We're going to my place now," Joel said, then started to walk.

Reyco hiked up her skirt and followed him.

All the shops were shuttered, and the whole street was kinda . . . wonky.

"I knew it was you, babe," Joel said. "Right away."

I mean, yeah. There wasn't anyone else around.

"I'm really glad we could meet up," Reyco said—and she was.

She was even into the way he called her "babe" (even though they'd never met).

"You come to Yokohama a lot?"

"Nope, never."

"I thought you'd be one of those girls in all black and stuff. I get a lot of girls like that. Tons of jewelry, chains jangling every time they move."

"They're still coming after you?"

"Yeah, I guess. But I like girls, so . . ."

"So it's not a bad deal, huh?"

"Not really, no."

Green Grass wasn't that popular—not now. They weren't even together anymore. But there were still plenty of girls who wanted to feast their eyes on this beautiful Angel of Rock.

Joel was wearing skinny pants that ran long over the tops of his buckskin slip-ons. Of course he was.

"How old are you?" Joel asked. Zero hesitation.

"I was . . ." Reyco started to say, then caught herself. "I'm eighteen."

Joel didn't seem put off—not at all. "You look around twenty-one to me."

There was something spiritual about this guy—but without the spirit. Complicated, but straightforward. It's a weird way to put it, but . . .

So why the hell do I feel so down? When I'm twenty-eight, I'll get a second crack at youth . . . I'll get pretty damn wild, too. Steeped in euphoric despair.

I guess I was sorta down in the dumps *back then*. When I was young . . . Ugh, what the hell's wrong with me? I'm a total wreck. All mixed up.

But looking at Joel beside me lifts me up. (Even though controlling my emotions is something I won't figure out for some time to come . . .)

I mean, check out the eyelashes on this guy. They're half an inch long—at least. Thick, too. I bet they get in the way.

And those big eyes. Deep blue tinged with gray. But every time we go under a streetlight, they light up yellow. Then, when the light's behind us, they almost look green. Eyes like glass—so vacant, so pretty.

You should be happy. On cloud nine. And just like that—there she was, walking on clouds.

("A Love Psychedelic: Part II" . . . Wait, what's the "II" for?)

"You live on your own?" I asked from up on my cloud.

What a stupid question. I hope no one's gonna be around to bother us, though. This is *our time*—just the two of us.

"Not until last month," Joel said, laughing a little.

We turned down a narrow street. This had to be the place. Joel put his foot on the first of the iron steps, turned to look at me, and whispered, "Shhh."

Then he went up—quietly. I followed him, focusing all my energy on not making any noise.

"It isn't locked," Joel said, then pulled the door open.

"Ever?"

"Yeah. Why bother?"

The windows were open. No curtains.

He put the bag down in the dark, then drank some water straight from the faucet. I copied him.

Without turning on the light, Joel took off his shirt.

(Here's hoping nothing weird happens . . . And I don't mean "weird" like somebody walking in on us . . .)

Weird?

Yeah, I know what's happening. Somebody's moving me around in time. And all I can do is act in a way that doesn't go against their will—whoever (or whatever) they are.

The dim light from the streetlamp outside was falling into the room.

"How are you feeling?" Joel asked, no smile.

"I'm good."

He wet a towel and wiped the sweat off his chest. (Yeah, that was August.)

Joel sat down on the bed and lit a cigarette. I watched as he took a drag.

"Come over here," he finally said. I moved a little in his direction—just a little.

"You scared? Think I'm gonna bite?" (Now he smiled.) "Funny . . . You're the one who called me."

"That's not it . . ."

Should I just tell him?

"What's not it?"

How do you even explain to somebody that time's out of whack? Probably better to just leave it alone.

"C'mere," he said.

I sat down on the bed, next to him.

"When I got clean, I put on some weight." Joel pressed his hand against his chest. "Does it bother you?"

"Not really."

"Not one to pull your punches, huh?" he whispered as he leaned in. Reyco swore she could hear Joel's thick eyelashes every time they moved. God, those eyes.

Reyco remembered.

First, I make this boy mine, then hook up with the rest of the band. After that, I move on to other bands, to the guys who catch my eye. Just like a full-fledged groupie. That's the course that's been laid out for me.

It occurred to Joel to set the mood, so he got up. "I'll put a record on. You're gonna love this one. It's a new British band. Well, the members are originally from the U.S. . . ."

Doesn't ring a bell.

As soon as Joel came back, the Stray Cats started to play. Reyco jumped into the air. "No way! No way!!"

"What's wrong?"

"This record," I gasped. "It doesn't come out until 1981."

"What are you talkin' about? This is 'Runaway Boys,' by the Stray Cats."

"Yeah, I know. That's my point . . ."

What the hell am I supposed to do? The room's pretty dark, but I can see an Agnes Lum poster on the wall.

"Time's all mixed up!"

I started to cry—just like a teenage girl.

"You're the one who's mixed up, babe."

Joel put his arms around me, and the second we touched, he must have caught it.

Now Joel was the one gasping. "Oh shit! We're off the rails! What's going on?"

I kept crying, and he held me. When my tears finally stopped, he looked at me with serious eyes for the first time all night.

"I remember now . . . How long have you . . .?"

"The whole time."

"That musta been heavy."

"Yeah, kinda."

"Why don't we go outside?"

"To see what year it is?"

"I wanna buy a calendar . . . But I guess the store's closed."

"It's 1971. Some version of 1971, at least."

"Damn." Joel dropped his shoulders.

"You want to go ask people what's going on, don't you? There's no point. You can't go around telling people the world isn't what it's supposed to be. Nobody's gonna listen."

"Yeah, pretty sure you're right about that. What's going on, though?"

"I don't know what caused it . . . But, right now, we're in my present *and* my past. We're in my time."

"So this is a dream of yours or something? Trippy . . ."

Yeah, maybe that was the best way to put it.

"And I bet I gave it to you when we touched. We must have been on the same voltage or something, mentally . . ."

Reyco suddenly felt a ton lighter.

"But it's alright. It's psychedelic. I'd dig a movie like this," Joel said, kind of chuckling.

"Wait, I just figured this out. This isn't my dream. Five minutes ago, I was so sure it was. If it is a dream, it's somebody else doing the dreaming."

"Hey, count me in. As long as it's a good ride . . ." Joel said as he held up one hand, his palm facing Reyco.

"Same here." She lifted a hand and put her palm against his. Pretty sure there was a scene like that in *Barbarella*.

Then the two of them had some fun together, and went to sleep. In the morning, the boy with blue-gray eyes made Reyco a croque monsieur and a cup of freshly brewed coffee. Then he walked her to the station. After spending the night so connected with Joel, Reyco was on the verge of tears when they said goodbye.

"Later," Joel said coldly—not like he was even trying to play it cool.

Then he walked off, returning to a time all his own.

— Well, this looks like our best shot.
— It'll have to work. Otherwise we're going to have to go even further back.
— The girl knows, doesn't she?
— I can take care of her.
— And what about the guy?
— He's already forgotten. He's not the type to get hung up on things.
— You sure about this?
— Yeah, it'll be fine. The characters won't suspect a thing, no matter what happens. That's the way they're made.
— You really think it's going to work?
— Like a charm. It'll feel more real than reality.

3

Reiko ran a hand over the pleats of her skirt.

August. A Friday afternoon in Shibuya. Nothing else to do. So here she was, waiting at the café.

(But seriously, what am I doing here? . . . Waiting for an older guy I met through work . . . A section chief in his late forties . . . I mean, who *am* I?)

Over the past two months, they'd met up every other week or so—and Reiko was already utterly bored.

(. . . I guess I've always been a little fickle, even when I was a kid, but it got a whole lot worse when I changed tracks— when I made up my mind to stop caring about looks . . . Even though I never *actually* stopped caring . . .)

On the fifth floor, up over Koen-dori. Girls and boys who all looked the same, coming and going. They all looked so baggy—so blissful. In front of Hachikō, a boy who got stood up by his date was desperately hitting on a girl passing by. As the afternoon presses on, the panic starts to show.

Shibuya. Far from Reiko's place, and far from the guy's office. That made sense . . . But why Koen-dori? Doesn't it make him sick to see the gaggles of kids walking around? What's going on in this guy's brain?

And what about Reiko? She was the one sitting here, wait-ing for this guy like some kind of chump.

Reiko started feeling more and more depressed.

She was happy when he called her up the night before. (Wasn't she?) Well, maybe not happy . . . But some sort of emotion in that general area. Then, the second she set foot in the café, that all went up in smoke.

Nevertheless. Here she was.

Eyes glued to the entrance.

She got here too early. Reiko pulled out the paperback she'd bought at Taiseido on the way over. *Groupie*. A trans-lated novel. She almost went with the latest issue of *Nutrition and Cookery*, but decided to go with something smaller instead.

She opened the book and started reading. Not bad. Right away, she could tell it was set in the seventies . . . Maybe a little earlier. The "psychedelic lighting" was a dead giveaway.

When Reiko looked up, there he was, sitting across from her.

"I'm ten minutes late," he said. "Sorry about that."

Reiko set the paperback down on the table between them. She'd taken off the brown paper cover they'd put on it at the bookstore.

"*Groupie?*" He said, reading the title out loud. "What's that mean?"

"You know . . . A girl who follows bands around, sleeping with the stars."

The words are heavy. It takes a lot of effort to get them out.

"Huh . . . Is that a thing these days?"

Reiko looks him straight in the eye. Geez, if he just had a better face. I mean, I'm not asking for much . . .

"It's nothing new. It was more of a thing in the past, really."

"News to me. So why do they do it?"

"Bragging rights with other girls. If they can pull it off . . ."

The waiter handed the man an oshibori. He gave his hands a quick wipe, then made a big production of wiping his face.

"If they can pull it off? You mean the girl's the one trying to get the guy into bed?"

"Yeah, of course," Reiko said with a little laugh.

"Ray-Co," the man said. The waiter bent forward, not sure what the man was saying. "I'll have a Raygun Cola," he said. The waiter nodded and walked off.

"That's what we call it back in Kansai . . . Ray-Co," he explained with a goofy smile.

Dumbass with a capital D.

"Yeah, I know."

"Same as your name."

Was that supposed to be a joke? *He* thought it was funny.

"Anyway, the guys are happy to oblige, right?"

Back to groupies.

"Oh, you'd be surprised. Competition's real stiff."

"Come on, there can't be that many of these groupers out there . . ."

"Groupies. And there are."

What a drag.

"Hnh. I had no idea. Maybe I should try my hand as a pop singer. Not that I know the first thing about music . . ."

Even if you did . . . At your age? With your face?

"You want the attention?" Reiko asked.

"Nah, I do well enough as it is. I'm a CCM," he said, leaning in over the table. "A certified chick magnet."

Where'd this guy come from?

But forget him . . . What about me? How'd I end up as an office lady? Everybody around me's mind-numbingly boring. I gave up the groupie life and studied my ass off to get into college, but why? For what?

"I saw in some magazine that girls go to the airport to meet foreign stars when they come to Japan . . . Are those groupies?"

"Nope, most of those girls are ordinary fans. There's a line, but who knows how clear it is . . ."

"I dunno, I don't get it. What are they thinking? There's no guarantee the guys are going to want to stay with them, right?"

Reiko didn't bother answering. She put the novel back into her bag. When she did, her fingers found something.

A tape.

"Hey, I brought this," she said, pulling it out to show him.

"That for work?"

"It's music."

"Oh, you listen to tapes?"

What else are you gonna do with them? That's what they're for, right?

"The last time I went out drinking with the young crowd from work, they hipped me to 'Saitama for Some Reason.' What an amazing song."

"Late to the party, huh?" Reiko laughed—all the while doing her best to keep from being mean.

"He went missing, right?"

"Who? Manzo Saita? They found him, ages ago . . . He's on For Life. These days, those guys don't put out anything but trashy novelty records. Ever since The Bonchi . . ."

Then Reiko realized. He had *no clue* what she was talking about. Not that he seemed to mind. Because he's a grade-A idiot.

When the waiter came back with the man's soda, he grabbed the straw and took the loudest sip. *Sluuurp*. This guy's slurps and smacks have been getting on Reiko's nerves since the second time they met up. Like nails on a chalkboard . . . She did her best to think about something else—to tune it out.

"So, where are we going?" Reiko asked.

With a big smile. God, I'm good at this. Too good.

But (Q:) What's the performance for?

(A:) So I don't have to spend my Friday nights alone.

"Ready to go?" The man took the bill.

"Yesterday was my birthday." Crap, why the hell did I say that?

"How old are you?" he asked, looking over his shoulder as he walked to the register. What an ugly way to turn around. Is a little attention to visual beauty too much to ask?

"Twenty-eight."

"Is that right? I'm forty-eight. We're exactly twenty years apart. Kinda perfect, huh?"

Perfect? I don't know about that—but he seemed satisfied in his own little world. Reiko went outside to wait, then they took the escalator down.

When they got to the street, they were surrounded by girls.

"Get a load of these dense-looking chicks. Not that they're fat or anything . . ."

"Dense?"

Oh, right. You have to explain everything to this guy.

"You know udon, right?"

"The food?"

"Know how udon's kinda dense? Compared to soba. These girls are like that."

"Huh . . . So what's a soba girl like?"

What the hell's going on in his head?

"Everything's got to be symmetrical for you, huh? Thesis, antithesis, synthesis. Nice and logical . . ."

"That's right," he said with a smirk. Is it any fun for this guy, being with me? If it is, I wonder *why*.

"So, where should we go?"

"Dunno. I haven't come here in ages."

"I've never come here . . . Wanna head over to Shinjuku?"

Then why'd he choose to meet in Shibuya?

"I know a place we can go there."

By this point, Reiko had given up. She was on autopilot. In "whatever" mode.

Anywhere would be *fine*—as long as it was nowhere near these hordes of trendy chickadees.

They walked toward the station, saying nothing as they went. This guy was one hundred percent okay with weird silences. It was normal for him. When they reached the corner, he leaned into the street to stop a cab. Reiko couldn't keep herself from checking him out. *Sizing him up*, really.

(What a shrimp. I bet we're pretty much the same height. His legs are shorter than mine. But at least he's no porker.)

Along with a dull pain, it hit Reiko. She was trapped in a life she could hardly call a happy one. She chalked it up to her own mindset. If she were more like Michiko from the office, she'd be happy enough. Michiko could get into any guy, no matter how repulsive he was. All she had to do was "decide" she was going to be into him.

For a few years, Reiko had been forming strategic alliances with women around her. She and Michiko had been playing friends for maybe two years now—she'd even told Michiko about this guy.

The taxi pulled up in front of them and the door opened. Reiko got in first, then the man hopped in after her.

The car headed down Meiji Dori. YMO was on the radio. The song: "Rydeen." Gimme a break, Reiko thought. This song was always playing on the speakers in the shopping district by her apartment. Nothing else, ever. The other day, when she was at the greengrocer's buying sweet potatoes, she started to wonder if the local station even had any other records, so she stood there for a while to see what would come on next. Sure enough, the second the song ended, it started over again from the beginning. Reiko remembered a flyer she'd seen for some joke band called IMO. She wondered if the name was supposed to be pronounced "imo"—like potato. Had to be. The album name: *Spud State Survivor*.

In Harajuku, the car stopped at a red light. "Tong Poo" came on.

"You know YMO?" As usual, it was Reiko who put an end to the awkward silence.

"No, what's that?"

"It's the name of the band on the radio."

"Oh yeah?"

Seriously, what rock has this guy been living under?

"YMO . . . Does that stand for something?"

"Mhm. Yellow Magic Orchestra. There's this drop-dead gorgeous guy in the band, Ryuichi Sakamoto . . ."

"Yellow Music Orchestra. You learn something new every day."

Ugh . . . Is it even worth saying anything?

Another silence. And this time she wasn't going to break it.

"Hey, you know a lot about music."

"Everybody knows YMO." She did all she could to keep from sighing.

The light turned green. When Reiko glanced out the rear windshield, she thought: (I know that place. Masahiko's played there.)

Masahiko? Who the hell is Masahiko?

There's a visual attached to the name. But the image is fading, just like an old dream. There's no memory there. When and where did they meet? Who was he? Who was she to him?

"A Love Psychedelic," Masahiko said.

(When? Where?) The words rang a bell.

Reiko pulled the cassette out of her bag and looked at the J-card. There it was: "A Love Psychedelic."

A song.

Shinjuku was getting closer . . .

When Reiko came to, the man was mid-sentence: ". . . if you stop and think about it. So time's just a human invention, see?"

She must have asked him something about time.

"Uh-huh," Reiko heard herself say, not really sure what she was agreeing with.

"It's nothing more than a concept."

"I wonder what made me ask you about time . . ."

"What made you . . .?" The man looked confused.

"My brain just went kinda fuzzy. Like I was coming into contact with another world or something . . . Did I look weird or anything?"

"Nah, not that I noticed."

With a guy like this, why bother asking?

"You don't notice much, do you?" There was an edge to her words.

"That's what my wife always says."

"That a joke?"

"No, milady—I speak only the truth."

I guess that's funny in his world. In his world, not in this one.

"Anyway, the girls at work are always saying it's exhausting when guys pay too much attention."

"Maybe those guys are paying attention to the wrong things. Or maybe the girls aren't quick enough to keep up. They sound kinda dense—like they just want a low-maintenance lobotomized lover."

Reiko shouldn't have gone there. She wasn't trying to hurt him.

When she's done talking, she gives him a long look, to see if he's okay.

But he is. He's fine, facing forward, talking to the driver. "Right there's good, thanks."

They got out and walked to Golden Gai.

Masahiko. He's a musician, I think. And he lives in West Shinjuku.

"Where was it again . . ."

The man was walking around, looking for the right bar, one hand stuffed in his back pocket. God, he looks idiotic. And those slacks aren't helping any. Beltless, the type that buttons up in the front. Gray with an ugly check. Old-school bell bottoms. And that polo shirt with its stupid little logo. (Why am I like this? My heart's made of stone. But am I sad about it? Not really. Not at all.)

Reiko started thinking about Masahiko again . . . Masahiko knows how to carry himself. It's a weird way to put it, but he's got grace. The way he handles things with care and lightness.

There was a staticky noise in Reiko's head. CLICK. CLICK. Almost like somebody changing the channel on the TV. CLICK.

There it was again. A clear signal—a connection.

Masahiko was there, looking at Reiko, just smiling at her. CLICK.

The man was ten feet ahead, a puzzled look on his face, turning back to look at her with his hand still shoved in his back pocket. Reiko caught up to him.

"I was testing you—to see what you'd do. Some people keep on walking." The lie just came out.

"Oh yeah?"

Hook, line, and sinker.

The place was a one-woman bar.

"I came here the other day, with the young crowd from work," the man said as he grabbed a stool. Reiko sat next to him, then put her bag down one seat over.

At the far end of the bar was a cheap little boombox.

"Mind if I put a tape on?" Reiko asked.

"Sure. There's a trick to it, though," said the lady behind the bar. "It goes the other way around . . . Yeah, just like that."

The tape opened with a real tearjerker: "The Setting Sun."

"This is a pretty old one, isn't it?" The lady looked up as she mixed their drinks.

"Sure is."

"What else is on this?" The man took a look at the case. "Huh, I don't know any of . . . Ooh, now we're talkin'! Play this one!"

Masahiko's so mature. But this guy . . .

Reiko abandoned her zero-star review before she could finish it.

"Which one?" she asked. With spiked kindness.

"'Kemeko's Song.' I love this one."

Without a word, Reiko got up and fast-forwarded the tape. The whole time "Kemeko" was playing, the man couldn't have looked any happier.

"Oh yeah . . . Uh-huh . . . That's what I call music."

Doesn't do a thing for me, Reiko thought. She couldn't keep herself from seriously judging anybody who dug this kind of junk. Just like that kid from work who wouldn't shut up about that brain-dead Snake Man Show routine on TV.

"Play it again," the man said as soon as the song ended.

Reiko wanted to scream—but she went along with it. "I bet you like 'The Drunk Returns,' too, don't you?" she asked.

"Oh yeah, I love that one!"

Go figure.

"I can't stand it."

"Why not? It's funny!"

"It's a gag song. It's *supposed* to make people laugh. I'm more into it when the musicians are serious as all get-out . . . When they pour their heart and soul into it, but you still wanna laugh."

"Like what?"

"Like Alice."

"The cartoon character? From *Alice in Wonderland*, right? Yeah, I know that one."

"No, from TV. *Alice in TV Land*."

"That's a show?"

"Nope. Just having fun."

"Hmph."

Mizuwari, pickled shallots.

"So, Michiko was going out with this really short guy . . ."

Nothing else to talk about.

"Michiko? Oh, right . . ."

"And, you know, I'm pure evil. I was talking with this other girl from work, and I was saying, 'I'd rather choke on my own tongue and die than go out with a guy like that . . .'"

But come on. Is this guy any better? I guess he's a step up — at least in status and stature.

"So what'd she say?"

He was listening, apparently, so Reiko kept going.

"Oh, she was right there with me. We were both like, if this was the last guy on earth, we'd just die virgins. We were totally serious, too. Then a minute later, it hit us, both of us at the same time. 'Uh . . . We're not virgins.' It was a full minute, though, I swear."

"Wait, you're not a virgin? I can't believe my ears!"

Omigod, somebody put me out of my misery! The lady behind the bar manages to muster a half-convincing laugh — but all I want to do is kick this moron to the ground and run out of this bar like my life depends on it.

But, for some reason, I can't. All I have to do is get up and say, "I'm going home." But there's this silent voice in the back of my head ordering me to stand down. A program I can't switch off.

The man got up. "Shall we?"

There was a hotel in the subway station building, and that was where they were going to stay. The same place as usual.

Reiko went over to the boombox to eject her tape, which had stopped playing a while back. Whatever's going on, the answer's here. On this tape. It's gotta be.

"We're not eating first?" Reiko asked as they walked.

"Oh, I couldn't care less about food. Guess I've always been a light eater. That's why I'm this skinny. And I don't wanna get fat. Fat people gross me out. Last thing I want to do is end up gross. Know what I mean? I can still wear the pants I bought when I was twenty-five. I've got amazing self-control."

"Yeah, except in the bedroom, maybe . . ." Reiko said, looking straight ahead.

"Hey . . ."

Serves you right. Sure, he's got no malice (same goes for Michiko), but he can really get under her skin sometimes. Not that she could ever explain that feeling to anybody else.

"What kind of guys did you go out with?"

"What, when I was younger?"

"I mean, you're still young now, but yeah . . ."

"I went for the really beautiful ones. I was a kind of groupie."

Joel from Green Grass. She went all the way to Honmoku to meet him. And then . . . something happened. That was ten years ago, but it's all a big blur now.

Even though he was the brightest of the stars.

Even though she was crazy about him.

And even now, when she sees pictures of Joel from back then, she can't help but sigh with emotion.

"So you were a sucker for a pretty face, huh?"

"Oh, the biggest."

What happened in Honmoku? We were together, in his room . . . And we were scared. But scared of what?

"So I guess at some point you had a change of heart, huh? If you're with a guy like me now."

Reiko knew what he wanted to hear.

She dodged: "I dunno."

"I mean . . ."

"You're my first older guy."

"For real?"

The way he said "for real"—the "real" shooting up like two octaves. Bet he picked that one up from the girls at his office.

"Oh, I take that back . . . Masahiko was a year older than me."

"Masahiko? Who's he? Your boyfriend before me?"

So, what? You're my boyfriend now?

"Uh-uh," Reiko said with a shake of her head. "The boyfriend before my last one."

Yeah, let's go with that . . . It sounds shallow and girly, but it'll do the trick.

The man wandered around, unable to find the hotel entrance. Reiko came to the basement-level tearoom sometimes, so she knew where it was, but she just followed after him, not saying anything.

They went up to the second floor, then the third.

"I know we've stayed here before, but . . ."

Geez, this guy's hopeless. If you gave him an electric kettle, he wouldn't be able to get the water to boil. Even if he had a hundred years to figure it out.

But the same shadowy voice in Reiko's head told her to go along with it.

They finally got to the entrance (Reiko told him where it was), then made their way to the front desk.

"A room for two," he said to the clerk.

"At the moment, we only have a room with twin beds," the clerk said back.

"That's fine."

"That'll be fifteen thousand yen."

The man handed the clerk two bills.

"Out of twenty . . . I'll need your name here."

The man grabbed a pen and wrote his name down. Reiko watched from maybe six feet away.

"Thank you, Mr. [- - -]."

It cut out! For the two seconds it took the clerk to say the man's name, sound ceased to exist—a total blank.

Possessed by a crushing anxiety, Reiko stepped forward to read the man's name off the paper, but the clerk had already taken the form away and handed the room key to the man.

He has to have a name! (Everybody does!)

The man walked to the elevator. Reiko followed him, in a trance.

We're getting closer now—closer to the heart of the mystery. Time is . . . And this hotel is . . .

"Room 2003," the man said.

"2003: A Space Case Odyssey," she muttered back. God, after a joke that bad, Reiko wanted to shoot herself into space.

The elevator doors slid open, and another couple got in with them.

I know Masahiko, Reiko told herself. So why isn't he the one here with me?

The elevator made its ascent. When they got out on the twentieth floor, Reiko felt the circuit switching in her head. This wasn't her first time on this floor.

Room 2003 . . . That faces the east exit. Why the hell do I remember that?

But when Reiko went into the room and pulled back the curtains, she saw the west side of the station.

"The world's turned around!" Reiko cried as she stood in front of the window. "This room's supposed to be on the other side! I remember!"

"Hey, take it easy," the man said as he took off his shoes.

"But look! The Triangle Building's over there!"

"So you misremembered. Nothing to get worked up about."

"No, I was here—with Masahiko!" Reiko shrieked hysterically. She'd come to the wrong world, and she knew it.

Reiko pressed her forehead up against the window and burst into tears.

"What's going on with you tonight?"

"It's this world . . . It isn't mine."

Now it really hits her.

Joel knew it, too. That night, when we touched. Time's out of whack. But he managed to forget—to put it behind him. (At least I think he did.)

"Come on, why so blue?" the man asked.

So even this doofus can be a little considerate.

"I'd rather die than be stuck in a time like this!" Reiko pushed against the glass. But it wasn't about to break.

"Hey, hey! Pull yourself together!" From behind, the man put a hand on her shoulder.

Reiko spun around and they bumped foreheads. The man pretended to stumble back. ". . . Fine, I'll say it," she said. "Don't you ever wonder why you don't have a name? Doesn't it bother you?"

It took a minute, but the color eventually drained from his face.

"You know why you don't have a name? It's this stupid ad-lib world! It wasn't like this before . . . Then salmon roe started falling out of thin air and some invisible being in the sky made sushi out of the stuff and ate it! I saw the whole thing with Masahiko, from his apartment!"

The man sank to the floor. Probably from the shock.

". . . I-I was living at the bottom of a lake, for tens of thousands of years," he said. "Nothing to keep me company except my thoughts. Yeah . . . I thought a lot about big concepts. Concepts like time . . ."

The two of them sat there on the floor, their faces pale. No music was playing.

The time criminal was sentenced to permanent deletion. Cloning him was strictly forbidden.

AFTER EVERYTHING

Snakes emerge from the ocean. The hard sky glitters a deep, uniform blue. Beneath its massive, perfect dome, deformed snakes like antediluvian lifeforms crawl up onto the land The sun, perfectly still in the dead center of the sky, is a single rotten eye. The snakes slither up over yellow dunes ruled by that merciless eyeball, their breath coming in gasps.

I know, you see. Even sitting quietly beside this stone stair, I know. Far in the distant past, the relationship between two people was sundered. Back then the sky was a dusky purple, and the gratingly sharp light fell on the iron handrail of a fire escape. The light had turned to ice and was burning. In truth, the purple of the sky was nauseating, stagnant. Far off a siren was blaring.

I believe I let my long, long girlhood pass in suffering. I was always sweating, dragging all that excess fat around with me. I was aware of my own stink.

Two people parted ways then. I needed to get to that place as soon as I possibly could—this was something I vaguely felt long after the fact. These irrevocable events proceeded exactly as scripted. And though I knew, I couldn't do anything about it. After all, I was a sorry excuse for a girl for a hundred years, maybe more.

The snakes keep coming. Here I am spending a peaceful afternoon sitting among the azaleas. Does everyone know about the snakes? About this endless stream of creatures who seem to be fleeing the ocean?

Two ladies leisurely descend the stone steps, a couple of real beauties in kimonos, strolling through the sunlight. One wears a flamboyant flower pattern on a black background. She looks sterner than the other.

"What's that hairstyle called?" her companion, dressed all in cream, inquires. Her voice is soporific, elusive.

"Don't you know?" the woman in black smiles.

"No . . ."

"It's called 'The Siege of Port Arthur.'"

At length their voices fade and disappear. Probably because it's just too hot. Like there's gold dust dancing in the air. No wind. Nothing moves.

I gaze at the path below the stone stair. The ladies' sons are crouched there, scratching something into the ground. Five and six years old.

The decisive parting happened long, long ago, and then it was all over. A mind-bogglingly long time passed, and everyone forgot about it. Things decayed completely, until there was no way for them to break down any further. And a long time passed after that process of decay had ended.

I've always been walking. And I have to keep on walking. Because I still haven't found my little brother. That boy, his body a specimen adorning the bright, happy sunroom of the facility, just *might* have been my brother. But staring at the internal organs neatly packed inside his splayed-open belly, I thought, no—this isn't the child I'm searching for.

Back when my skin was still humming with filthy life, I lived in a big house with all my siblings. Twelve, maybe eighteen—anyhow, there were a lot of us. One of them went missing, I believe, and I think one of my older sisters killed herself. No one much cared about any of it. And I gave up on having a single stream of memory, too. I'm pretty sure our beautiful, demented mother had already picked up husband number five somewhere along the way. Thanks to her unstinting efforts, my siblings must have ballooned to a staggering number at this point.

The tangle of snakes fills the beach to overflowing. Their glistening, livid backs entwine, secreting mucus on one another. They begin to erode the land.

The two beauties are standing, chatting cheerfully, while their sons play together cheek to cheek. One throws his soft arm around the other's neck and whispers something in his ear. The younger boy giggles. I'm able to see every single one of their overlong eyelashes with perfect clarity.

Time is passing at a stupendous rate. With an unchanging viscosity. Things just sluggishly weather away to nothing. That purple sky will never come again. Whatever happens, no one will be surprised. No one will notice; after all, they've long abandoned the act of remembering. Maybe they can't even die.

Maybe the boy I'm looking for isn't a human being. Day followed night, and night followed day. Wounds closed, then opened again, then dissolved to the point that it was impossible to discern their original form. And yet if that child is somewhere (and I'm convinced he is), surely it's beyond him to be alive and waiting.

In town, the people are beaten down by the sun's rays. They crawl across the ground, clawing their way through the tepid air. Knowing full well the end will never come, they simply endure the pain. He had been staring at my naked back with eyes like razors. I was forever enduring the pain, so I could never think about anything else. I took off my clothes and did my piecework, then once again gave my love to him.

Such is the film that unreels before my eyes as I sit among the azaleas. I was a plenty good girl, so he made me a lot of promises. Why? I have no idea. I was always one hundred percent submissive, obedient to anyone and everyone. Because something irrevocable had happened. Because I couldn't stop it from happening.

Below the stone stair, the six-year-old is gouging out the other boy's eye. With something like a metal chopstick. Torrents of blood gush over the boy's chin and onto his shirt. Their mothers are still chatting. I stand up. I can't stay here. Got to keep searching.

Tens of thousands of snakes surge onto the highway. Everyone watches quietly, with eyes like hollow pits.

THE COVENANT

"Hurry up and turn off the light," his wife said, her back still turned toward him. "How am I supposed to sleep? I have to be up at six, you know."

The implication was clear: *unlike you.* He let out a long sigh and picked up a cigarette off the nightstand.

"Turn it off? Please?" His wife was getting annoyed.

"Just a little longer . . . Is that really so much to ask? I've got some thinking to do." He lit the cigarette with a match from a coffeehouse matchbook.

"Oh yeah? What else is new . . . What are you always pondering, anyway? Pretty sure it's not how to find a job. All you ever think about is ESP or 'unexplained phenomena' or whatever."

Not being able to get to sleep seemed to be making her cranky. Then again, his wife was never sympathetic to such topics: the face of a dead friend filling the sky above the train platform, a woman's head floating impossibly among the crowd. It happened all the time. To him.

"So what does it look like?" she had asked him once.

"Well, it's bizarre. Just a disembodied face kind of hanging there. But it happens all the time, so I try not to let it bother me. I mean, right this minute, I can see clean through you to the bones, from your shoulders down to your ribs."

He always went on like this. His wife suspected that it was what had gotten him fired, however indirectly. Not that she ignored this part of him, let alone looked down on him for it. In his case, maybe it wasn't ESP but simple delusion. His mental state was very unstable. He was even hospitalized once after he'd spent a whole week raving about all kinds of things that made no sense. But she had no such gifts. It made her feel somehow left out. What a drag.

He lay there smoking.

As far as his wife was concerned, he could sit there contemplating forever. She didn't mind, so long as it didn't inconvenience her.

He stubbed out his cigarette and switched off the lamp. The light coming in through the curtains was surprisingly bright. They lived on the second floor, which made it worse.

"Can you hear it?" he asked.

"'It,' what?" All she could hear were the sounds of sirens and the voices of drunk college students going by below their window.

"Oh, okay, sorry. For the past three days someone's been beaming these transmissions into my brain . . . I wonder what it's all about."

"Yesterday, when we were in Suginami, didn't you say all the people who had died that day were walking along a road right underneath us?"

"Yup. That was one for sure. Mostly old folks, but there was the odd younger person mixed in, too. Though they weren't so much walking as floating. They hadn't yet realized that they were nothing more than souls now. And at night they started wandering around aimlessly. I was so focused on them that I couldn't pay proper attention to this signal. It's a distress signal. And it's getting gradually stronger. At first I thought it was coming from somewhere inside Japan, but the feel isn't quite right. I wonder if it isn't coming from another planet."

"In the Milky Way?"

"I'm not exactly sure. But probably, yeah. It's pretty exhausting, but I'll try and focus my awareness on it for a while." He sat up and leaned against the headboard. Folding his arms, he closed his eyes.

She got out of bed and went into the kitchen. She thought about making tea but decided against it, since she was about to go to sleep. Instead she got some ice and poured herself a glass of juice, then grabbed the cheesecake out of the fridge. They hadn't paid that month's rent yet. The super was *not* pleased.

Getting back into bed, she opened her mouth wide and shoved some cake in. Then a sip of juice. He was still sitting with his eyes closed, same as before. Being with him used to be terribly draining, but she'd gotten used to it. No need to get worked up. Best just to let him be.

She ate a piece and a half of cake. Half a piece was plenty for him. Then she smoked a cigarette, a habit she'd just taken up.

". . . Got it." At last he opened his eyes and uncrossed his arms. She handed him the juice. He ignored the straw and drank straight from the glass. She returned the straw to the tray on the nightstand.

"They come from a distant planet, and they need help. See, there were these amoeba-like organisms lying dormant in their polar regions for a long time, but when their planet's axis suddenly tilted, the organisms began to proliferate with terrifying rapidity. They've engulfed seas, mountains, plains, cities . . . they're threatening to envelop the entire surface of the world. At first they were just single cells, but when split in two they recombined again right away. They oozed steadily out from the poles, driving the intelligent life on their planet into the regions around the equator—swallowing up a lot of people in the process. The amoebae from the two poles linked up and became one giant cell engulfing just about the entire surface of the planet. The high equatorial mountains are all that's left for what remains of the population. Their messiah is on top of one of the peaks, in a white robe, praying—that's the only thing left for them to do. This savior is desperately seeking aid from other planets. I want to find a way to help them. Okay, here I go again."

While he was again focusing his awareness, his wife wolfed down the rest of the cake.

She could hear more sirens in the distance. Lot of fires tonight, she thought to herself. Mind you, they did live less than half a mile from the fire station. She could also hear what sounded like an ambulance.

"Their planet is very far away," he murmured after about half an hour. "The transmission I'm receiving was sent almost five thousand years ago. The situation on their planet has probably changed by now. Still, I'd sure like to rescue them. Though I don't think my mental powers would be up to it. To saving a whole planet, I mean. Let me try again."

Another thirty minutes passed.

It was already past 3 a.m. She worked at a little bar, so it didn't matter too much, but there went her morning of housework. Even so, she was fascinated, and sat watching him intently. He was illuminated by the faint light from outside. His eyes were shut tight and he was wrinkling his brow.

She got up again and went to the bathroom; she'd drunk the rest of his juice as well.

Before getting back into bed, she took down a book from the shelf: *Eleven Children Who Remember Their Past Lives.* She absolutely loved this kind of nonfiction, but he thought such books were stupid and wouldn't touch them. He had no interest in anything but his own powers, whatever lay within the bounds of his own abilities.

Back in bed, she turned on the light and began to read. She became more and more absorbed.

"It's all okay," he finally declared in a relieved voice. "Crisis averted. A sort of tempest arose and unleashed a hailstorm that drove the organism into retreat."

"Wait, but it came from the poles in the first place, didn't it? And it's vulnerable to little clumps of ice? That doesn't make sense."

"No, see, the hail was falling with tremendous force. And over a massive area. We're talking about a hailstorm beyond anything we could conceive of on Earth. Like a storm of blades falling from the sky. The amoeba got slashed to ribbons. The people were smart, though, and they hid in underground shelters."

"... Uh-huh." She didn't really get it but was more or less satisfied. "Well, that's nice." She left it at that. She had developed a habit of dealing with it this way whenever he talked with such conviction about his ESP, especially when it was totally illogical.

"You're reading *that*? Well, guess we've all got our interests," her husband said. But who was he to talk? He was the one who was always saying he could pinpoint people's past and future lives, like some kind of fortune teller. And what was wrong with an interest in reincarnation, anyway?

"Tell me about my past life," his wife said.

"Let's see now," he began with an earnest expression. "You were a little green tree frog. Or maybe just a fly," he said conclusively, brushing her off.

"What about you?"

"Me? The son of God. Pretty sure I was Jesus Christ."

"Every mental hospital has a couple of patients who think that, from what I hear. Who think they're Jesus, or the emperor. The older ones think they're General Nogi or Douglas MacArthur. Some of them even think they're Hitler, apparently."

"But I really am the Messiah. I've never told anyone this before, but when I was seven, I saw God. Back then we lived in an apartment building with a courtyard in the center. The road in front of the building ran along a river, with a baseball field on the other side. I was playing in the courtyard with my dog when a figure wearing an outfit straight out of Ancient Greece descended from the sky, stopping about six feet off

122

the ground. At first the dog barked at him, but then suddenly shut up and sat obediently. I'm pretty sure it was either God or a space alien. If it had only been me, I'd say it was just a daydream . . . but my dog was there, too, and he was definitely reacting to something.

"This guy, his entire body was kind of translucent, and he said to me, 'I will bestow upon you the power of the Messiah.' He wasn't speaking Japanese, or it wasn't that I heard his voice, exactly; it's more like he was inside my head and I could instantly know what he wanted to tell me. Then he showed me all these things that were going to happen in the world, kind of like a news reel. He disappeared after about fifteen minutes, and my dog, he just sat there and stared."

"Well, then, what was this special power he bestowed on you?"

"Well, I mean, that's—"

"So I was a tree frog and you're Jesus Christ?"

"It was a joke."

"Then use your . . . psychic powers or clairvoyance or whatever and tell me about my previous life, please."

"It's incredibly tiring. I just finished receiving an extraterrestrial transmission, you know? I'm totally worn out. Plus, I don't want to know about myself or the people close to me," he said solemnly. "I mean, we're talking about *truth*, about something nobody knows. It's too much."

She pretended to listen, but she only heard about half of what her husband said, and even that evaporated more or less right away. She was busy thinking about how to portion out her next paycheck. They were in a lot of debt; she would put fifty or sixty thousand yen toward paying it off, and the rent was forty-eight thousand, which left . . .

"I wonder where their planet is, though," he mused.

"61 Cygni." She said the first thing that came into her head. It could just as well have been Alpha Centauri.

"No, I don't think so . . . And given that their telepathic communication was able to reach Earth, at least a few dozen of them are probably here already."

Her mother darted glances at the TV as she put on her makeup, lurid blue eyelids peeking out from behind her giant compact. "Akiko, you seen my false eyelashes?"

The girl looked back at the middle-aged woman in exasperation.

"I bought some the other day. I'm sure I put 'em in the drawer, so where the hell are they?"

"How should I know? You're such a mess, Mom." Akiko turned back to the eighteen-inch screen. Not that there was anything particularly interesting on. She just didn't feel like talking to her mother.

"Ugh, look at Miss Stumpy there. What a freak, I mean, come on." Her mother's gaze was fixed on the TV, powder puff frozen halfway to her face. "Guess some people are just born with short little legs . . . But no need to flaunt them on TV. Why would you embarrass yourself like that?"

Akiko looked back at her mother, but then returned her gaze to the screen. It was too much hassle to say anything. And why did the old hag always put on so much makeup? She couldn't wait till she got to the bar? Her mother uncapped some lipstick and began to apply it, one eye still on the television. She didn't use a brush, so it strayed a little outside the lines. Then she went over those parts again to make them darker. She had told Akiko once that this made her thin lips look more sensual. To which she added: "Wouldn't look so good on a girl with naturally thick lips like yours." Always had to get that dig in.

After the lipstick came the perfume. Akiko looked at the clock beside the doll display case. It was just after six. It would be another hour at least before her mother left.

"Akiko, call the liquor store for me. Two cases of beer, and the same whiskey and brandy as always. Three bottles each. And some wine. Sachi should already be there, so tell 'em not to leave the bottles outside the shop like they always do."

Akiko stood up and did as she was told. The liquor store owner asked about mineral water, and she told him to throw some in. After she hung up, she said, "There's no way Sachi's there yet."

"That girl's a hard worker—she's there alright. Cleaning behind the bar, I expect. I have faith in her. Just about the only person in the world I *can't* trust is my own daughter." Her mother dismissed Akiko's remark in her usual offhanded style. Akiko had been standing by the phone, but now she went into her own tiny bedroom. What she really wanted to do was climb inside the built-in wardrobe, close the doors, and hold her breath. But if she did, her mother would start yelling, "You little lunatic!" with that terrifying expression of hers, so she thought better of it.

The room was dark. Darkroom blackout curtains hung from the ceiling. Akiko sat down on the edge of her single bed. She opened the drawer, and there was the gold-colored lighter she'd gotten from the middle-aged man. Underneath it was her diary. She opened it and read the entry from the day before. After the date were written a strange series of numbers and symbols:

666—9 ◉☆ Distance
Finally discovered the truth. Now I just have to prove it. I found out how in "the Room of Revelation." All I have to do is put it into practice. 6 and 9 are dancing.
These numbers have profound meaning.

Akiko closed the diary. Her thoughts were so idiosyncratic that no human being would be able to comprehend them. The notion made her happy. Her mother might've been sneaking peeks at her diary for all she knew, but the woman was too feebleminded to comprehend what was in it. She was of a different species, after all.

"Hurry up and get in the bath." The hoarse voice came through the door.

"Later," Akiko mumbled.

"I'll shut off the valve, then!" Her mother must've finished with her makeup. Akiko could hear her opening the bureau. "What to wear, what to wear. Maybe this lamé number? Ahh, what a mess. My necklaces are all tangled up . . . Guess I'll have to wear the ivory one. But it's so dull. Maybe the one that looks like a string of gold leaves would be better. It's dark in there, no one'll be able to tell it's fake. Or maybe the opals—Akiko!" She'd been lying on her bed listening to her mother's muttered soliloquy. "Come here and tell me which one looks better."

"Just wear whichever one you want. You've been in the nightlife biz long enough." The girl stayed where she was and buried her face in the pillow.

"Come on, just tell me which one looks better."

"What's wrong with the leaves? They're nice and gaudy!" Akiko raised her face and yelled.

The sliver of sky she could see between the curtains was filled with the dusky blue of twilight. Beloved night was almost here. Night, without her mother. Night, alone. Akiko had been alone ever since she was a child. She'd never had friends. She'd been a taciturn, expressionless, polite child. Her good grades had made her something of a teacher's pet, but she never cared about any of that. After many long years of resenting the fact that no one loved her, she had conceived a vague hatred for this world.

About two years ago, even that had stopped bothering her. She didn't care anymore that her mother saw her as nothing but a burden. It was only natural that no one understood her. A forgone conclusion. So she hadn't felt a thing even when a boy she went to school with tried to gas himself after she ignored the love letter he'd written her. *I guess he must've convinced himself he was in love with me*, was all she thought. He didn't understand a goddamn thing. It was himself he was really infatuated with. No one could ever understand me. Seeing as I'm not even from this planet . . .

The boy had been back on his feet in no time, and about two months later he changed schools. The few classmates who knew the whole story blamed Akiko for being so cold. But everyone forgot about it pretty much right away.

People forget everything so quickly, Akiko thought to herself. But there's one thing that I, at least, can never forget. A promise made before I was born. I was given life so I could fulfill that promise, and to that end I'll spare no sacrifice.

"Akiko, come zip me up." Her mother was calling her. It seemed she had at long last decided what to wear. In the living room she found her mother in a sparkly dress, her plump back bared. Akiko zipped up the dress and fastened the catch at the top.

"Guess I'll have a little snack before I go. I'm already dressed, so go make some tea for me, will you? And there's some pizza in the fridge, heat that up too?"

You could just go to the bar and dine out on some customer's dime, Akiko thought, but she kept quiet. Lately her mother always wanted to be shoving something into her mouth. Maybe she'd gotten gluttonous in the face of old age? These days she was constantly eating, no longer a bit concerned about getting fat. When Akiko had mentioned it to her classmate Nana, she'd said, "She's frustrated, *obviously*. Miyako says her mama's always gorging herself, too."

"How about yours?" asked Akiko. Nana smiled faintly.

"Well, she's fooling around on the side. She dolls herself up to look young, then goes out on the town with some student . . . twenty-one, maybe twenty-two years old. Divorce has gotta be right around the corner."

It was almost time for her phone date with Nana. But her mother was still just sitting there, smoking up a storm. Get out of here already.

Akiko poured her some iced tea.

"Thanks, this is perfect. It's so hot today." Her mother fanned her chest. Her eyes, as ever, were glued to the screen.

Akiko covered the surface of a frying pan with two sheets of aluminum foil, on which she arranged the pizza, cut into six equal pieces.

"If you're going to use the stove, be sure to turn the vent on."

"Duh." Akiko pulled the cord, then sat down on the kitchen chair. "Hey Mom, are you my real birth mother?" she asked absently.

"Well, you're a strange girl," her mother replied, her back still to Akiko. "What kind of a question is that? Of course I am."

"Who was my father?"

"The man I divorced a year after you were born. Now he's with that woman, and they've got two kids together."

Akiko turned so she was sitting wrong way round on the chair and folded her arms on the back. "You sure someone else wasn't my father?"

"What the hell kind of nonsense is that? What, are you asking if I had another man?" Her mother turned to look at her for the first time.

"No, not at all . . ."

"He's your father, sorry as I am to say it."

"Mom, before I was born, did you see a shooting star or a UFO or anything?"

"Hmmm, I don't remember. It was seventeen years ago, after all . . . But people think they see that stuff all the time, don't they? Because of optical illusions and what have you. What, you want to think you're somebody special? Like I experienced some kind of revelation, or had a dream about the sun flying into my womb before you were born . . .? Everyone your age would like to believe the same thing."

"You just don't get it, Mom."

"You were born at the hospital. The city hospital, just down the road. It was a terribly difficult birth, and my body was in tatters. They sewed me back up but I spent too much time walking around while I was still in the hospital and I popped my stitches. At any rate, your father was too busy hanging around with that floozy—he never once came to see me. My mental state wasn't too good—how's that pizza coming?"

Akiko put the pizza onto a plate and brought it out to the living room. Her mother tucked a handkerchief into the front of her dress in place of a napkin and picked up a slice.

"Mom . . . How come I don't have any siblings?"

"I was pregnant at the time of the divorce, but I got rid of it." Her mother's eyes acquired that gentle look they always did when she was recalling the past. "Mm. Would've been nice to have one more, but I had to work. Are you lonely?"

"No."

"Then what's the problem? Since you're an only child, I can afford to buy you whatever you want."

Akiko had no use for "things." She just wasn't interested. When she was in her third year of middle school, her mother had bought her an expensive sweater. Akiko hadn't even pretended to be pleased. "You ingrate!" her mother had screamed, before bursting into tears. "I work my ass off day and night. And all for you! How can you be so heartless?"

130

After that, Akiko began putting on a show of being pleased. And once she did, she discovered there was nothing to it. She would say, "It's beautiful," or, "It's just what I wanted," or "Hooray, thanks," and her mother never seemed to notice how hollow it was. No one did.

Akiko was aware that she came off as morose, so she forced herself to appear cheerful. She would keep it up all day at school and be completely exhausted by the time she got home. But it was impossible to maintain the performance forever. No matter how sunny she tried to be, she never made a single friend.

Last fall, she'd been sitting at the library reading Unica Zürn's *Man of Jasmine*. As she read, she gazed at the poplars outside the window. The wind blew and the trees bent. Beyond them, the men's track-and-field team was practicing in the crystalline sunlight. The leaves of the poplars were tinged with yellow but showed no signs of falling. They appeared fragile, yet they defied the wind.

Through another window, she could see a line of cypresses. Was it the wind that sculpted them into a shape like a flame? When Akiko had wanted a book of Van Gogh paintings, she hadn't said anything to her mother. The only times she ever asked her mother to buy her anything were when she needed something for school, or when the holes in her shoes had gotten so big that on rainy days her socks and feet would end up covered in mud. That was about it. When she'd wanted a book of Georg Trakl's poems, she'd kept quiet about that too. Unless it was something she wanted so badly she was willing to kill for it, she would never ask for anything. Her mother had no feeling for painting or poetry, and seemed to think that as long as a young woman had makeup and pretty clothes, she was all set. Her mother had bought her nice-smelling face powder, mascara, eyebrow pencils. For her sixteenth birthday, she'd had a baroque black pearl set in a silver ring for her. "Once you've got some money, you can have it set in platinum." But before the week was out, Akiko lost it down the bathtub drain. It had been too loose. A size nine or ten would've fit perfectly, but her mother had ordered an eleven. It had slipped off her finger while she was soaping herself up. Her mother's feelings were hurt, and since then she'd only bought Akiko cheap imitations.

For a while Akiko didn't notice that another girl had sat down at the same table; she was too wrapped up in the cypresses.

"Do you ever get the feeling those trees are fake?" Nana said quietly. When Akiko looked up, the girl had her elbows propped on the table, showing off her lovely profile. Akiko just stared at her classmate without replying—it was exactly what she'd been thinking. "Then again, all human beings are just actors. Everyone's a fake. It's one thing if you're aware of it, but some people seem convinced the role they're playing is the real them. They're the worst."

"Who do you mean?" Akiko asked.

"The ones who've turned into the characters they're playing? That's pretty much everyone, isn't it?" Nana's voice was calm. Akiko felt strangely drawn to her.

"What about you?"

"Me? I'm different," Nana said casually. "And so are you. I've been watching you for a while now. Thought maybe you'd be someone I could talk to."

"But you've got tons of friends. Boyfriends, too."

"As an accessory for my lifestyle, sure. Just out of necessity." Nana's quiet voice made a deep impression on Akiko. "Wanna come to my house later? If we tell my folks we're studying together, they'll be thrilled. Because they don't understand a goddamn thing . . . My room's detached from the rest of the house, which makes all kinds of things easier."

Akiko agreed immediately.

The two of them gazed out the window at the quiet golden autumn for a long time. Somewhere the school chorus was singing "Zigeunerleben." It was a languid afternoon.

There was a piano in Nana's room. She lifted the fallboard, and after playing two or three classical pieces, she started in on some traditional jazz: "This is Bud Powell. 'Cleopatra's Dream.'" Even Akiko could tell the song required serious skill.

"Where'd you learn to play like that?"

"From the record. I just listen and imitate it. It's fun. Should I play 'Lucille' next? I do the Everly Brothers' version. The beginning is all harmonies. You know the words, right? Oh, then the sheet music's right there."

Akiko spent the whole afternoon enjoying Nana's playing. She's got talent, she thought to herself. When she said it out loud, Nana laughed.

"People who can play like this are a dime a dozen in the clubs on the edge of town. I'm nothing special. But who cares? I've got a goal in life."

"What is it?"

"Maybe something you can relate to. See, sometimes I wonder if I'm really a human being at all. But I think it's just

133

that I've lost something. I don't feel anything. I can't empa-thize with anyone. So, I'm thinking about falling in love. If I could feel all that jealousy and pain and whatever else comes with it, maybe I could get my human emotions back."

"Self-healing?" Akiko threw out a term she'd read in a book somewhere.

"Something like that. Right now I've got my sights set on my mom's lover. Mama's wrapped around his finger, but that's because she's a fool. Since I'm never going to love anyone, I figure it'll make a good primer. And if I do end up falling in love for real, well, so much the better. I'll become a human being!"

"And what'll you do then?"

"I don't think about that."

Apparently, Nana had been raped by her brother when she was twelve and he was sixteen. Her memories of it were hazy, though. Both girls felt a faint hatred for the male of the species: Nana because of her brother, Akiko because of the father who had abandoned her.

"I come from a distant planet," Akiko confided. "This was thousands of years ago now, but the planet was dying, and in an attempt to save us, our Messiah cast a bunch of spells on me so that I could be reborn as an alien on a faraway world. My body effectively died, and I was reborn here, now, on Earth."

"When did you find out?"

"About a year ago. It was told to me in a dream. After that, whenever I focused on the night sky and prayed, I would see a shooting star, or sometimes a UFO. My brother was supposed to come to Earth the same way, but I guess he failed. Older or younger I don't know, but either way, a member of the opposite sex I could completely rely on."

"Not an older brother, then," said Nana. "I'm sure of it. I bet he's about two years younger than you, don't you think? I've got a younger brother myself, and he's adorable. I totally depend on him, for everything. Older brothers disgust me. I'd like to kill them all." Nana scowled, which she almost never did.

"He's my younger brother *and* my older brother, and my lover, and my betrothed. We were promised to each other in a covenant, thousands of years ago. A promise is a vow between people. But when God is involved, it becomes a covenant. Like the Ark of the Covenant: that's a compact with God. A covenant is sacred. But these days the word's been stripped of its meaning. Now it's cheap—just a name for insurance brokers and trucking companies. The thing that links me and 'him' isn't God, though. It's fate. I'm sure of it."

"Sounds like you've got it made," Nana said. "Compared to me, anyway. I suppose I'll just wind up as a delinquent."

Ever since then, they'd been best friends.

After about six months, they added a third member: their classmate Miyako. She'd been baptized at thirteen and was planning to enter a convent. This girl was pure and innocent, but because her family ran a boarding house, all the students who came from Tokyo became her friendboys (that's what they called male friends when there wasn't even a whiff of sex in their relationship). She tried to see the best in people.

The three of them did everything together.

In junior year they all got put in the same class again, it being the only one for non-collegebound students in their year. Miyako was planning to enter the convent after graduation, and she had so many siblings (six) that her parents didn't raise much of a stink about it. Nana was completely absorbed in her self-proclaimed "phony" love affair, and her household was on the verge of collapse. Akiko's mother had gone to college, but after all the setbacks she'd suffered, she'd come to believe that "women don't need an education."

Her mother finally left.

Akiko dialed Nana's number.

"So, seven-thirty at the usual coffeehouse? I'll let Miyako know. We're meeting that middle-aged guy around, what, nine? Hey, let's get him to buy us a bunch of stuff. He loves swanning around with a gaggle of young girls on his arm, seems to think it'll make him young again, so he's a total pushover."

"That idiot is the perfect sacrifice," Akiko said in a low voice.

"Exactly. He thinks we hang out with him because of his status and money—because of his 'male gravitas,' in other words. What a sap. He actually believes a bunch of high school girls would go out with him based on his personal charm. Moron. Women just want to use human men for their own ends, and that goes double for us."

"Might not be true of Miyako, though."

"I know. I'd be lying if I said I didn't feel a little awkward about it. She's not as twisted as we are. At this point it's too late to drop her, though, right? I'll call her once we get off the phone, but I kinda hope she's not there. I don't want that girl to see how dirty the world can . . . Hey Akiko, do you think I'm getting soft?"

"Not a chance."

"You and me, we *have* to despise human men. I mean, if that hatred isn't fully realized, love can't take a distinct form either. Assuming love even exists, that is. We lost our feelings somewhere along the way. But maybe Miyako doesn't need that hatred."

"Just try calling her anyway?"

"Okay. We'll see what happens."

Nana was always confirming with Akiko: "We're friends, right? If we weren't, there'd be no one I could be real with. Even that student I'm dating, it's not like I can let him see all of me. But he's head over heels. He was talking about leaving Mama. I had to stop him. I told him not to do anything crazy, that we had to keep our relationship a secret. Plus, he gets money from her. I'm sick to death of him."

Abruptly, Akiko declared: "That middle-aged guy will be our sacrifice. It came to me in a vision. It *absolutely has* to be that way. It's our destiny, the Covenant says so. It's preordained. I'm gonna do it. Do you want to stop me?"

"Stop you? I've always let you do what you like. By which I mean I've kept out of it, I guess. What I'm saying is, do whatever you want. I don't think I'd feel much of anything if you did kill him. I suspect I'd be better off having an affair with a man who had a more . . . nineteenth-century 'disposition.' I'm fed up with saccharine words and sentimental atmospheres. I need a man with a burning lust for life, like Julien

Sorel, only who'd look after me. Good luck finding anyone like that, though."

Akiko washed her face and changed her clothes. She put on a layer of foundation and dusted it with baby powder. The stuff her mother had bought her was pink and didn't suit Akiko's sallow complexion. She drew in some light eyebrows, added mascara, and voilà. Having checked her twenty-one-and-a-half-inch waist in the big mirror by the front door, she went out, satisfied.

The three of them sat at a table next to a tank alive with tropical fish and chatted for a while. Mostly about how things were at home.

"Mama's worried that her student might have a new girlfriend. Not that she'd ever in a million years dream it was her own daughter. The lady"—only Nana and Akiko referred to their mothers this way—"constantly throws money at him, but it all ends up in my pocket. So let me get the bill."

"You're flush tonight? Then yes, please. That sound good, Miyako? Whoever's got money pays?"

"I've been working part-time too, you know. At the beach-side spot my family runs. You came once, Akiko, remember? So I can—"

"Don't worry about it," Nana cut her off. "You save your money, Miyako. You've been volunteering and all, that's gotta be tough."

"Oh, right. I still have to go buy a knife." Akiko stood up. Miyako didn't ask why. There was a lot about Akiko and Nana that remained mysterious to her. But the strange thing was that, no matter what they did, they somehow seemed

138

purer than the other girls at school. In fact, that was precisely what had held their threesome together this long.

"There's a home goods store right near here. The place we're meeting him's about a twenty-minute walk. So we've still got half an hour."

The three fell silent and sat watching the angelfish. Akiko took the poetry collection out of her bag and began reading "Sebastian in Dream."

"At first I thought it was 'Sebas-chan,' but I think the German pronunciation is more 'like Sebas-tee-an'."

Miyako: "Is that from the martyrdom of Saint Sebastian?"

"What else?" Akiko turned the page.

"I don't like that picture. There's something . . . carnal about it. Also, I don't know . . ."

"Homoerotic?" Akiko bailed her out.

"Yeah, sometimes it looks that way to me. But maybe that's just my own impurity before God."

"The only one who's impure is whoever painted that picture." Nana brushed the whole thing off as lightly as ever. "A naked man stretched out with a chest full of arrows? It's a wet dream for all the gay masochists out there."

"Still, this poem is great." Akiko started reading again.

The air conditioner was on though it was almost autumn. Nana had spent the previous fall riding around on a motorcycle in a leather jumpsuit. She'd adopted the look because she was a beauty with long legs (and knew it). This being the boonies, rumors started flying instantly, but thanks to the fact that her dad was a bigshot in town and her mother's half-brother was a full-fledged gangster, she never got into trouble. The police just turned a blind eye. Nana was hell on

139

wheels, but Miyako sensed something pathetic in her. She was beside herself with worry about both her friends. Akiko was a picture-perfect honors student, but there were times when everything she talked about seemed to be describing an imaginary world, and her robotic coldness did bother Miyako.

She felt she had to do something for them. But I'm so weak, can I really save these two? she wondered, with (what she believed to be) the perfect pure-heartedness of a maiden.

"Hey, this bit here—*With compassion a bearded face bowed down*—do you think he's talking about Jesus?" Akiko put her finger on a line in the open book and showed it to Miyako. Miyako read the whole poem. Given the references to "Saint Peter's churchyard," "Holy night," the "rosy angel," "Easter bells," it certainly seemed to have a Christian theme. But Miyako couldn't rightly say. She told herself she lacked the sensitivity for poetry, and heaved a deep, sad sigh. Akiko kept on reading for a while.

"Alright, time to go." Nana stood up.

At the home goods store, Akiko bought a paring knife and a chef's knife. They passed a drugstore on the way to meet the middle-aged man, and she bought a KAI razor as well.

The man was there already. He was wiping away the sweat, so he must've just arrived.

"Man, is it hot. I feel like I'm melting." His head was an almost perfect cube, though his perfect baldness may have contributed to the effect. He mopped the top of it with his handkerchief. "It's true what they say, you know: it's the really virile ones who go bald, ha-ha-ha. I tear through my work, and my appetite for you-know-what just keeps on growing, but I guess I'll have to hit middle age *some*day."

The girls ignored him.

"You girls hungry? I know a great little Italian place near here. Let's start there. But first, I brought you all a little something. Nana, honey, I know you said you wanted a new motorcycle, but the things are pretty damn expensive. I couldn't believe it! This'll only cover about a third, but take it for now. The rest, well, good things come to those who wait . . . I'm expecting a real windfall next month. Akiko, sweetie, with the right makeup, you could be a top-tier model. I had them put this together at one of my beauty parlors. Take it. Don't be shy, now. There's a half-off coupon for the salon in there, too."

He put a hard case like the kind models use on the table in front of her. Akiko didn't want it, but it was easier to just accept.

"Miyako, now this was a tough one. I mean, I get such a pure, innocent impression from you. But then I figured you're probably into accessories just like everyone else, so I brought you a few. It may be small, but that's a real sapphire in the pendant there. If you bought this at a jeweler's, it'd cost a pretty penny. But being the nice guy that I am, I lend money to a lot of different people, and my desk is practically overflowing with diamonds and rubies and emeralds they give me as collateral. A guy like me, it's like they just drop into my lap. There's a watch for you, too. I figured this kind of craftsmanship would suit your style. Delicate, not too flashy."

Miyako looked at her friends. Both of their expressions said *take them*. Blushing, she reluctantly accepted the gifts.

The man looked so pleased he might burst.

The four ate dinner together at the Italian restaurant. The man was putting on a great show of being lively. He even tackled his meal with vigor. Nana ate quietly, like a proper lady; it had been Akiko's habit since she was a child to eat slowly, as if the food was disgusting; only Miyako was conscious of the others' expressions as she timidly tucked into her portion.

The girls left first and stood waiting around outside the entrance. The man was paying.

"Miyako, your curfew's ten o'clock, isn't it? You'd better head on home," Nana ordered curtly.

"But I feel bad. I can't leave a guy like that alone with the two of you."

"Don't worry, we've got everything under control." Nana hailed a taxi and forced a 10,000-yen note into Miyako's hand from the wad the man had given her.

"That girl's a human being," Akiko murmured as the car drove off.

"Yeah."

"Don't you think it's about time we cut her loose?"

"That's up to her."

"Heyyy, sorry to keep you waiting. That asshole at the register screwed up the bill and was trying to charge me some outrageous sum. I figure he's doing it on purpose, so I say, 'Get me the manager.' And he says, 'I'm sorry, I made a mistake. You had just the one half-bottle of wine, I believe.' That's when I got mad. They weren't gonna admit they'd been trying to fleece me! So I say, 'Is this how you train your staff? Unacceptable.' Really letting 'em know who's boss,

142

right? The little shit turned pale and started trembling. I'm telling you, you can't be too careful."

He liked to throw his weight around, no matter the situation. So the cashier was tired and made a mistake about the wine, so what? What would that come to, one thousand yen at most?

The two girls stood silently, filled with loathing.

"Where's little Miyako?"

"She went home," Nana said coolly.

"Ahhh, that's a shame. Oh well, shit happens. That girl, she's kind of uptight. Always gotta watch what you say with her. Not like you two—you girls get it."

They didn't tell him it was just an illusion. Instead, their contempt for him grew. By leaps and bounds.

"I've got a bar near here. Wanna go have a drink there? No need to worry about getting ripped off. Makes everything nice and easy."

The place in question was two stories below ground. When they came in, the bartender nodded and just said, "Boss." The girl grilling squid tentacles looked their way but didn't say a word. The only other customers were three business types.

"I'm a wine guy myself. What'll you girls have?"

"Gin fizz," Akiko said, playing the naif.

"How 'bout a screwdriver for you, Nana, sweetheart? It's pretty much like orange juice."

It was the oldest trick in the book. But Akiko and Nana had already tested their tolerance for alcohol, twice in Nana's room and once at a party. "That'd be fine," Nana replied. She was well aware it contained vodka. And both of them could hold their liquor. Nana could handle pills like nobody's business, too. One morning when she came to school, she told Akiko, "I took forty tablets of bromisoval last night, but then I got caught up in a book and didn't end up sleeping at all. Now I'm beat. Think I'll go to the infirmary." She slept all morning, ate her lunch, and finally showed up to class in the afternoon. Akiko loaned her the notes for the classes she missed.

This was the middle-aged man's first time properly drinking with the girls, and he wasn't about to let the opportunity pass him by. He nursed his wine while at the same time pushing the two of them to get plastered. Akiko and Nana both drank at a leisurely pace, though. For the second round, Akiko switched to a nice weak scotch and water, making it last for a full half hour. Sure, it was her job, but her mother could really put it away, and Akiko had a genetically high tolerance. Nana had admitted to Akiko once that she'd been drinking and smoking and popping pills since middle school.

Maybe because it was so expensive for how shabby it was, or maybe because of its poor location, the bar didn't seem terribly popular. After the business types went home, the only other customers were a young couple and one guy drinking alone. But the middle-aged man kept up his bluster to the end. "Let me tell you, I think of this place as my home away from home. Forget making money—it's nice and quiet in here, and nobody bothers you. Now that's a refreshing feeling. Makes you feel like royalty, you know?"

At eleven-thirty, the girl working the kitchen went home. After that Akiko started acting tipsy. Nana appeared dead drunk, but this too was an act.

"You can go home for the night," the man said to the bartender. "I'll lock up."

"Have yourself a good time." The bartender cracked a grin and took off his apron. The middle-aged man went around behind the counter.

"Have another drink. I'll look after you."

Akiko's scotch and water was much stronger this time. She spilled half of it on the floor, then filled it back up with water. Nana did the same.

It must have been past midnight.

"I'm done." Akiko put her head down on the bar. Nana "stumbled" toward the bathroom.

"It's gonna be a real pain for you girls to get home from here, huh. How 'bout this: I know an inn nearby, what if you stayed there? I'll just take you there and then head home."

"That'd be great," Nana assented, deliberately slurring her words.

"Then let's get going . . . Just gimme a minute."

"You okay, Akiko?" Nana whispered without a hint of a slur, once the man had disappeared into the bathroom.

"He's the only one who's drunk," Akiko whispered back.

"Should we do it after we get to the inn? Gives us more options for an excuse. Like he was going to rape us or whatever."

"Too much trouble. I just need to shed Earthling blood to show that I'm from another planet."

"Roger."

"You put that powdered sedative in his drink, right? The cyclobarbital or whatever it's called? I was watching, but he didn't notice a thing—drank it right down. Looks like he only just started drinking wine! He has no idea how it's supposed to taste."

"A pharmacist I know stole this stuff from the hospital for me. Should be pretty strong."

The man came out of the bathroom and collapsed into a sitting position on the carpet. "Whoa, wasn't expecting that . . . I was having so much fun drinking with you young ladies, I guess I got a little ahead of myself. But don't worry, I'll be fine if I just lie down at the inn for half an hour. The night's still young."

Standing behind the man, Akiko whipped the chef's knife out of her bag and drove it straight at his heart. The bones got in the way. The man cried out in surprise. She yanked the knife out, and this time struck at his carotid artery with all her strength. Blood fountained to the ceiling. She cut both the left and the right. The man just sat there, suffering. The drugs must've been working. He couldn't fight back.

"Think that'll do it?" Nana seemed totally calm, but Akiko thought maybe it was because she was in shock.

"I think so."

"Your clothes are covered in blood. And your face and hands."

Akiko went behind the bar and washed her face and hands. She took off her clothes, which had been drenched by the spraying blood, and changed into a dress she'd brought along for the purpose.

"I don't think anyone heard him. The place on the floor above us is closed and everything."

Akiko shoved the knife and blood-soaked clothes into her bag.

While they were making their way up the stairs, Nana promised her in a small voice, "I'll never tell. That bartender, though . . . he might say something."

"I'm not worried. Even if they get onto our trail. I'm just glad Miyako wasn't there. The burden would be too much for her."

Out on the street, they parted ways as usual.

When she got home, Akiko headed straight to the bath. She crammed the bloody clothes into a corner of the garbage bag, out of sight. The knife she washed over and over again, then wrapped it in umpteen layers of newspaper and put it in the bag as well. No one else got onto the elevator as she rode down from the sixth floor to drop the bag in the dumpster.

Akiko was wired, so she took fifteen of the sleeping pills Nana had given her.

She'd done it. She'd finally done it. Delight welled up inside her. She put on her pajamas and got the vodka from the cabinet. She drank it straight.

Opening the curtains all the way, she saw the starry sky spread out before her eyes. Akiko knelt down. O he who is to come from our homeworld in accordance with the Covenant, I have carried out my mission. Please come for me soon. So that you will know me wherever I may go, let me now carve the crucifix of my oath.

Akiko opened the front of her nightgown. She drew the razor straight down from her throat to between her breasts. Lightly. Then likewise across. But the wound would heal too quickly this way. Over the straight lines she began to carve a series of small Xs. At length the pain came, but she couldn't stop now. It was the first time she'd ever taken this kind of pill, but Nana had assured her, "It's long-lasting, you'll sleep like a baby." She took another ten. Then she returned to her task. It hurt. But this much she would have to bear. When she finally finished, Akiko was exhausted. She wrapped the whole thing up in bandages so her mother wouldn't find out. After shoving the blood-streaked nightgown under her bed, she took out another one and put it on.

Akiko lit a cigarette and smoked it as she drank the vodka. The ashtray she kept hidden in her room was made of metal. Suddenly, she felt the urge to burn something. And it had to be white. She went out to the kitchen and found some paper napkins. She burned them in the ashtray. Beyond the wall of smoke, the visage of the man from her homeworld appeared and smiled at Akiko. The pain was gone. She was suffused with joy and knelt once more.

She didn't fall asleep until seven in the morning, and by the time she opened her eyes again it was already evening.

"So you played hooky today, huh?" her mother called out to her as she lay in bed. "When I got home I figured you were already at school."

"I caught cold and it was so uncomfortable that I couldn't sleep. Tomorrow's Saturday. I'll go to school on Monday."

"You sure you don't need to see the doctor?"

"It's just my throat. I don't have a fever or anything, plus there's no cure for the common cold. I just need to sleep."

A little after seven, Nana called. First she made sure Akiko's mother had left, then asked, "Are you okay?"

"I feel great. But forget about me, how're you?"

"I'm just wondering how I can be so unfazed. I almost can't believe it. Though maybe I'm happy that I feel so numb. Or maybe that kinda thing is just no big deal, you know? I was way more shocked that time two gangs of delinquents fought over me. Two of them were seriously wounded. And all because I was getting some on the side. Ever since then I haven't been surprised by much of anything. That stuff doesn't make me feel pain anymore—or feel anything, really. It's all ancient history at this point. Do you need me to come over?"

"Nope, I'm very happy right now. I feel more joyful than I ever have in my whole life, it's making my head spin. But . . . I know you'll be there if I need you. And listen, the cops might come around, but if they do, tell them: 'It all happened so fast, I was so surprised that I couldn't stop her. And when I got home I was too scared to go to the police. But I told her over and over again to give herself up.' Got it? Insist you had nothing to do with it."

"But . . ."

"Just do as I say. Please. If you don't, the act will lose its purity."

". . . Okay." Nana's voice was as calm as ever, but there was a hint of melancholy in it somewhere. It was so subtle that if they hadn't spent so much time together, Akiko would have missed it.

After she hung up the phone, Akiko removed her bandages. They were stuck to the dried blood. But having been carved so deeply, the mark would definitely last. Akiko touched her chest, satisfied.

It wasn't her first time at a mental hospital. Sachiko stepped into the lobby carrying a small bouquet of the lovely white flowers she liked, mixed with baby's breath. She didn't know what the flowers themselves were called. They had cruciform petals, and were the kind she imagined a blushing bride might carry down the aisle.

Akiko was arrested at school on Monday. The bartender's testimony had been the clincher. Nana admitted being present at the scene of the crime. In an emotionless voice, she gave the exact testimony Akiko had told her to give. She figured this was no time to start acting saintly. Nana was so calm, in fact, that the detectives whispered to each other, "Seems like there's something wrong with her upstairs." When Akiko was called to the principal's office, she immediately fessed up. But her madness was advanced to a whole other level. The psychological evaluation returned a diagnosis of schizophrenia. As a result (along with the fact that she was a minor), Akiko was involuntarily committed. Her mother came to see her at the beginning. Once was enough for her, though, and after that she gave Sachiko from the bar carfare and Akiko's 10,000-yen monthly allowance, and asked her to visit her daughter.

Sachiko had always been interested in mental hospitals. Her husband had been in one once, after all, and she didn't feel like they were to be avoided, the way most people did.

The nurse directed Sachiko to the locked ward, telling her, "Give the money to the attendant there for safekeeping. That's right, she can use it to buy things from the commissary, and to pay for any calls she makes from the attendant's room."

The hospital was on a hill, well outside of town. There was no fence or wall, and a number of patients with milder conditions were walking along the paths out front and wandering among the groves of trees. When she was seventeen, Sachiko's aunt had lost her mind, but the hospital she'd been committed to had been a horrible place. Iron bars everywhere. When Sachiko went to see her, patient and visitor were put together in a small room and the nurse locked the door from the outside.

Turning at the end of a long corridor, she came to the locked ward.

"She killed someone and she's a suicide risk, so for the first fifteen days she was in a single. But now she's been moved to a room with five other people. I'll go get her, please wait here."

The AC was on. Sachiko took out a cigarette and lit it. Outside the glass door, in a garden too big to really call a garden, clumps of cosmos grew here and there amid the overgrown summer grass.

First the sound of two locks opening, then there was Akiko. She gave the same impression as she had the two or three other times Sachiko had met her: very quiet and introverted. Now, though, there was a restless light blazing in the girl's eyes. Was it due to her confinement?

"Gimme a cigarette," Akiko said. "They won't let me smoke inside. Uh-uh, not because I'm a minor. I guess they're afraid I'll put my eye out or attack the other patients with it."

Akiko began anxiously pulling on the cigarette. Beyond the glass door, there was nothing preventing escape.

"Is it comfortable here?"

"Comfortable enough, I guess. Pretty soon they'll let me move to the open ward. Once they realize I'm not a danger to myself or others. But I have no intention of doing anything like that again. I killed that man because I was commanded to, because it was my mission. This was something I had to do, too," and she indicated the large, cross-shaped scar extending from her throat down to her chest. "But that's all over. I couldn't even kill a cat. Now, I just have to wait."

"For what?"

"For him to arrive in his flying saucer. From our home-world far, far away. He's coming for me. He departed thousands of years ago. I wonder if he knows I'm here, though. He must, right? After all, sometimes he comes out of the wall and speaks to me in that gentle voice of his."

Sachiko was so shocked that she dropped her cigarette on the floor—because the night her husband had talked about receiving that "extra-terrestrial transmission" had come rushing back to her. She probably shouldn't have mentioned it. But Sachiko could never keep anything hidden, and she told Akiko the story in detail, adding, "Promise me you won't say a word to the doctors."

"Wow!" Through a veil of welling tears, Akiko's eyes looked huge. "That's it. That's it exactly. I mean, those of us from other planets, people with telepathic abilities, we all get treated like we're crazy here on Earth. Not that it matters to me, I'll be going home soon."

"So you really believe it? You're sure he'll come for you?"

"Of course. I'm certain of it. I mean, this is what I was born for."

"There's always the chance he might die in an accident or something on the way."

"It's possible, sure. But during the thousands of years he's spending in cryosleep on his journey here, he dreams of this unfamiliar Earth. And those dreams reach me sometimes. That's how I know he's still alive. Hey, maybe I am crazy after all."

"You're not crazy," Sachiko said, partly just to comfort her. "Just a little weird. And you know what? Plenty of people in this world are weird. My husband, for instance. Me."

"Nana's a weird person, too. She doesn't even have visions, like I do. She's a good, sweet girl, but there's something in her so cold it'll freeze your blood. She says she can't see people as human beings. However well she gets to know them, however much she likes them, suddenly they appear to her as totally unfamiliar lifeforms. She once told me, 'I can't look at your face. It scares me to look at it.' She said my eyes and nose and mouth looked all disconnected, and whenever I spoke it was just my mouth that was alive and moving. So she avoided me for a while. And because of all that, she skips school a lot. She says she wants to go back. But she's not from somewhere else like I am, she's a human being. What a luxury! She doesn't know what it really means to be alone."

"Nana's the girl who was there with you?"

"Yeah. I wrote her a letter, but I don't want the doctors or nurses to look at it, so would you deliver it for me? Her house is close to the bar. Even if you could just put it in the mail for me I'd appreciate it, but I somehow get the feeling it'd be stolen."

"Sure. I'm surprised they let you have pen and paper, though."

"I asked if I could do some drawing in the attendant's room, and I wrote it then."

Akiko reached into the breast of her summer sweater and pulled out the letter. It was just the folded paper, no envelope. Nana's address was written on the outside.

"I wonder how she's doing. I'd like to see her. But lately, I dunno, I've started to feel like we're strangers. I've been thinking so hard about all kinds of things, and I've come to new truths, but she has no interest in what goes on inside other people's heads. I mean, she doesn't even care about herself. She lives like she's already dead. Oh, and I also wrote a letter to 'him,' but I don't know how to deliver it. Burning it would probably work best, but I can't so long as I'm in the locked ward." Akiko looked down. "Plus, I have to write to him on paper napkins. White paper napkins are his favorite. Hey, don't you think there's something eternal about the number eight . . . ?"

By the time she left the hospital, Sachiko was terribly tired. She stopped by Nana's on the way to the bar. After running her eyes over the letter, Nana said, "Got it. Please get rid of this. You can read it first if you want."

This girl's pretty damn loony herself, Sachiko thought. When she got to the bar at six-thirty that evening, she read the letter.

You hanged yourself in the distant past
You had a cramp in your distinctive legs
You hauled along your distasteful sins . . .

It went on and on like that. Must be some kind of word game. Sachiko burned it.

In the middle of September, a satellite crashed in the woods just outside the mental hospital. The area was consumed in flames, and the remains of a burned body of indeterminate sex were discovered among the ashes. Akiko, who had been moved to the open ward, had disappeared that same afternoon. The authorities concluded the corpse was hers.

Nana ran away from home and took up with the head of a gang of delinquents in Yokosuka. She was feared by the other members for her ruthless nature.

Sachiko quit the bar and started working during the day. Her husband had finally found a new job. And gradually he stopped talking about things like telepathy and precognition.

THE WALKER

I couldn't tell you why, but I'd been walking for ages, and I was worn out and hungry. I felt as if I'd been wandering for a hundred years, maybe even since the dawn of time.

Then, when I was one step from oblivion, there in the middle of a field, in a place where the pale sunlight gathered and fell lightly as a scarf, I came upon a shabby little udon cart.

A girl of about fifteen, her hair parted and tied back with a rubber band, was frying up some squid tempura.

"Think I could have something to eat?" I asked weakly.

"Of course, that's what we do."

The girl seemed tired, too. She had the forlorn look of someone toiling for a crime syndicate. A picture-perfect country bumpkin.

"How much?"

"That depends. For fifteen yen, you get a quarter helping of udon. For thirty-five you'll get twice that, plus a tentacle."

"Well, isn't that something." I didn't have any money on me, but I was enthusiastic nonetheless. How could I not be, with the prospect of a meal before me? "I'll take the thirty-five-yen special then, thanks. And do me a favor, throw in some scallions and a shake of chili powder?"

"Sure, no problem."

The scrawny girl whipped up the noodles for me with arms that were themselves like squid tentacles. I downed the whole thing in an instant, drinking every last drop of broth, then sighed.

"That was truly delicious."

"Yeah?"

"Squid tempura udon—one hell of a dish."

"Yeah."

"The thing is, though, I don't have any money."

This time she didn't say "yeah." Strands of hair the color of withered grass blew into the girl's face, and her doglike eyes clouded with tears.

"What'll I do? If I go home like this, I'll get a tongue-lashing."

"No one has to know," I said.

"Uh-uh. He checks everything. Every morning he marks down exactly how many balls of udon and exactly how many tentacles I take with me. He'll beat me half to death."

"If it's that bad, why don't you run away?"

"I can't. I'm afraid of him." At the thought of her employer, the girl's reedy body began to tremble.

"Who is this guy?"

I pictured a man with a glass eye, stalking the halls of his gloomy manor on the scrubby heaths of Wuthering Heights.

"He's my husband. We've got a kid too, so I can't just leave."

"That so?" I said, in my best imitation of Humphrey Bogart. "Well then, have this. It's worth plenty more than thirty-five yen."

I handed her a silver-plated ring set with a translucent green stone. The girl eyed the trinket dubiously, as if I was trying to pull one over on her. But when she put it on, an awkward grin spread slowly across her face, like a baby's first smile. "It's real pretty, huh?"

She let out a long sigh, then thrust the hand wearing the ring behind her back.

"You won't change your mind, will you?" She glanced up at me furtively from sly, gray eyes.

"I told you, it's for you."

"First time I ever saw something so pretty. Listen, I'm gonna have to hide this. My husband'll take it from me."

I was so tired. Which was only natural—I'd been walking since before the birth of Christ, at least.

"I don't suppose there's anywhere around here I can take a rest."

"Hmm. Not unless you go into town."

"Town, huh . . . Is that where you live?"

I was counting on the girl to pack up her cart and head home. The wan light of dusk had enveloped the area; it couldn't be long now. But she just stood there, gazing idly into space. The sun had long since set, and its last glimmers were reddening the ridgeline of the mountains.

"Aren't you going to go home?"

"Somebody else might come."

"Do you get many customers all the way out here? More likely to get foxes, aren't you?"

"I get customers. I mean, you're here, aren't you?" she said brusquely, then lapsed back into silence.

Was there anyone else left like me? Someone who walked and walked, who couldn't think of anything but walking? Someone who'd been walking *since long before her own birth*, who could do nothing but keep on walking.

On and on, through war after war, as people die and others devote themselves to reproducing only to die in turn, until the merciless blazing sun grinds to a halt halfway across the massive dome of the heavy blue sky, and the Earth turns hard and cold.

The world will cease to spin, I suppose. The sun in its death mask will burn away the last traces of life clinging to the surface—the lichens, the insects, even the bacteria—with tongues of flame. And the Walker, the last person left, will she continue her great wandering circle through the sun's mad tantrum?

"Where are you headed?" the girl asked me, with the blank look of an animal.

". . . To find my brother."

Why that was what came out, I couldn't say. But once uttered, it became a conviction. I was walking in search of the brother of my blood, seeking the other half of myself.

"Aww, I'm sorry, lady. Makes my life sound not so bad. I have a nice husband, cute kid, business is good—profits are never less than a hundred yen a day!—so I really can't complain."

The girl's newfound compassion scored me a cup of hot, weak tea.

Once night was fully upon us, she packed up the cart and set off in the direction of what I assumed to be the town. I walked along after her. It was that "town" alright, the kind everybody knows. The lamps from the bakeries and candy shops illuminated a street that seemed a little too wide.

"Uwaa!" The girl raised a happy cry and began to run, jouncing the balls of udon heaped on the cart. Two or three fell to the ground like clods of horseshit.

"You came to meet me? I'm so glad. I love you, I love you!"

The girl threw her arms around a slender youth, little more than a boy. He held the hand of a child who toddled along beside him. Outside a bar, a middle-aged man sat on a stool, smoking and taking in the scene.

"Hey, not in front of everybody . . . C'mon, save the mushy stuff for later." In a queerly squeaky voice that had only recently changed, the boy tried to maintain some semblance of whatever passed for his dignity.

"How'd we do today?"

"Look at this."

Even though she'd said she needed to hide it, the girl (with an innocence that I could only assume was feigned) showed off the ring I'd given her.

"What the hell is that?"

"This lady ate thirty-five yen's worth of noodles, but didn't have any money, so . . ."

And how it happened, I (once again) couldn't really say, but next thing I knew, the boy was on the ground.

I suppose he pounced on me, trying to knock me down. But he was a shrimpy little fellow, so when he lunged for my waist, I lashed out in a fit of fury, kicking him in the gut with all the strength of my mighty thighs.

"Pay up! When you eat something, you gotta pay for it, everybody knows that."

The boy raged at me from where he lay.

"Feh, you little runt."

I turned to leave. I had to keep walking, after all.

Just then, a car came barreling down the road and ran over their child with decorous aplomb, as if this were the sole reason for its existence. His severed head rolled across the ground and stopped at his parents' feet.

"How lovely," I said. The girl laughed. Everyone opened the stone voids of their mouths and laughed.

SOFTLY, AS IN A MORNING SUNRISE

They were met by a group of large, pink, rabbit-like beings arrayed in a semi-circle, swaying to and fro with forepaws tucked behind their backs. The creatures' placid faces gave the impression they were faintly smiling.

"Hey there," Pete hailed them. "You represent the intelligent lifeforms on this planet?" He made like he was going to kick one of the pseudo-rabbits, but it hopped back, and from a slight remove broke out into what did, after all, seem to be a grin.

"Don't be so disrespectful. That could be their emperor, for all you know," teased Sabu (a man who liked other men) from behind lightly tinted sunglasses. "Ever heard of lèse-majesté? Could be curtains for you, chop, chop." He stepped down from the ship in his jumpsuit.

"They'll cut off his balls?" Junko let slip. Her mind was always in the gutter. Still and all, she was the captain.

Naoshi silently adjusted the holster at his waist.

It wasn't all that uncommon to discover a new planet, and the Terran government couldn't afford to dispatch a scientific research team to each one. Meanwhile a number of corporations had established regular shipping routes between Earth and its Moon, Mars, and two or three other key planets.

Junko used to work for Stardust Space Services, but she'd been obliquely cautioned for sexual impropriety and quit in a fit of rage. Naoshi had been her coworker there, and one morning she came storming into his apartment while he was asleep, demanding that he quit, too. He agreed immediately. She did the same with all the guys she'd been seeing at the time, but Naoshi was the only one who went along with it. "That's what I love about you," she said as she embraced him. "So amenable." He'd been wanting to quit for a while anyway.

Pete had been a trainee at New Worlds CosmoLine, and Sabu was peeling potatoes at a spaceport restaurant. Pete's family was wealthy, and he didn't actually need to work. He'd be the first to admit he was a selfish, negative guy, whose relatives didn't think much of him. He also said it was getting tougher to be at home. When Sabu heard Pete had resigned, he just kind of ended up quitting too. When a boy like *that* left, it always threw him for a loop.

Together they cooked up a get-rich-quick scheme to collect unusual animals for Earth's leisure class. Using the money Pete's late aunt had left him, they bought a scrapheap of a freighter and named it the *Goodbye Again*. Pete was the one who came up with the name. He fancied himself something of an ironist. He was also—and this he was less inclined to own up to—something of a bad drunk.

Pete and Sabu were sick of life on Earth. You'd get hassled by the cops every fifteen minutes just for hanging out around town. Not that they looked like freaks or anything—it was just that wandering the streets without a purpose, and more importantly without a permit, was practically a crime. And acting like you didn't know that would make you seem like an escaped mental patient.

Junko told Naoshi that anything untoward got recorded in MOTHER, the nerve center linking the computers used by the various government ministries. The reason no one needed to carry an insurance card or driver's license anymore was that every citizen had been assigned a standard identification number, and the police or hospitals could now access whatever information they needed instantaneously—one ID sufficed for everything.

"Oh, come off it," muttered Naoshi anxiously.

"Do you know why I left the company?" Junko shot back. "Because I knew too much, and the Intelligence Ministry had their eye on me."

By careening off around the frontiers of the known universe, they could escape all that. The one thing the *Goodbye Again* needed was a crew, so they hired Junko and Naoshi, no questions asked. They were running away too, after all.

"How do we catch them?" Pete asked.

"The nerve blaster should do the trick," Naoshi replied.

"Assuming they have nervous systems."

They started walking away, and the pseudo-rabbits saw them off with picture-perfect smiles.

"Not much of a find, are they," Sabu said. "I can't quite picture them as pets. Then again, if there's someone who wants to live with that lizard from the planet Mirin, I suppose all bets are off." Sabu trailed after Junko. He always tried to stay out

165

of harm's way, keeping as far as possible from any potentially dangerous creatures. But for some reason, if someone was going to get hurt, it was always him. *Why's it always got to be me?* he often lamented. They'd gone after that lizard at the behest of a certain elderly gentleman back on Earth, and it had bitten Sabu in the thigh. He said he'd been on his guard, but when it lunged at him he was overcome by "some kind of momentary apathy," and found himself unable to move. One of his eyes was artificial for much the same reason: before he got the job at the restaurant, he'd worked at home engraving rings, and one day a moon sapphire came flying out of the polisher; he'd seen it coming, but he still hadn't been able to get out of the way.

"Watch out! A lizard!" Pete was just trying to spook him.

"I wonder if they're actually smiling. They don't seem to have any other expressions." Junko proceeded into the jungle, hacking at vines and tendrils as she went.

The storage capacity on board ship was limited, but this planet, composed as it was of a single continent with abundant lakes and rivers, was unlikely to support an overwhelming diversity of species. Combined with the planet's seemingly moderate climate, the job was looking to be a breeze.

"Hear that?" Naoshi said from the rear, pausing to listen.

"I hear it." Pete pursed his lips.

"That's no bird. Sounds like a baby." Naoshi looked up.

". . . Maybe," Pete replied without conviction.

With a sharp cry, a bird resembling an archaeopteryx glided by overhead.

"Sounds more like a cat," said Junko.

"Let's go see," said Naoshi.

"Hang on. It might be dangerous. We should go back to

the ship and get the amphibious rover." Junko only disagreed with him because she wanted to make sure everyone remembered that *she* was the captain.

"Don't be so dramatic," said Sabu. "If a lizard pops out, I'll take one for the team."

That decided it.

The jungle thinned out as they advanced, until suddenly there it was: an infant, holding itself upright with the help of a large tree stump. It was very plump, and dressed in woolen clothes that had a vaguely Phoenician look about them. Its cheeks were drenched with tears, and it stared at the four of them with wide, startled chestnut eyes.

"It's a human baby." Sabu let out a sigh of relief.

"First coin lockers, now this? People abandon their babies in some pretty strange places . . ." Pete thought this was a clever thing to say. He was the only one, though; no one else so much as chuckled.

"It can't be a human baby," breathed Naoshi.

"It sure looks like one." Junko tilted her head. The infant smiled sweetly and cooed at them, slapping the stump in delight.

Naoshi moved toward the child like he was being pulled in by a tractor beam, scooping it up with total disregard for Junko's cry of warning.

"Oh, come on. It's not dangerous." The child snuggled happily into the crook of his arm.

"But what if its parents come back . . . That animal we saw earlier, the one that looked like a horrible, fiendish gorilla? That might've been its mother," said Junko. "The revolting smell, those little hairs growing out of its slimy black skin . . . I never saw anything so awful. *That thing* might come after us." Her firm opposition had less to do with the child itself, however, than with the fact that she sensed something strange in Naoshi's attitude.

"We're armed, remember."

"Even the thought of fighting that thing gives me the chills. Come on, put the kid down and let's split. It's not ours, after all."

"Sure, but that doesn't mean we can just leave it here. Not when it's been *abandoned*."

"I was just kidding," Pete put in. "Its parents are probably off gathering firewood or something, and they'll be back for lunch any minute."

The infant was now sucking its left thumb with a tense look on its face. Every time someone spoke, it turned its head to stare at them.

"Listen, Naoshi," Sabu began reasonably. "It might not be the human race we know from Earth, but it does seem like a human child. We can't just cart it off like that. It's not an animal."

Naoshi responded with a muttered "Mm." But he wasn't convinced. "And we can't just leave a baby here on its own. It's not like it just got lost—it can't even walk! Any parent that would dump it in a place like this clearly doesn't care what happens to it. But that doesn't mean we can just stand by and let it die."

They looked around at each other.

This wasn't the first difficult decision they'd faced. There had been the debate over whether the aforementioned lizard's bite was poisonous, for instance. They'd stocked two or three different kinds of antivenom on board, but there was only one left: an extremely strong one. If they used it and Sabu hadn't in fact been poisoned, there was a risk he'd go into shock; it depended to some degree on his constitution. Junko insisted the lizard was poisonous, and administered the antivenom. It was a good thing she did.

And sometimes an animal they captured would die because they couldn't figure out what to feed it. They were still having trouble with the man-eating starfishes from the planet Bali. The creatures would leap up out of their tank with a splash and try to sink their teeth into any living flesh that came too close. The crew had tried hanging meat on wires above the tank, but it wasn't working out too well. They had to be careful not to lose a finger every time they fed the things.

Another bird glided by overhead.

"So what do we do?" Pete asked. "We need to be starting back soon."

The infant tugged at Naoshi's hair and squealed with glee.

"Do you seriously mean to abandon it here?" There was a surprising amount of emotion in Naoshi's voice.

Junko narrowed her eyes at him. "You keep saying that. What, you abandon a baby before or something?" Naoshi was speechless; he tried to muster a retort, but nothing came out. Junko carried on like the captain she was. "You're being too empathetic. It's ridiculous. Sure, the poor kid's situation is real unfortunate. And you're right, it doesn't seem danger-ous. And we've got plenty of food back on the ship. But if we take one of the inhabitants of this planet with us, it could cause problems down the line."

"It won't," Naoshi insisted.

"You don't know that."

"Even if it did, it's not like there's anything resembling an advanced civilization here. You saw for yourself when we entered orbit. There's nothing but a handful of tiny settlements. No way do they have the scientific knowledge to start an interstellar war."

"You're assuming it has to be an Earth-type civilization. Who knows, they could live underground."

A small animal ran past and scampered up a tree. Suddenly a great flurry of leaves rained down on them—an endless avalanche of leaves that just kept on coming, blotting out everything else. It was all they could do to keep the detritus from getting in their eyes and mouths. By the time it stopped they were buried up to their chests.

"What the hell was that?" growled Pete.

"Falling leaves, I'd say," Sabu said playfully, as they hauled themselves out with a bit of effort. "Wonder if it happens every day around this time . . ."

"This'd be enough fuel to barbecue a human being. Bonfire night, stars are bright, little angel dressed in white . . ." The baby clung to Naoshi's chest.

Junko wasn't pleased, though she couldn't say exactly why. Was she jealous? She tried the thought on for size.

She set off, and the others followed behind.

Night fell over the unfamiliar planet.

They assembled in the cabin of the ship to discuss the situation. The debate dragged on, right up until Sabu put dinner on the table.

～

"What is this?" Junko asked, even though she knew perfectly well.

"Fried man-eating starfish. We can't eat synthesized rations for *every* meal."

"Another one died?"

"From the shock of the landing. But there are still twelve or thirteen left."

"All the same . . . Dammit, it was a tough job poaching those starfish, and we can get surprisingly good money for them."

"Those Balians sure are aggressive, though, huh. And so cool under fire . . . They'd probably make great soldiers." Pete tried to steer the conversation in a harmless direction. Naoshi listened, a dark look playing about his eyes.

"They already do," Junko replied. "Most of the Foreign Legion is Balian." She searched Naoshi's face as she spoke. He'd been totally hung up on that baby since the moment he laid eyes on it. There *had* to have been something in his past. And she could more or less imagine what it was.

Naoshi sat on the bed beside the sleeping baby. Sabu gathered all the linens that would serve, and set out two days' worth of diapers. Something like a very long bandage had been wrapped around the baby's midriff up to that point, and it looked terribly cumbersome to change. In fact, it seemed like it hadn't been changed for at least a week: the pee and poop had seeped all the way through, and the child's bottom was red and peeling.

"Let's just grab some of those rabbit-looking things and call it a day. They seem easy enough to catch. I'd love to get my

171

hands on that golden love child of a chipmunk and a flying squirrel we saw run up that tree right before the leaves fell on us, but the traps are broken. Pete, how long do you think it'd take you to fix them?" Junko was sitting cross-legged on the floor.

"All three?"

"One would be enough."

"In that case, maybe half a day? We're a little short on parts, but I'm sure I can manage."

"Tomorrow night, then?" Junko had a gentle smile on her face. It was best to be wary of this particular expression—it meant she had something up her sleeve.

"Sure, no problem."

"Okay then, tomorrow we'll bag ourselves some pink rabbits. I wonder if grass and twigs'll do for feed?"

"They were eating dirt earlier," Sabu reported. "And still smirking the whole time. There's something creepy about them."

"How much dirt do you think we can stockpile for the trip back to Earth?"

"Hmm, it isn't all that far, so maybe enough for four or five of them," Sabu replied. "Those two emerald sheep died, and the other one's on its last legs. We'll be eating mutton chops again in no time . . ."

As she listened, Junko glanced over at Naoshi. She couldn't allow mutiny, but he was a vital member of the crew, as well as her current lover, so she had to be careful he didn't decide to stay behind on this planet. "We should be able to catch five of them in a couple of days. What do you think, Pete?"

"Piece of cake."

"Right then. We'll remain here for five more days, beginning tomorrow. On day three we set out the trap for that other little fella. Day four we begin preparations for departure."

"Roger." Pete stood up and made his way down to the lower deck. Sabu headed to the galley.

This left woman, man, and baby alone in the small cabin.

Junko stood before Naoshi and drew the zipper of her jumpsuit down her chest, revealing the form-fitting woolen undergarment beneath. Naoshi watched like a man who had lost his appetite. The flesh-colored union suit covered her entire body from wrists to ankles. She undid five of the buttons running down the front of it, then knelt and wrapped her arms around Naoshi's neck.

"Something wrong?" Junko looked up at his face with a mocking twinkle in her eyes. Naoshi looked away.

"You're a shallow, cruel woman," he mumbled. "You could never understand how I feel."

"Mm-hmm, mm-hmm." Junko wore her usual cynical smile.

"So I'm done."

"With what?" she asked, her voice dripping with honey.

"It's not like I'm such a great crew member anyway."

"Oh *yes. You. Are.*"

"Don't make fun of me. I thought about staying here, but I'm not confident I'd be able to survive. Tomorrow I'll start sleeping down below with Pete." This very much constituted a threat. Without a man, Junko grew irritable and prone to lapses in judgment.

"There's no bed for you."

"There are two down there."

"Sabu's using the other one."

"He is? Damn . . . Well, I'll be just as happy next to the galley storage compartment."

"You think I'm a nymphomaniac, don't you. Fine, do whatever you like. But the baby . . ."

Naoshi looked at her for the first time.

Just then the child woke up and started crying. It was a helpless, forlorn wail. Rubbing its eyes, the baby tottered a few steps toward Junko then began to topple over. She reached out and caught it up in her arms. Once resettled there, it stopped crying. It opened its hands and tugged at her flesh-colored undergarment.

"Cut that out. Ugh, I don't like this kid."

The baby seemed to be having a ball, though, and just kept tugging harder. It was impressively strong. When she finally got it to let go of the cloth, it grabbed her hair instead.

"Dammit, that hurts!" Junko shouted, and set the baby back on the floor. It sat down with its legs splayed out in front of it and beamed, so infectiously that Junko couldn't help but break out in a grin herself. When she stole a glance at Naoshi, he was desperately trying to hide his look of triumph. Junko pursed her lips, sat down on the bed, and folded her arms.

"There's still room in the cargo hold," she said.

"Nope, it's full up with sheep and sea creatures."

"Ohhh? Maybe we'll have to keep it down to three pink rabbits, then."

Naoshi was silent.

"Any objections?" Junko asked sternly. In a tone that said, *You're on thin ice, watch how you answer.*

"To what?" Naoshi replied weakly.

"I want this runt belowdecks, not in the living quarters. It doesn't have to go in with the sheep; there's a lot less hay than there used to be, so there's plenty of space in the hold. We can toss it in there."

"But how can we see to its needs down there?" Naoshi argued.

"Sabu will take care of it. After he feeds the animals."

"That doesn't make me feel any better."

"Sabu's a kind man. He's got a gentle side. It's not like you could take care of it anyway, you're the pilot."

"Once the ship enters hyperdrive, I don't need to be in the cockpit *all* the time. It'll be fine."

"I can't have that baby turning everyone's lives upside down," Junko said in her captain's voice.

"They've been upside down from the start." Naoshi followed the baby as it crawled across the floor. It stood up when it got to the hatch, put both hands on the door, and started rocking back and forth. Naoshi opened the door and helped it over the threshold. Then the two set off, ostensibly in the direction of the galley. The layout of the *Goodbye Again* was very unorthodox; the strangest things were in the strangest places.

Opening the door a crack, Junko watched them proceed down the corridor like a man and his beloved pet. When they came to a thick pipe cutting across the floor, Naoshi lifted the baby up like a puppy. It crawled along at an impressive speed, its bottom swishing from side to side as it went.

Junko returned to the bed without closing the door. She turned out the light and crawled inside her sleeping bag. She was curiously angry.

A man she used to know popped into her head. He'd been a leader in the student movement, and in his glory days he'd appeared in the papers and on television. When she knew him, he was working as a day laborer. He'd been a simple, sentimental man. He beat his woman, who was pregnant, and she left him. After she had the baby, he was consumed by self-recrimination. He told Junko that when he ran into the woman two and a half years later, the kid took one look at him and burst into tears. "I must have looked like a monster."

"The kid was probably just shy," Junko replied.

"You don't know what you're talking about."

She thought now that the man hadn't been angry with himself because of the kid; it was his own youth he regretted, back when he'd been a milk-and-water zealot. The kid had simply come to symbolize that period of his life.

Naoshi's past was probably similar, Junko thought. It irritated her that he wouldn't just come out and talk about it. What was the big deal?

She pondered who was worse at letting go, men or women, and arrived at the conclusion that it was men, by an overwhelming margin.

Naoshi and Sabu were laughing in the galley. It suddenly occurred to her that Naoshi might quit after this run. He was always talking about living the simple life: *The world's just too complicated these days. New Zealand, maybe New Caledonia, somewhere I could take it easy. It doesn't even have to be Earth. Meele, maybe. The climate's mild and the people are friendly.* Was he running away from his youth as well? Junko recalled how readily he'd quit Space Services when she put the squeeze on him.

She could hear Sabu saying something in that smug tone of his. And . . . Pete was there, too. He sounded like he'd been drinking. Sabu must've given it to him. Little did Junko know he'd arranged with Sabu to smuggle a couple dozen bottles of whiskey aboard.

Some crew, thought Junko angrily. No respect for the captain. Without me they'd never even make it out of the atmosphere! But what can you do? Crewmen are hard to come by. Just assembling a ragtag team of losers like this one (she was of course not including herself) meant sifting through the intergalactic garbage.

In the galley, Naoshi was playing the flute. The tune was a jazz standard with a sad melody: "Softly, as in a Morning Sunrise."

"It's a song about how this guy feels on his way home from spending the night with a prostitute," Naoshi had told her.

There was a part in a novel she read a long time ago where a black woman and a white man are living together. The woman's older brother had been with a white woman, but he treated her horribly and ended up committing suicide. In the kitchen, the black woman sometimes sings, "'Cause the sun's gonna shine in my back door someday." Why *back* door? the white man wonders.

Naoshi is a defeated man, Junko thought to herself, *who craves some kind of stability.*

Pete was hollering about something. A bunch of space trash, sitting around getting hammered together. She could hear the baby's babbling mixed in with the other sounds. *Manmanmaman, waaa, pappappa.*

It really was just like a Terran baby.

Clear skies again the next morning.

The pink rabbits turned out to be just as lethargic as they seemed, and the crew were able to catch twelve of them. They let the old and decrepit ones go.

Naoshi started to get antsy after a couple of hours. Probably fretting about the baby, who they'd locked in the cabin before leaving the ship. Three hours in, he started saying, "Let's head back for an early lunch."

"Something's been bothering me," Pete whispered so that only Junko could hear. "Think I could borrow the rover for a couple of hours?"

"What's up?"

"You saw those smoke signals or whatever they were this morning, didn't you? They were coming from a village not too far from here . . ."

"You're worried about witchcraft now?"

"No, listen, I have a hunch it had something to do with that baby. Sabu and I went back to the place where we found it, and a little further on we discovered something strange. It seemed like some kinda makeshift sacrificial altar."

"Show me."

Naoshi and Sabu had loaded the pink rabbits, rendered unconscious by knock-out gas, into the amphibious rover, and were about to head back to the ship. Junko told Sabu to come back for them in a little while, then let Pete lead her into the jungle. He brought her to a spot where the trees had been felled to create a small clearing. A flat stone in the center was adorned with white-leaved branches unlike anything they had seen so far in the area. Atop the stone lay a thorny vine, covered in small talismans with magical formulae of some kind written on them.

"This looks like blood," said Junko, peering closely at the faint traces of something sticky on the rock's surface.

"Pretty sure it is," Pete replied calmly.

"The kid's blood?"

"I haven't checked yet, but probably, yeah. Though that would mean the kid had been wounded here, and it wasn't bleeding at all when we found it. Or maybe I'm wrong, maybe they slaughtered a lamb or something. There isn't enough blood for that, though, so who knows, maybe one of the people at the ceremony cut open their finger . . . Either way, it seems significant."

"But the child . . . Why would they . . .?"

"That's what I'd like to find out. You know that little table Sabu insisted on putting in the galley? The baby was playing alone in there, and this morning I noticed teeth marks on the legs. Little ones."

"But the kid doesn't even have teeth yet."

"I know."

"You sure *you* didn't do it while you were drunk?" Junko asked in her usual acid tone.

"I'm sure."

"But you *had* been drinking."

"Yeah, I had," Pete replied, undaunted. "Not as much as usual, though. Plus, the marks were tiny, and they looked like whatever made them had fangs."

"Oh, come on," Junko shook her head. Then it occurred to her: "Could it have been the silver fang-rats we picked up on Bali?"

"It's possible. But I don't think so. The three of us were in the galley with the baby, and afterward Sabu and I went below. There's no way the fang-rats could've gotten up there, and even if they *had* chewed through the mesh of their cage, someone would've noticed."

"Okay, okay, we'll look into it. They should be back for us any minute . . . and I assume they'll bring the baby. Did you actually go to the settlement?"

"No, I wanted to take some pictures of this place, and I happened to spot it through my telephoto lens from the roof of the rover. Seems to be a relatively primitive village, but the women were washing something that looked like plates."

The pair returned to the rendezvous point just as the amphibious rover pulled up.

"Hey, how're the rabbits?" Junko asked in a cheerful voice. The gas ought to keep them knocked out for a while.

"Still smiling," Sabu replied coquettishly.

Naoshi was expressionless. The infant, bouncing up and down on his lap, was the picture of innocence.

"That thing is a malignant tumor," Junko muttered to Sabu as he got down from the vehicle. She was referring to the baby, naturally.

"Good grief." Sabu's eyes twinkled behind his sunglasses; even the artificial one seemed amused. "It really is a horrid little beast. Puts absolutely everything in its mouth, tries to break anything it can get its hands on, opens cans of food and

180

dumps them all over the floor . . . Am I going to be expected to follow it around and clean up after it from now on? I'm not a maid, you know."

"Even if that kid is human, it sure as hell doesn't seem like it," Pete chimed in. "Funny little freak. Like an adorable mutant. Though maybe I just don't hang out with very many babies."

Naoshi was staring at them uneasily. He could tell they were talking about the baby, but couldn't make out what they were saying.

"Pete's got a pretty wild theory . . ." Junko began in a hushed voice.

"Yeah, he told me," Sabu said. "Took me out to the jungle to see that weird altar."

"Who discovered the teeth marks?"

"It was me," Sabu said, looking grave.

"So, what are we dealing with? A vampire?"

"Could be. Last night Pete and I slept down below, but in separate rooms. Naoshi and the child were over by the pantry . . ."

Naoshi got down from the rover with the baby.

"Did you bring lunch?" Junko changed the subject as he approached.

"That was Sabu's job . . ." There was a hint of tension in Naoshi's voice as he trailed off. Had he picked up on the fact that he was being left out in the cold? Though he talked like that most of the time anyway.

They sat down to lunch.

Suddenly Sabu let out a shrill cry as an enormous tree came crashing down. Naoshi stepped back, clutching the baby to his chest, and Junko and Pete jumped clear, but once again Sabu failed to get out of the way.

He was trapped beneath the fallen tree—or so it seemed. With an awesome display of strength, he heaved the trunk off himself and crawled free. It was so thick that two adults wouldn't be able to join hands around it.

A vampire, *and* a man with superhuman strength! For an instant Junko felt as if all the blood was draining from her body.

"Ha-ha, look at me, I'm Superman! I can leap tall buildings in a single bound!" Sabu was hamming it up, puffing out his chest and striking a triumphal pose. Pete slipped the toe of his boot under the tree and lifted it like it was nothing.

"It's hollow."

"This jungle is full of surprises." Naoshi smiled for the first time.

After lunch, Pete and Junko went to the village. As the amphibious rover approached, a smoke signal went up. There was a great commotion as the villagers ran to hide inside their houses.

"What was that all about?"

"We just startled them. Let's go the rest of the way on foot."

But every door remained firmly shut. The log houses seemed to be constructed with the same kind of hollow tree that had fallen on Sabu, and the roofs were thatched with grass.

This planet's sun had a bluish tinge, probably because of the composition of the atmosphere; it was similar to Earth's, but just different enough.

"Looks to be a public square over there." Junko walked off ahead of Pete. Assembly ground might have been more accurate. It was a circular area paved with flagstones, in the center of which stood a low table supported by four stone stanchions. On top lay a branch festooned with fresh white leaves, looking for all the world as if it had been placed there only moments ago. It was the same as the ones on the stone altar in the jungle, and was clearly freighted with magical or ritual significance.

"Bingo," Junko murmured.

Pete glanced at her sharply. "Seems like that baby is pretty damn important to Naoshi."

"It just represents a break with his past, a way for him to balance the books. He's as drained as the rest of us are." Junko tried voicing her conclusions of the night before.

"Well . . . what do you think?" Pete asked hesitantly.

"A demon-child?" Junko suggested, even as she felt a new thought percolating.

"Maybe so. Or maybe our arrival scared them, and they gave it to their gods as an offering."

"I think it's best if Naoshi stays here," Junko muttered absently. Then she turned to look at Pete.

He didn't respond. Probably just being cautious, Junko thought.

There were three wells in the village, and a number of long benches that might serve for communal meals.

"Let's head back. Doesn't seem like there's anything else to be gained here."

The two of them returned to the rover.

~

The crew spent the evening busy with their various tasks.

Junko secluded herself in the cockpit and hailed the nearest base station. She had begun to wonder whether this planet was, in fact, previously undiscovered. She gave its approximate location, and after a while received precisely the response she'd expected. The planet had been discovered thirty years ago, but due to its remoteness from Earth and lack of mineral resources, it had quickly been forgotten again. Its inhabitants were cowardly and hidebound, and the consensus was that the shock of the Terran arrival thirty years earlier had only served to reinforce their superstitious nature.

Junko propped her elbows on the control panel and lost herself in thought. A certain conviction took hold of her. It wouldn't do to be suspicious of her crew, but . . . She raised the base station a second time. Then she returned to her cabin.

The infant was there, playing by itself. She picked it up, but it let out a horrible wail when she tried to inspect the inside of its mouth.

"What are you doing?!" Naoshi came bounding in.

"Nothing, I just—"

"I can no longer trust you, Captain." His face was pale.

"There's no reason to get so worked up," she shouted. Why was he so intense when it came to this baby? And, "I can no longer trust you"? What was that all about? Had something else happened?

"Oh no? Then who let the fang-rats out?"

"Let them out?" Damn, she'd meant to look into that.

"You heard me. The key to their cage was in the galley the whole time. Where I was sleeping. The culprit made a very careful hole in the mesh, then put it back the way it was afterward." His shoulders were shaking. Was he putting on an act?

"Making you the least likely suspect. Listen—anyone could've pulled a stunt like that."

"I see how it is . . . If you're that suspicious, I'll stay behind."

"Come on, that kid doesn't have fangs. Someone's up to something. It could even be you." She was careful not to raise her voice. The door was shut, so it was probably fine.

There was a knock, and Pete came in. "Apparently, one of the starfish bit Sabu."

"How? There's wire mesh over the top of their tank. Those things are poisonous."

"Seems the mesh was torn open when we got back today. Sabu's saying it's the curse of the demon-child. He's terrified." Pete was pretty pale himself.

"I'm on my way." Junko descended to the lower deck.

Sabu was bandaged up and lying in bed.

"How you feeling?"

"There's no medicine," he replied feebly.

"Impossible. What happened to the reserve medical supplies?" Junko was momentarily at a loss.

"Gone," Pete reported, his voice steady once more.

"What—"

"It's a curse. We're cursed. We did something we shouldn't have. Do you believe in sorcery, Captain?"

She couldn't manage a reply.

"You think it's just some old wives' tale?" Pete was getting worked up again.

"Never mind that, what do we do about Sabu?"

"He's bewitched, so there must be some way of breaking the spell. An incantation or something . . . The point is, it all goes back to that baby."

"Pete, you bastard!" Naoshi bellowed.

"Look, when you leave Earth and travel into outer space, you have to forget everything you think you know," Pete said. "Remember that planet with the freakish inhabitants, the ones who kept regrowing their arms and legs? For them, that was perfectly normal." He was beginning to sound like a college professor.

"So?"

Now they would come to it. The conviction Junko had felt when she made her earlier inquiry to the base station came bubbling up once more.

Pete had a desperate look in his eyes. "So, if we want to save Sabu, we gotta go to that village. Right now. If we don't, he'll die."

"D'you really expect me to believe all this?" Junko was riling him up on purpose.

"Are you really that pigheaded? Don't you care if Sabu dies?"

Junko was furiously calculating in her head. She'd taken stock of their remaining fuel earlier on, and . . . "Fine, we'll go."

"And leave Sabu behind?" Naoshi asked her.

"Well, he is in rough shape," Pete replied instead.

"I'm okay for now," Sabu's voice rose feebly from the bed. "I'll come with you. I didn't believe any of it at first, but now I'm scared to be alone."

"No: that starfish poison will take about a week to circulate through your body, but the more you move around, the more the process'll speed up," Junko said cautiously. "Alright, the rest of you, we leave in ten minutes."

Naoshi was white as a sheet. The baby, meanwhile, was having a ball. Pete seemed keyed up behind the wheel of the amphibious rover, and they raced over the ground at a rapid clip.

After five minutes or so, he stopped the vehicle. "This about good, Captain?"

His voice strengthened her resolve. "Mm-hmm. Kill the lights and take her into the shadow of those trees."

Before they left the ship, she'd told Sabu to send up a flare if anything happened.

Now they waited amid the gloom.

"What's going on?" asked Naoshi.

"I looked into Sabu's record, and didn't find much to speak of," Junko replied quietly. "Apart from the fact that he's wanted for murder, of course."

"Then . . ."

"This has all been a farce," Pete cut in.

"Oh Pete, I'm sorry. I suspected you at first," Junko told him.

"I'm well aware of that. I'm sure it all looks pretty suspicious, up to and including sinking my entire inheritance into that rust bucket. If you'd killed someone, what better way to escape than by zipping off into space?"

A flare went up.

They drove back to the ship at breakneck speed.

Sabu greeted them with a raygun in his hand. "Sorry about this. I was hoping to take off before you got back. I'll send a distress signal, and the rescue ship should be here for you in a couple of months."

Hearing this, Junko suddenly felt sorry for him. "You almost pulled it off, Sabu. But I emptied the fuel tanks."

Sabu's face twisted madly. "But I . . ."

Pete dashed up and snatched the gun from him. "Always the short straw. First the lizard, now this." He patted Sabu on the shoulder as the man began to sob quietly. It didn't seem like he'd been planning this from the start; he must have hit on the idea after Naoshi took in the mysterious infant.

"Glad that's over!" Naoshi held the baby up and nuzzled its cheeks. "Now we can make a life together, you and me. New Caledonia, New Zealand . . . We'll live softly, as in a morning sunrise."

Junko was not happy about any of it. This meant the *Goodbye Again* was losing two of its crew. She felt bad for Sabu, but she had to send him back to Earth . . . No, wait— what the hell did she care? This wasn't Earth. The laws of that stifling little planet didn't mean a thing out here.

"Listen, guys," Junko began, addressing herself to Sabu and Naoshi. "I'll still be needing both of you on our next voyage." Sabu looked like he couldn't believe his ears. Naoshi's face turned sour. Junko grinned. "I'm the captain of this ship, remember. And she still needs a crew, even a motley one like this. None of us were able to make it work back on Earth, anyway. I'm talking about extraterritoriality. Anyone have any objections?"

"What about the baby?" asked Naoshi.

"Forget all that old-folks bullshit about New Caledonia, you guys can live just fine right here. We can remodel the cabin; we'll make it work somehow. And if this ship gets too small, we'll trade it in for a new one. Sabu'll be in charge of childcare. He seems to have more of a knack for it than you do, Naoshi."

"You really mean it?" Pete looked relieved. The other two were so happy they couldn't get a word out.

"In return, I just want you to keep in mind that orders are orders . . . and I'm the one giving 'em, got that?" She felt genuinely good.

Naoshi took out his silver flute and put it to his lips.

Night descended quietly over the planet.

MEMORY OF WATER

A dark, ominous lake formed at the bottom of the auditorium and across the main screen in front. The door to the ground floor was shut. The guests climbed a spiral corridor to reach long, thin balconies that were attached to the walls like patch pockets. The seats were all occupied, and the balconies seemed ready to collapse under the weight into the deep waters below.

She was seated on the third floor.

Her palms and the backs of her legs were sweaty. She'd dared to venture out, but now she was regretting it. Maybe she shouldn't have come after all. It wasn't the kind of place to brave alone. Some company might have been reassuring. But that company didn't exist. She had no family, no friends, no acquaintances. No one out there had any time to be with her. No one even noticed that she was wholly alone.

She'd been alone for quite some time. Alone, always. She slept alone, she woke alone, she idled away alone.

Her parents had died long ago. She'd stopped feeling any of that wistful sorrow about their deaths. She did have a job, once. When she quit and started living off unemployment, she became sick. She was quarantined for five years in a single room. Doctors or nurses rarely came to see her. Her symptoms lingered on and on, so she was thrown out to make way for new patients. She still hadn't fully recovered. Her living costs were covered by money from the government that was automatically paid into her bank account. This was conditional on her visiting the doctor once a week, but she often skipped it. No one had ever complained. Even when she did go in, the doctor merely asked a handful of routine questions. No one truly cared about her health.

There was nothing she was obliged to do. She'd long been stagnating this way, where it didn't matter if she was dead or alive. She'd been useless ever since her life began. Nobody needed her, so she had no idea of how to interact with other people. She was used to their indifference by now.

With a great deal of effort, she'd spurred herself on to come here today. A strange invitation had landed in her mailbox a week prior. She almost never got letters in the mail. Very occasionally there'd be envelopes containing ads for products, insurance deals, local community events, which she kept unopened on a shelf in the kitchen. When they'd piled up too high she threw them away. Everything felt like too much effort, maybe because she so often came down with fevers.

The promo she received from this theater arrived in a black envelope decorated with gold curlicues. Looks like a funeral, she thought. Her long-dormant curiosity had been roused.

It appeared to be a first-time trial of something. An event, the invite said. Not a show, not a film—and calling it a "viewing" made it sound like something was for sale. They must have ended up using that word for lack of anything better. The blurb went on and on: "based on the psychological profile of a woman with multiple personalities," "schizophrenic hallucinations and delirium," "the darkness of human existence," "the cracks and fissures in life itself." Made no sense. There were quotes from various eminent figures but none of them seemed to know how to respond to the piece. She wondered if it might be a talk on psychoanalysis, but that didn't seem right, either. At the very least she could tell that large-scale 3-D visuals were involved. Plus, the admission fee wasn't too steep.

She decided that she really must go out, for once. Still, it was a real struggle to put on some shoes and a coat. She'd lost all her drive, and some days even found it tough going out to buy food. She no longer felt any desire to do anything. It took a lot of energy to overcome this oppressive inertia. She'd wear herself out doing exactly that, which then made it nigh-on impossible to get it together to do anything else. She had to tire herself out just to overcome her own filthy mood.

She knew she had to stay put and bear it for a while. She grabbed the handrail and looked down. Something rose up from the black lake, like poison vapors from a witch's potion. Feeling limp, she stopped looking.

A fever was coming on. Her mouth was dry. She was never in good physical health, but her ailments had never pushed her close to death, either. She carried a backlog of constant, uncomfortable fatigue. She'd abandoned all hopes of full recovery. By now, it was just the normal way her body operated.

She realized she shouldn't have come, after all. She should've holed up at home, taken her mystery meds, and stayed in bed. Giving herself up to the emptiness was scary, but also safe. Whereas just being in this place felt like an inescapable nightmare.

"It's like it's real," said a girl sitting behind her. "Gives me the creeps."

"Yeah, it's pretty convincing. But it's not real," her boyfriend replied.

"Don't they make 3-D TVs now? Is it like that?"

"Probably. I mean, if you get the light right you can make it look like that. Still, it's so high-fidelity, it feels live."

"Fidel-a-what? What's that mean?"

"Maybe we should call it a 'simulated experience.' They could be trying to approximate the feeling of being on hashish or mescaline."

"You sure are smart," the girl marveled.

"If you try to touch it, you won't feel anything there. It's an illusion."

"You know about such complex stuff," the girl said, smirking and moving closer to him.

She closed her eyes and let her head drop back. She felt like she was falling. It could have been just one of her woozy spells. But there was a light glowing from behind and suddenly she saw a galaxy in the distance. Moving slowly, getting closer. Then came a vague memory of living alongside someone, years, hundreds of thousands of years ago. Right back at the start of this galaxy, wherever it was in the cosmos. Who could ever remember. We stood together on the shore of a primordial sea. The sky was red behind us, strange-shaped shells and fish washed up at our feet. The world was our stage and it bent to our imaginations. Endless impersonal, unsentimental, synthetic landscapes lay before us. The skies turned artificial violet now and then, and buildings bleached by a fierce light carved up space into flat boards.

There were no signs of life and the sun had dimmed. Time had stopped there. To think that moments ago there'd been disaster sirens wailing everywhere. Or wait, maybe that'd happened somewhere else. The final war was over by the time we appeared. It was the end of the world, the end of time. Neither of us could ever die. We'd achieved permanence and come to a standstill. Like we'd fallen into the center of a strange, invisible wheel. What a peculiar distant memory to have!

Her seizure ended.

She took a breath and opened her eyes. This was happening to her about twice a week now. Hallucinations, perhaps. Had she gone mad? The thought of it didn't make her feel any particular way. She didn't care. A strange nostalgia followed these seizures. A faint, sweet pain crept back if she recalled them once they'd passed.

As always, she wondered whether what she saw had really happened. Her mind might have just cooked it up, but surely it was too vivid for that. She was tormented by visions of something she'd already lost.

The theater went dark.

"She had waited a long time," a sexless voice from the speakers intoned. "A long, long time, waiting, simply waiting, so long she lost all sense of what she herself was."

The lake started slowly shifting. The audience fell silent.

The cold, synthetic voice continued.

"She no longer knew what she was waiting for. Eventually at the very core of her character there formed a single eye that was always watching, gazing, relentlessly."

The water began to bubble.

"The eye became evil."

The water was now bubbling furiously, spitting and spluttering.

"What's going on?" she heard the girl behind her say. "Maybe there's an underwater volcano?"

"But see, there's no *water* to be *under*."

She couldn't hear the girl's fawning response over the sound of water gushing up more and more aggressively— though it was still only a section of the lake, the rest of the surface remaining calm.

"She is angry. Trembling with fury. She has waited an eternity yet still it has not come. A wicked, unstoppable resolve has stirred within her. She has been seized by an extreme anger. She seeks her victim."

The column of water reached a formidable height. There was a strong gust of wind and the water assailed the audience.

A few people jumped up and rushed for the door. Some screamed. One person yelled warnings about an accident. To think, being scared by such a strangely unrealistic rainstorm.

She heard someone reassure, "It's alright, it's not real."

The lake was whipped into a rage.

She was immobilized amid the violent water and wind.

～

"Well, how splendid. Getting caught up in a disaster in a movie theater!"

"Yes indeed, a rare experience. I shan't be taking loans to go traveling anymore."

"I wanted to taste the danger. With the guarantee of no injuries, of course, and without putting my life at risk at all."

"What's weird is, I'm not the slightest bit wet, even though we were drenched in water."

"That's the whole charm of it, no? You don't want to catch cold. And I only just bought this fur!"

But she was wet through. The persistent spray from the lake felt like mucus, sticky and viscous. Why was it only her? She wanted to scream, but her body was frozen still. She couldn't escape, she couldn't even move. The evil eye had fixed on her. Why only her!

The chaos of the lake was terrifying.

She started to feel unwell and vaguely nauseous. Her cold sweat and the sticky water made her feel faint. She trembled. She was in pain, she couldn't breathe. Slowly she keeled over. Something dark, like a spider, flew out from the lake and struck her on the head.

She ventured into the corridor once most of the audience had gone. No one had come to her aid. She was just lucky not to get trodden on. Her temperature swung between hot and cold. Her stomach quivered. The gentle slope down was pristine and empty.

A group of men covered with feather decorations were quietly performing a dance.

One of them called out to her, "Madam . . . Miss!"

"Wasn't that fun! A thrill beyond the insipid flavors of daily life! Make sure to come again next week!" He handed her a printed flyer.

"Next time we'll be doing a rain dance! Ushering in a downpour through a fantasy of light and sound!"

She looked down at the piece of paper he'd given her.

"An unprecedented concept! Implanting root hairs directly into the scalp! Wigs are a thing of the past!"

Must be a collaboration with this theater, she thought.

"Come see us make a spectacular rain pour down!"

The man spoke with manic energy. What would they make the rain pour down upon?

She folded the flyer and put it in her coat pocket. Her clothes weren't wet, but her skin was still sticky. The water from the lake only got to her. But why?

She said nothing and walked out. The men resumed their slow and mournful dance.

There was a cafeteria near the train station. She was about to pass it by when she abruptly resolved to go in, and stopped walking. Then she wavered. She wasn't sure if she was hungry or not. It was early evening, soon it would be the time to eat. She'd be home before dark. With that logic in place, she finally went through the door.

The cafeteria was empty. The only customers were two teenage girls. Or maybe they were younger. One was overweight. Her skinny friend had a face like a bird and was putting on makeup.

A dull-seeming boy slouched behind the circular counter. He was probably dying to knock off and go do something more fun. Every now and then he glanced out the window. Whatever he was hoping for wasn't there, and his lips parted in disappointment.

She murmured something and sat down on one of the high chairs. It took a lot of nerve to come out somewhere to eat like this. Cooking for herself was hassle enough, but eating out was a differently troublesome task. Because it involved talking to other people.

"Um, a coffee, please."

See, you managed to say something! She was surprised at how something so mundane could strike her as so impressive. Surely she could have always managed that much.

The boy moved around sluggishly before handing her a steaming paper cup with a little pot of milk on the side. She mumbled a thank-you. She felt like she was doing something bad.

She added the milk to her coffee, a fixed routine. She felt like an actor on stage. It's not like anyone was watching, and yet whenever she went into town she became highly self-conscious. Maybe it was a sort of social phobia toward an unspecific other. Her movements became painfully awkward.

These days it took her such determination to do the least thing. She could barely decide anything herself. Choosing between products at the supermarket was an ordeal. Her mind went blank, she lost all sense of what to do.

If a shop assistant suggested something, that's what she bought. She often found she didn't like it afterward, but still didn't have a clue as to what she *would* like. There wasn't anything she wanted. She just needed various items to "live," apparently, so it was in line with that "common knowledge" that she bought her clothes and bowls and books. She did sometimes ruminate on how very passive she was. At the same time, she just didn't think it mattered whether her towels were yellow or blue. Who cared if her plates were decorated with pictures of flowers or old European peasants? Why, they'd be fine with no pictures at all, for not even a hopping bunny on the end of a spoon made things any more interesting. She was basically uninterested in "reality." She didn't care how it was. She lived in apathy, yet had no wish to die. She was waiting for someone else's command.

She glanced across the counter as she drank her coffee.

The skinny girl had an attitude about her. She took out a square compact, rubbed her finger over the powder inside, then smoothed it onto her eyelids. Silver sparkled above her eyes, as if she'd put on a mask.

"This stuff's great. Nice and dry, lasts forever."

The fat one took more cosmetics from the bag on the chair and followed suit. As she applied her makeup, she only looked uglier and more ridiculous. The girl really was awfully fat. She wore a coat and kept her chins buried under a fluffy scarf, so she was sweating, too.

Watching these two girls had got her chain-smoking, out of nerves. She took a long last drag on a cigarette, stubbed it out, lit another. Her tongue and throat were raw but she couldn't stop. She felt so strangely ill at ease. Then again, there wasn't anywhere in this world where she did feel comfortable. She herself must lack something, something everyone else had and didn't even question.

Thoughts like this threatened to lead her into a labyrinth. She decided to focus on the girls. What sort of families were they raised in? (But what was a family, again? She couldn't remember at all. She wasn't even sure if she'd ever had one herself.) Were they attending school properly? (And what's a school? Oh, that's right. She remembered being somewhere like that, centuries ago. She'd had no friends and everyone shunned her. Having to do the same as everyone else was torture. She was too scared to go into the classroom when she was late for class, so she'd go and hang around the back gates. She'd kill time until her mother left the house, then she'd head back home and just go to sleep.)

She sighed, guessing there was no way she could understand those two girls. Perhaps she was a different sort of human being than most other people. Still, why was time so strange? She sometimes felt like she was dreaming. She sometimes lost hours, days of memory, hopelessly uncertain of where she'd been and what she'd been doing during those periods.

She'd finished her coffee. She had to order something else to keep up the act.

"Uh . . ."

She murmured quietly while she read the menu on the wall. Why was she so nervous?

"A pizza, please. And some juice."

She couldn't help being so timid. The boy's face didn't change. He only moved his hands.

"You've put on some weight," the skinny girl said.

"Yeah, but there's a reason." The fat girl was fidgeting with her napkin.

"Why don't you go on a diet?"

201

"There's a *reason*," the fat one repeated patiently. The skinny one started applying some lipstick.

The pizza and the juice arrived.

She began to eat. She'd never put something in her mouth and thought it tasted "good." She took no pleasure in food. Eating was just one of the things she had to do. Her life would be easier if there were more things like that.

She did wonder whether she found this so difficult because of some other illness. She had no idea what kind of illness that might be, but it separated her from other people.

She wasn't hungry at all. She pushed the pizza into her mouth as if under duress.

"Why isn't it dark yet?" said the skinny girl. "We're going dancing tonight. Have you got an outfit with you?"

"Sure. Wonder if I'll find a guy who'll make me shake."

"Hope there's someone cool. I got my heart broken the other day. That's the third time."

"I got pregnant again. The reason I gained weight."

"I'm gonna dress up pretty wild tonight."

Through the window she saw it had turned gray outside.

She feared the dark. She got scared spending the night all alone. She'd take even a visit from a ghost or a ghoul once in a while. Those sorts of beasts most likely didn't exist. Nor was there a heaven or a hell. Once you die, you're just physical matter. That's all. Nothing of you remains. You don't take anything away. Everything disappears. There were no dead people coming to pay her a visit.

So, what about that memory of hers? It was hazy, sure, yet she could even remember how the other person's hand had felt. Maybe the memory belonged to a past life. Not that she believed in reincarnation. Or maybe it was herself, in a different world. But what did "a different world" even mean?

She'd finished eating the pizza. The juice was long gone, stained ice cubes were all that was left. She took out her wallet and mumbled a request for the bill.

Once she'd paid she had to leave. The two girls were still plastering their faces.

She walked toward her apartment. Nobody turned to look at her. From her teenage years to her early twenties she did sometimes catch a man's eye. When she was in middle school, a boy from her class killed himself. He did it because nothing came of his unrequited love for her (obviously, since it was unrequited) and he hadn't had the courage to tell her about it. For a long time she herself was unaware.

Some years ago, one of her former teachers had knocked on her door and told her. He'd left the school and joined some religious group. He was standing in the next election and wanted her vote. That was the main reason for his visit.

She didn't know who the boy was, didn't recognize his name or his face. She couldn't remember, no matter how hard she tried. He must've been a pretty idiotic kid. But she herself was still scared of males, even at her age, which was a lot more idiotic. Had that kid in middle school dared open up to her, she'd have probably immediately gone into her shell and closed herself off anyway. She was an autistic type as a girl, and even now, in middle age, that hadn't changed. In fact, it was worse. Anyhow, that kid was dead and gone. She wasn't moved in the slightest by the death of that singular boy.

～

She'd been waiting for the world. Secretly she wanted to be loved. Maybe that intense desire had created the memory. It was back when the Andromeda Galaxy was formed. Or maybe after the Earth had ended.

She was hollowed out by lost memories of youth. She could neither laugh nor cry. She was just a vacant, living being.

She wondered what was happening out in space. She'd read somewhere that the universe was continually expanding. Galaxies were moving away from each other at terrifying speed. There was no end to the universe. No matter how far you traveled, even if you carried on for tens of thousands, millions of years, you'd just find endless space. A long, long time passes, until eventually there's no more time. Everything is the beginning and the end, a single moment is simultaneously a billion years. Start and end are one. There is no past, no present, no future. This is eternity. Knowing infinity is discovering your own universe, your own God. Most people didn't think about or even notice this kind of stuff. She knew it was there. But she didn't know where or when "there" was.

Her reverie broke as she approached her apartment.

She got undressed and put on a plain flannel nightie. The gown was a calm blue. She was putting her clothes away when she found a tight skirt in shocking pink. Why? Why did she own something like this?

It certainly wasn't anything she'd choose. She always bought clothes that didn't stand out, often in old-fashioned granny colors. She had no memory of ever buying it. This had happened several times before. Surely someone hadn't come and left it in her room. She locked the doors whenever she went out.

Uneasy, she closed her wardrobe. The phone rang. She jumped and spun around. She picked up the receiver and an unfamiliar voice spoke to her in a familiar way.

"Hey, how's it going?"

Who could it be? She gazed up at the ceiling, trying to jog her memory. Maybe it was a doctor from the clinic? But not at this hour . . .

"Man, what a mess that ended up being. I took you home and you told me to stay over. You were blind drunk, vomiting and screaming the place down. Terrible scene."

Really, who was this? Maybe he had the wrong number.

"Uh . . ." she began, but no other words followed.

"When I tried to put you to bed you threw up right in my face."

What was he talking about?

"So, what you up to? I'm just kicking about."

He spoke lightheartedly. He was being way too familiar. Was this a prank? Or what if he was someone she'd actually met somewhere? She decided to grant him the bare minimum of courtesy.

"Nothing much," she replied softly. She wished he would say his name. He just kept blithely chattering on. Who was he? She racked her brains. Maybe she should hang up. Or would that be rude?

"I'm here, same place as always."

She could hear faint voices and music in the background, the clinking of glasses.

"Wanna come join?"

"No," she replied, wishing she could disappear.

The man scoffed. "Right, you wouldn't come alone. You're always with *that* one."

What was he on about? She was shaking. There was something unpleasant in his voice.

"No way I can convince you?"

"No." She frowned.

"Fine. I get it. See ya."

He hung up. She put down the receiver. Just who was that? She was exhausted. She walked over to the bed, her head hanging. Sleep, she thought. Sleep and forget.

She got under the sheets.

Once she turned off the light, images began appearing in her mind.

The lake at the theater, the violent water. They were also one woman's psychological state. The lake had revealed a person crazed by anger. A woman who had been waiting a long time, she thought, like me. But that woman wasn't as feeble or as empty as me, which was why the evil eye had appeared.

Strangely, her skin wasn't clammy anymore. It felt that way before, because she'd gone a bit funny. Small triggers from the external world gradually took their toll. Maybe she'd go see the doctor and get some tranquilizers.

She fell asleep.

Alter-She woke up. How could *she* have gone to sleep this early? She wasn't a child. She fucking loved life. She was going to enjoy it as much as she could.

Alter-She thought about her other self. She felt sorry for her, so monkish, incapable of doing a thing. She always walked around with her eyes on the ground. She scrutinized the expression on the face of the ticket attendant as she went through the gates at the train station. She was consumed with worry that she might be committing some rude misstep. Petrified that someone might voice a complaint to her. She'd even let someone behind her skip ahead in the line for a taxi. She never went out at night. She never danced or listened to music. She wrapped herself up in a blanket in her silent room.

Alter-She knew everything her timid self did. She was apt to lose her temper over it. That girl couldn't handle some situations, and that's when she, her alter-ego, intervened. One time when her other self was approached by a drunk guy, Alter-She came out and slugged him with her handbag. He ran away. She was satisfied and handed back to her timid self, who was in a daze, with no idea of what had happened.

Sometimes she'd find herself overcome by an immense tiredness. It was so bad that she'd not get out of bed for ages. That was when Alter-She emerged and spent the night out painting the town.

They shared one body. But they were so different that returning to one personality wasn't possible. Alter-She was born during a tough adolescence. She cut school and went traveling. When she returned to her meeker self, the latter was horrified to find herself in a place she didn't recognize. The memory gaps distressed her. When she finally got home, her mother flew into a towering rage. This was way too frightening for her, so Alter-She took over again. Her mother hit her. She scrambled across the table and ran away, ran away to meet a boy.

She opened her wardrobe. She took out the pink skirt and remembered her other self quailing at the sight of it. She chuckled. A pair of silver stilettos were tucked out of sight, right at the back. Thankfully the other one hadn't found them. She needed to get better at hiding things in future.

Alter-She got dressed and did her makeup. She felt euphoric. She thought of calling up a man she hadn't seen in a while. They'd only been on a few dates, but it was clear they were very similar, almost like twins. He wanted them to get married, but she hadn't responded. This was because she'd remembered her other self: eternally uneasy, always frightened.

That woman was scared of everything. High places, wide spaces, oceans, lakes. When Alter-She put up a poster of some southern seascape, the other promptly tore it down in tears. She drew her thick curtains, turned on the light, and spent the whole day like that. She felt threatened by the light outside.

By contrast, Alter-She wasn't into sealed-up cocoons or remote country nooks. She preferred things free and easy. Vast skies and seas. Water.

What would happen if she got married? Her timid self would be overwhelmed, no doubt about it. Pity held her back. Although she deplored her other self's way of life, nonetheless she knew she was a well-meaning, if tragic, person.

She had to show that gross guy on the phone who's boss. To hell with being polite!

She made her empty bed, grabbed her bag, opened the door, and left her miserable little nest behind.

~

"How have you been doing lately?"

The doctor had his arms folded on the desk. She'd not met this one before. He asked the question with real concern and care.

"Well, you see, I get ever so tired. Even when I do nothing. Sometimes I get so exhausted that I spend the whole day in bed. I can't even fix myself something to eat."

She summarized her case, eyes downcast. This doctor seemed a kind man and she felt she could tell him anything. Anything, well—there were limits to that, of course.

"Your physical health is much improved," he said in a low tone.

"Yes, but you see, there are these ... I don't really know where they come from, but I get these fevers. I'm so very nervous about them."

She feared the doctor might think she was having him on. She mustn't confide too much, so that he didn't flat-out reject her.

"These fevers are constant, you mean?" he asked seriously.

"Yes."

"Perhaps it could be psychosomatic?"

What a sensitive doctor. The old one never spoke with her this way. Whenever she opened her mouth with him, he silenced her. "Only answer when I ask you a question. No time for unnecessary chatter." What's more, he really doled out the drugs.

"You say you're nervous. How do you mean?"

Her body shivered. She couldn't respond. The doctor's eyes were on her. She didn't feel exactly pressured, but still she began sweating. She had to say something.

"Oh, it's nothing. Nothing serious. Honestly."

He looked at her doubtfully. He mustn't know. He probably wouldn't believe her anyway. He'd probably hate her.

"You don't need this much medication anymore," he said, after glancing through her medical records. "You're healthy, so why not engage in a little more activity. How about going on a trip, for instance?"

Travel: to a place she didn't recognize. Long ago she'd found herself all alone somewhere, with no idea of why or how she'd gotten there. The fear she'd felt then had never left her.

"I just don't feel like it."

("You must be kidding," she didn't say, "I'm far too scared.")

"From now on it's about your frame of mind. It's not good to carry on doing nothing."

"Yes, I know. But I can't."

The doctor wrote out a prescription.

"Well, this should help you relax a bit."

What was he trying to say? Did he know about her constant anxiety? She considered telling him everything, but she wasn't sure how to express it. Maybe this doctor would listen. About how strange time and memory were for her.

"I'll see you next week," she said.

The doctor smiled at her. The phone on his desk rang.

He picked it up. "Yes, I'll be right over." His voice was bright and clear.

"Wait!"

She was shaken, her voice trembling. She didn't want anyone to know, but she wanted him to understand. But he just handed her the slip of paper and turned away.

210

Alter-She watched the doctor open the door and leave. She stood up, prescription in hand. Just because he's a doctor doesn't mean he cares. No need to be so disheartened. Pull yourself together. She took her other self along and made for the exit. Still, for the doctor's sake, she went by the pharmacy.

While waiting on the couch with other patients, Alter-She thought about the job she was going to interview for that day.

She was doing it because there were so many things she coveted and needed money for, no matter that her other self was strictly frugal. She just hoped that that timid self didn't interfere on the job. Imagine how distressed she'd be if one day she suddenly found herself holding a serving tray in a café! She was useless, she quit everything before she started.

That lake from the theater came to mind. She'd been petrified. She had this phobia of lakes and water, so she'd taken illusions for the real thing. She believed she'd seen something evil and been assailed by something dark.

Her alter-ego, being far more in tune with reality, experienced nothing of the sort. She wanted to stop living with her other self. Unaware that she was, in fact, the source of her pitifully timid self's desires.

She felt dreadful the moment she woke up.

She was exhausted. And she'd discovered another new dress lying about. Why was this happening? It made no sense. It felt like there was another person in her house. There was an envelope containing some cash on the bedside table. She had no memory of it, and so no inclination to use it.

I'd be better off dead, she thought. She was incapable of anything. Nothing good was ever going to happen.

She clutched her head and crouched down in the bed. She couldn't go on living, not with thoughts like these. Not when something horrifying, some wicked intent was after her.

Perhaps she should follow it, then, perhaps she should surrender. How boring, to carry on living. Not just boring, but downright hard. Being a martyr for something else was a lot easier.

It felt like she was separating away from that bright memory, too. That self, satisfied and content for all eternity, couldn't be her. It seemed like some other person's story in some whole other world.

She reached for her medicine and took some. This stuff wouldn't help at all, she knew. It wouldn't rescue her from gloom, not one bit.

She heard a knock at the door. She cowered. Maybe it was someone selling newspaper subscriptions. Or bibles. She almost never answered when someone knocked. Too much trouble to open the door and speak with another person. If it seemed no one was home, they gave up and left.

The knocking persisted. She got up and went to open the door.

A skinny man she'd never seen before.

"I knew you'd be here! Started panicking when it seemed like you were out."

His smile was luminous, like a thousand suns in one.

"Uh . . ."

She stood there dumbly. She had absolutely no recollection

of who this man might be. And yet she felt strangely fond of him, like a sort of nostalgia.

"Took me a hell of a lot of sweat to find this place. You're so vague about where you are."

Why had he come? Didn't seem like he was selling anything, but who knows.

"Can I come in?"

He reached for her arm. She pulled away.

"What's wrong? Is me being here bothering you?"

A look of doubt crossed his face.

"Oh, no . . ." she said distantly. All she could do was stand with her head bowed.

He came inside and closed the door. Mustn't be rude, she thought, since she did feel like she'd seen him somewhere before.

"Bit low today, are we?"

He sat down in a chair and looked at her. She couldn't remember where they'd met, but it seemed like they must know each other.

"Would you like something to drink?" she offered faintly, and began making tea.

"You're acting like we've never met."

He bent his head down toward the ground and gazed straight up at her. She became flustered, her ears burned.

"Why are you being like this? Don't you like me anymore? Are you hiding something?"

The kettle boiled. She picked it up at an angle and burned her other hand.

"I . . . I'm not feeling too well."

She'd seen that face somewhere before.

"You're talking very strange," he said, cocking his head to one side. "Was I wrong to come?"

"But—!" she burst out at the top of her voice, "I don't even know you!"

As she yelled them the words shot through her head and echoed through the room. But she did know him, she was sure of it. She was just scared.

"You don't know me?" His eyes widened. "You don't know me . . . Are you serious?"

"Yes, I am," she replied.

He said nothing. His head was bowed in thought.

"You really don't know me," he said, mostly to himself.

Another person inside her whispered, *you can't say things like that.*

"Don't say things like that to me," he said quietly. "Sometimes you're so cold and distant when I call you on the phone. Like you're being now. I'd just chalk it up to a bad mood, but I was a bit suspicious too, frankly. I thought maybe you were messing with me."

She watched the movements of the long lashes that lined his tapered eyelids.

"You can be so opaque with me."

There was anger there.

Why was this man angry?

"You can be so cruel . . ."

His voice dropped.

"The way you say things sometimes, it can't just be a woman's mood swings."

She wanted this stranger to leave her house. He seemed to know things about her that she didn't. She didn't want him making a scene. Just like that dress, those shoes, he was another thorn in her side.

"So that's final, is it? You don't know me."

He looked up. His words could have been threatening, but he made them sound utterly sweet and gentle.

"Yes," she replied, finally.

"Got it." He stood up. "I'm done."

She felt that distant memory stir once more within her. Even after the end of the final war . . .

"Sorry I disturbed you. I guess we won't meet again."

He reached for the door.

No, no, no! the other person cried inside her. *How can you say that? Are you really prepared to lose him?*

"Well, take care of yourself."

After this muted goodbye, the man disappeared and the door closed.

She slumped down in her chair. The details were foggy, but she sensed she'd just lost something hugely important. That memory of another person in another world now came back to her vividly. He was always with her. Right from the very distant past. For an unfathomably long amount of time. They were together in a world where time had already ended.

Why hadn't she realized sooner? She was always miserable, up to her neck in emptiness, and so she'd ruined her dreams, those dreams that weren't dreams.

She was empty now, and couldn't cry. She knew it was that evil thing that'd done this to her. She hated this world. She hated the way she was. She felt she shouldn't go on living. (Not that she'd been living until now. She'd been sustained by someone else's emotions in another world.)

A hole appeared in the wall. Several holes. Water started spurting through. It's because I don't want to be alive, she thought impassively. She'd bow to that evil thing's will.

The water was now gushing inside.

Time to leave this goddamn woman, Alter-She decided. *She only sours any compassion I show her.*

She didn't even put shoes on before opening the door. She just couldn't stand living with her. She went down the stairs. The soles of her feet hurt. Whatever. She'd considered helping out her other self—who'd no doubt breathe her last breath still deep in the pits of despair. But he was leaving. She had to hurry. She was losing the best part of her life (and of her other self's life, too).

The level kept on rising. Strangely, the water didn't flow out under the door or through the windows. It was gluey, sticky, and now it came up to her waist. The room went dark. The lights had gone off. She needed to call someone for help. But who was there?

Until now someone had been inside her, sustaining her. She sensed she no longer had that. Such was her punishment for hating the world. This world rejected her and wouldn't love her and she hated it back. That's why she was guilty. It was no worse than she deserved.

More and more water. Her chest was submerged, then her shoulders. Where had that someone gone? They were never coming back. They were a dream she herself had created, but now they'd left and found their independence. Could an earnest desire, a dream, really move by itself like that?

She just didn't know, and anyway she couldn't think about anything anymore. The water had risen over her head. She drowned and died, a lonely woman on the second floor of an apartment building.

A dog-walker ambled down the bright street outside. It was a brilliant afternoon, enough to fill anyone with joy.

Alter-She was running. She was so excited that she failed to notice that she'd penetrated another world, plunged into it. She was on the shore of that primordial sea. A mushroom cloud rose up beyond the horizon. That's how the final war ended. From now on, there would be no more time. She was caught in eternity. A pure world with neither sorrow nor sin.

She stopped running. She knew that someone very close and very familiar was approaching.

I'LL NEVER FORGET

"How about going to Earth?" said Jebba.

"Why would you suggest that? Everyone died, okay? I don't want to remember all that."

Mari took some perfume bottles from behind the counter and lined them up.

"Hey, Terran women love this stuff. The way Meelian men smell is a bit of a turn-off, apparently. But I hear these scents work a charm."

"I don't care about that crap. Look, not *everyone* died." Jebba lowered his voice.

"You mean you and your family survived. I hear your little sister got engaged to a Terran. That's something. They say getting involved with a Terran like that is a shortcut to success. And here's me all alone. Have been for six years now."

Outside, a soft breeze blew in the paved streets. People were walking about leisurely in the sun. They found it so easy to forget anything these days.

"Seems like they pulled out some of the occupation forces," Jebba said quietly.

The shop was busy, though it was only the early afternoon. Full of Meelians from the sticks who made a pastime of visiting department stores.

"True, you don't see Terran troops about lately. Guess we've got more corpo types coming over instead. We've all forgotten that short little war."

Mari remembered her heartbreak at nineteen. He'd turned a corner and vanished, one quiet midsummer afternoon. Her cold sense of loss had crystallized into a big stone now lying deep in her chest. That's all she had to show for her time on Earth.

Her parents departed shortly after they returned to Meele. Six months later, her elder brother Sol killed himself on a spaceship bound for Meele.

Before she knew it, she'd lost her land and her home. She now worked as a happy-smiley sales assistant, living in an apartment by herself.

"Can't believe it's been six years." Jebba shook his head.

"Why did my brother die? Not at liberty to say? Maybe he'd become a Terran at heart . . ."

"He was definitely cornered. And pretty frustrated. But it was mostly because he was more honest than anyone else. That's all I can say."

"What about the murder charge?"

"You're joking. Luana's alive and kicking to this day. She was even given a second holiday home on this planet. Doing pretty well for herself, actually."

"Didn't he get married?"

"Yeah, seems like he did."

"Who to?"

"Someone who's in a mental hospital or something. I don't know exactly. They say she's related to the former director of the Space Bureau."

"Really."

"Look, don't worry about it, you're going to Earth for work."

Jebba sat upright, straightened his back.

"What kind of work?"

"As a fashion model. It's fine, nothing to fret about. You look so young, see. Plus the products are aimed at women in their early thirties. Man, those thirty-something fillies . . . They have it good."

Jebba's face lit up like he was about to appear on TV.

He'd set up a subcontracting company for one of the galaxy's three major advertising firms and made himself Chief Producer. (In Mari's opinion, it was a ridiculous idea. Being the country soul she was, she disdained the advertising and leisure industries for their frivolity. She found it tough enough having to stand there in a perfume shop, even if it was to put food on the table. So imagine how she felt about becoming a fashion model!)

"No way! I'd never do something like that."

"I'll be by the soda fountain upstairs at six."

Jebba smiled and left.

Mari scowled at him. Right on cue, her Terran boss appeared.

~

"Okay, let's rewrite her CV and make her an 'Earth-born gal.'"

"No need for that. Let's have more arrogance, a lonely, solitary air. 'The galaxy is my hometown,' how about that. 'She's come this far doing things her own way.'"

"What are we selling? Perfume and soap sets? Isn't she a bit too unsophisticated for that?"

"It's an asset. Like, she doesn't have a TV at home . . ."

About half of the men talking were Terran, the other half were Meelian. They really were spouting drivel.

"Now of course, she's never been involved in anything scandalous. But I'd like to see something, you know. Maybe she has a man, maybe she doesn't. But I feel like she should."

"Yeah, there's something dirty about a woman past twenty-five without a man. Is there really nobody?"

Puzzled, Mari stared at Jebba.

"Sol comes to mind. He was a very quiet guy, silent like the best boxers are. A true Meelian, basically. The kind of man we don't see around anymore."

He smiled faintly.

"That's just how it seems," one of the Terran men said in consolation.

"We've all forgotten it, haven't we? What happened after that unconditional surrender."

"I'll never forget. We should be more persistent. There's no way that war won't stay with us in some form. And I don't just mean for one generation. It'll be passed down, like a sort of spiritual heritage."

The different faces, the green and the cream-colored, looked at each other.

"Jebba, was Sol involved in any political movements?" one of the Terrans asked.

Jebba glanced at Mari. "Well . . ."

What was her brother involved in? What was he trying to say? What was he trying to do? And what about her empty youth, insubstantial and lost from the start?

Mari resolved to go to Earth. She wondered what it was that she'd already lost before her time, and whether it was something she should pursue.

~

This woman had faint wrinkles across her pallid face. Her figure and movements had lost all their freshness. She now led an orderly, regular life.

She took time over her skincare routine. She lathered on a thick coat of face cream, sighing to herself.

She was no longer attractive. If she walked down the street, no one would turn to look at her.

She couldn't hide her misery completely. For the most part, though, she possessed a high level of self-control that stopped her from wailing and crying.

She stripped naked, put on a bra correctly sized for her withered breasts and, though it was hardly necessary, a tight yellow corset. She then got dressed with elaborate care. Eyeliner, then eye shadow. Hair pinned up with a pearl-studded clasp. Once she'd applied her perfume, her hands moved to undo her buttons, one by one.

She welled up with tears and got into bed. She drew up the hem of her skirt and felt between her legs. There she found a dreadful hollow, as always—centuries had passed since it was last brimming with slick green mucus.

She fingered her lips, her breasts, then went limp. No one would touch her there.

She'd been sleeping alone for such a long time. That man never showed up anymore. Not in her fitful daytime sleep, nor in her endless dreams at night, which only left her exhausted.

If only he'd appear and hold her in his arms. Yes, even just once (though once wouldn't be enough). If only that Meelian man could bat his thick green lashes and gaze at her with his gentle, cloudy eyes.

She seriously wondered if she mightn't be a sex maniac. For a start, why had she been put in a place like this? She was afraid to ask. And so she never felt like talking to the doctors. Her mind was forever somewhere else.

She wrote a letter to her sister.

I'm always good, so please, buy me nicer things. I want those candles that smell nice when you set them on fire. Red, orange, pink, green. Violet loungewear. And to keep me occupied at night, a needle and thread and beads in all sorts of colors. Also, tell Dad to send me a bit more money.

She didn't know her dad had died not long before. Emma wasn't getting any special treatment at the clinic. She was interned there because when the spaceship was captured, she couldn't say anything about that "important man." And this then sent her over the edge.

How much love did Sol leave behind before he went? In that final moment of consciousness. The only thing he conveyed was that he'd never once made anything up.

His heart had grown weak. Emma knew he depended heavily on her. He'd treated her like a blood relative.

Emma smiled bitterly as she sang that old song, "If you were gonna fool me / Boy, I wish you'd fooled me till the end . . ." That boy did fool me till the end, she thought.

She was suspected of being a spy, too, but since she genuinely didn't know anything and instead burbled strange descriptions of things like how his heart embraced and held her, they'd put her in a mental hospital.

It's not hard to imagine someone falling to pieces after being institutionalized. Emma became hollow, dulled, depressed, and said she only slept four or five hours at night even after regular sleeping meds.

She cooked up past sins for herself and believed she'd be punished for them one day. Her sense of time turned toward that judgment day and spiraled, returning in circles to her days with Sol on the one hand, and on the other absorbed in the world of justice, right and wrong. She was diagnosed with schizophrenia.

They were heading for Earth on a *luxury* space liner. Mari knew that because Jebba kept marveling at how "luxurious" everything was. Some very chic passenger started playing the piano in the rear. It felt like a cocktail party.

"Spaceships can end up in tatters, you know. We're doing pretty well with this one." Jebba was in high spirits. They were even showing romantic films from the 1930s.

"All this would've been unthinkable before the war. You know, I've got a soft spot for old movies. Have you heard of Garbomania? Or Marlene Dietrich?"

Mari said she hadn't.

"How can a dame in her thirties like you not know them? Listen, we're making this trip with another goal in mind."

Just as Mari had thought. She put down her cocktail glass.

"I mean, I'm also fine with Terran culture flooding in. Sometimes I'm so moved I think I'm gonna come. I visited Earth when I was a teenager and went crazy for some of the music and the way they use words. Seriously, I almost jizzed everywhere. Hey, you know 'Once Upon a Time in Yokohama'? 'Course you don't. See, it's one kind of invasion. They slowly, slowly give us a little taste. Then in the end they rape us. And afterward they say, 'I love you.'"

A velvety voice singing a medley of Frank Sinatra songs came from behind the piano.

"Cultural exchange is all well and good, but I do feel like we've had enough. We want our old calm back. Our land, our longstanding culture, our families."

Mari bowed her head.

"Did people ever mistake you and your brother for Terrans? Mari and Sol ... Sounds like something in Spanish. You know, *mar y sol*, sea and sun. There used to be a singer called Marisol, too. I'm pretty clued-up, ain't I? *Blue light, Yokohama* ..."

Jebba was slightly drunk.

"So this is a political movement? Wonder how that'll go," Mari said coolly.

"Doesn't matter how it goes! It's about our attitude to life. We'll be no worse off if it flops."

"But how many half-Terran kids are out there now? It's too late to cut ties and seal ourselves away."

"I'm not saying we should do that. Don't you care about our homeland being destroyed?"

Jebba spoke with passion. He's a smooth one, Mari thought. She said nothing. He'd survived the war despite his circumstances.

"Been a while," a Terran woman nodded to Jebba. She wore a black dress and a black veil over her face, her hair tied back in a chignon with a fake rose pinned to the side.

"Hey, it's Luana!"

The two hugged.

"My, my, very classy. Bleeding those diamond mines dry, eh?" Jebba made a teasing dig at the wealthy-looking lady.

"It's uranium these days. Seems you're keeping busy too, Jebba. This is my husband. We've also been through some turbulence since that war, you know."

What silly people, Mari thought.

"I'm sure, I'm sure."

"We got posted unexpectedly. We're returning for a holiday."

Luana's lips were fashionably pearly. They reflected the lights when they moved.

"What a tragic thing Sol did. He just lived for pure love, didn't he?"

She let out a cackle.

"Weren't you and Emma fighting over him?"

"No, no. Apparently Emma had a miscarriage after that. Then she ended up in a mental hospital. They really loved each other, you know. Straight out of *In the Realm of the Senses.*"

Tired of hearing their nonsense, Mari tried to return to her seat, but Jebba stood up and blocked her path. With no way out, she signaled for another cocktail.

"They were totally prepared to die with that 'exodus to glory,' weren't they? Some people actually did die."

Luana waved her hands Hollywood-style as she spoke.

"But it wasn't glorious. Who knows if we aren't more miserable now than we were then." Jebba's face was serious now.

"People are miserable as long as they're alive, Jebba. After all that, my husband and I met and got married. His work happened to have a connection with Meele, you see. Now we're very happy. It was our wedding anniversary the other day . . . He got me a diamond bracelet and made me head of this new venture. It's an up-and-coming cosmetics business."

Luana appeared nervous, performing almost desperately, suggesting in a roundabout way how strong her pride was and how she didn't want anyone bringing up the past.

Jebba and Luana could easily have denounced each other as traitors. They only didn't because it suited both of their interests not to. It was clear they were both on shaky ground.

"We're using her for our first campaign." Jebba pointed at Mari.

"Oh, my goodness." Luana clocked her.

"Spitting image, ain't she?"

Luana murmured her agreement with Jebba's comment, lowering her voice as she did so. As everyone does when they speak of the dead.

"She's good though, isn't she? She'll help us sell. Looks fresh."

They were haunted by the past, smeared in shame, yet despite it all, carried on living.

Every person has one thing they can never forget.

Mari placed her now-empty cocktail glass on top of the piano. She returned to her own seat and drew the curtains. The inside of her eyes burned white. Perhaps she was over-tired.

Ever since her heart was broken aged nineteen (he was a Terran), she'd kept on always losing people, losing things. Her present life was just a quiet, discreet retreat. Who knows how it'd come to this.

"Hey, look, you've been a great girl. I'll never forget you."

That's what he said, patting her on the head.

Never forget?

Did he really say that? He'd never forget?

The guy had forgotten her long ago, for sure. And he'd have fathered two kids by now.

People on her planet almost never forgot, whether they promised it in words or not. That's why her parents and her brother reached their emotional limit and departed from this world.

She was alive because she was still empty. Vacant folk like her had to keep living, to fill that void.

Mari suddenly had the idea to go meet her. That woman had been living alone these whole six years. Why did she keep on living?

She heard Luana, drunk, come over and drop into the seats ahead of Mari, beyond the curtain.

"What? Oh, you're all liars!" She went on, "'I'm the husband,' you said? God, why do you talk like that? Pisses me right off. I'm sick of this already. Divorce me, quick. I'm sick of being alive, even."

"Geez," she heard a man's voice say. "Will you keep it down?"

"Why don't you keep it down! I can't stand hearing your voice."

"What are you talking about?"

"Just the sight of your face fucking ticks me off!"

Mari heard a slap. Silence. After a moment, Luana started sniveling.

"What d'you do that for? You're horrid, bullying me like that."

"You're the bully."

His voice remained serene.

"You just take advantage of people's weaknesses! Acting like you own the place! Look, it was a whole six years ago now. Back then I wasn't necessarily on Meele's side either."

"But Sol wouldn't bring you along in the end, would he?"

"It's not like he didn't care about me. He even became a murder suspect for my sake."

"You cheating whore . . ."

"You're the cheater! Just then I had to jump in before you tried it on with that damn model girl. Take my eyes off you for one second and you've got your hands on her tits!"

"That's not what happened."

"It was about to happen, that's why I stopped you!"

"Have you still not forgotten him?"

"I told you, it wasn't like that between us. He wasn't someone I'd forget or not forget. You're gonna use that against me for the rest of my life, huh?"

They were talking about Mari's brother. Seemed like the core of this couple's relationship was a sort of mock jealousy.

"What do you mean, use it against you?"

Neither spoke for a while.

Mari heard clothes rustling together. Were they going for it now? Seriously?

"It's okay, I get it," Luana whispered. "I'm sorry." She was breathing heavily.

"I wish you'd said that from the start." His voice sounded gentler.

They were a strange pair, these two.

They each prodded at some past infidelity, real or not, and that's what formed the basis of their relationship.

"Don't," Luana whispered softly.

"Don't." This time she sounded more tense. After that she must have given in, as now only short gasps were heard.

Mari opened her eyes. All she could see was the cream curtain in front.

What a shameless couple, she thought. Mari had never acquired any sense or intuition of the depths of sexuality. She'd no idea that these sorts of couples existed, that relationships could be like this.

For her, pure love alone was right and good. Anything else was unacceptable. What's more, she had only a conceptual understanding of pure love. She'd never experienced what it was, exactly.

There had been that man who got on his bicycle and left her, one afternoon during the height of summer, when she was nineteen.

It was so long ago now.

A sense of loss, or maybe more like a vacant feeling, had pervaded her life ever since.

It hadn't been love.

Lately she'd come to understand that, and had begun moving forward.

"I'm sorry, hon. I'm a bad girl, huh?" Luana spoke to her husband in a low, fawning tone.

He grunted in response.

"Please just don't mention Sol again, okay?"

"I know you always want me to mention him. That's why I do it."

Luana didn't respond. After a long while she said flatly, "You're such a smartass," followed by other equally inane comments.

Mari smiled and closed her eyes.

"You're running through a park in the morning."

Jebba was brainstorming ideas.

"Then you tie your hair up in a ponytail, hop on a bike, and . . ."

"Don't wanna." Mari shook her head like a little girl.

"What?"

"The thing with the bike."

"Why not?" Jebba lit a cigarette. The boy who broke her

heart: he'd left on a bicycle. Mari couldn't bring herself to admit such a ridiculous reason.

Luana was wearing jeans. The meeting was in her living room. The afternoon sun creaked past the window.

"You don't know how to ride a bike?" Jebba asked.

"That's it."

"No worries. It's fine, Jebba. Don't force things." Luana waved her hands about.

A woman brought some chilled drinks through to the team.

"Listen, I'm not asking for a thirty-year-old schoolgirl. Now *that* would be forced. Can you give me a 'gal in her thirties' kinda vibe? She's not embarrassed about age."

"She goes to nightclubs?" Luana asked.

"You bet. But wearing jeans and a poncho. She goes to the club with a man but leaves by herself. Can you swim?"

"Yes."

"Great. I'd have been worried if you couldn't do that either."

Faint laughter went round the room.

If you listened carefully, you could hear little noises all the time in Luana's house: a beep here, a clunk there. The air conditioning turning on by itself, off by itself. All sorts of switches coming on and off automatically. One room had a device for eavesdropping on phone calls; another had a device to protect phone calls from eavesdropping.

Mari thought it would be unbearably lonely to live by yourself in a house like that. When she mentioned this aloud, Luana was surprised.

"I couldn't stand being in a house without any devices installed. I'd be so scared! How would you know when a burglar was about to break in?"

Mari realized that this was Terran culture. Everyone lived in a house like Luana's: a secure safety-deposit box, guarded by infrared surveillance cameras.

Anyone who didn't was deemed to belong to the "underclass."

"I can't be in the underclass, can I?" Mari asked Jebba. She told him about her one-room apartment on Meele: she didn't have a 3-D television, or a dishwasher, and she'd never once put a lock on the door.

"Nothing wrong with keeping that in our concept. But it seems a tad hippyish, you know? Hippies are another kind of privileged class."

"So what about the poor people?"

Mari tried asking a Terran sort of conceptual question.

"They live in hostels, they're in hospitals, prisons, children's homes—those folks are in public institutions like that, right? By the way, you know, I was raised in an orphanage."

"Sure, Jebba."

"Fact. My parents split up when we came to Earth. My mom got custody and then she got hooked on drugs."

Mari couldn't believe what she was hearing.

"She died in hospital. I was there when she passed. I was sixteen. My dad latched onto a Terran girl, had kids and joined the Terran Defense Forces."

"You've been on your own since you were sixteen?"

"Yup."

Mari suddenly felt more respect for Jebba. She figured she was really laboring under the weight of her own solitude, so when she met someone who was even more alone than she was, she couldn't help but idolize them a bit.

This also meant that anyone who managed to have one relationship, even if it was a marriage like Luana's, was not alone. Luana was certainly lonely, but if you can get attached like that, you're not totally alone.

Mari suddenly realized she wanted someone who could offer that attachment.

"So I've got twenty years of solo living under my belt. If I share a place with a girl or something I just get annoyed. I like being with someone for a while. But together the whole day? Man, I just get so tetchy. I do everything for myself, too. Laundry's all automated. For food I either eat out or order in. When I wake up, I just clean up the bathroom and head out."

"Don't you feel lonely when you come home and nobody's there?"

"Nope." Jebba didn't hesitate.

"But when it's all dark and cold . . ."

"You're thinking about apartments back on Meele. Terran homes have automation devices installed."

"Oh, right."

"Actually, if I forget to turn off the holovision set, I think there's someone else there and I panic. It's just an image, of course. I remember you could buy these Welcome Home devices too. They were marketed at single people. 'Welcome back, honey! Tough day, huh? Did you eat? Wanna take a bath first?' . . . And there were these little bots called 'Woof-Woofs' for people who wanted a dog but couldn't be bothered feeding it or whatever. If you had one it would just sometimes trot out and bark a bit. Then some idiot built on that idea and made a 'Baby-on-Call' device, but that didn't work out so well. People's preferences about babies differ of course, but the sticking point more than anything was that a child has to actually grow and develop."

Luana was sipping some Meelian juice and checking her nails, looking bored.

She lived in a house full of automation devices, sometimes seeing her husband, doing her own work as she pleased, going out when she pleased. She and he were together before going to sleep, and if they felt like it they'd drum up some episode of infidelity from six years back, get mad at each other, and do it. Otherwise they somehow ignored their inconvenient bodies.

Must be hard to learn how and when to ignore your body like that. How did she get through a whole day when neither of them left the house? Breakfast, cleaning, lunch, bath, dinner—just going through that cycle?

Mari wondered what they could even talk about after six years together.

"Alright, let's trial the concept for two months," Luana said, breaking the silence abruptly.

"That's it? We're done?"

"If she's popular we'll use her for our jeans ad next. Why not hang around on Earth for a while? This one will sell."

Luana's face went blank. She seemed bored.

Jebba also fell quiet.

Mari hung her head. She was tired. The air conditioner was working fine, but maybe there was something wrong with the air in here. No, she'd been wasting away ever since she'd set off for Earth. She hadn't been able to sleep much the previous night. She'd got caught up thinking about love, guilt, solitude, and before she knew it the dawn had come.

She felt faint.

It shouldn't be like this.

"Mari, why don't you take a break? You look pale," Luana said indifferently before she left the room.

Maybe a nap would perk her up.

Mari took herself upstairs and into one of the bedrooms, where she dozed off. There were signs that someone had been sleeping there well into the morning. It was probably Luana's bed.

Mari remembered later that during that short nap she sensed her blood moving from her toes to her head, then draining out of her body.

She'd had such a strange, brief dream.

She woke up from it immediately.

It felt like her mind had been controlled by someone else.

She'd dreamt about a man with a drawn-out, greenish face.

His eyes were dull and his eyelids sagged, making him look deranged. He wore a short white robe that covered his head and was tied with a cord at his waist, but the cloth didn't cover the rest of his body. A red cross was drawn on the white robe, signifying that he'd been cast out.

His penis was exposed, hanging droopily. He was powerless and impotent. Mari was embarrassed that his parts were on show in this dream. The little toe was missing from both of his feet—seemed like they'd been cut off on purpose—and he was tied down into what looked like tiny five-centimeter open-toed clogs.

One hand was lifted to his green face, holding something like a bent straw or pipe between his lips.

Mari started interpreting the dream as she woke up. He was:

(1) Someone punished by a king;
(2) Someone with a decaying mind;
(3) Someone with a decaying body;
(4) Someone who had soaked up another person's brain;
(5) Someone guilty of adultery; or,
(6) Someone whose torso had been abruptly cut in two and the upper and lower halves had come apart.

In any case, he'd been made to wear that shameful outfit because he'd sinned in some way. Mari felt sorry for him in her dream. She didn't know what he'd done, but it seemed cruel.

His body had grown soon after he'd been made to wear the short robe over his head. Mari thought he really ought to be covered up (it wasn't a pretty sight).

Mari couldn't shake the feeling that someone had sent her the idea of this man. And the telepath who had sent it over as a fleeting dream was definitely a woman, one who loved this man very much. She was deeply attached to him. She felt that this naked, deranged man belonged to her.

The man was a Meelian.

His name was Sol.

As Mari got up she felt her head swim. Her lower body felt sluggish, like she'd just had sex. Or more like when she'd wanted a man to hold her, to be inside her—fervently wanted it, but he wouldn't do it.

A woman who was having dreams like this must wake up feeling both embarrassed and oppressed.

She was incensed that she couldn't hold and touch with her own skin this man she'd lost forever.

She'd dreamt of him for years and years, thought of him over and over again, yet she still couldn't remember his face.

In spite of all this, he had certainly committed some crime against her. Nothing to do with any punishment from a king, she thought.

This is because, for a time, he was her god. Once he'd died, there would be no god who could punish her. That in itself was some kind of offense, for a woman so obsessed with right and wrong. He had become feeble-minded and died screaming. No god would do such a thing.

And so she was troubled by contradictions.

Her body was dry and shriveled after seeking one particular man for so long. To still be alive in spite of this was torture. Why did it have to be him? She didn't understand.

Her love had lost its object and was driving her deeper into madness.

She was Emma.

Mari tried saying her name. She didn't know her at all. But when Sol was dying, he called out, "Emma."

Was Emma a telepath?

It was the first time Mari had experienced anything like this. Was Emma tormented in her madness by these sorts of visions and daydreams? Constantly?

How unbearable, to have such dreams all the time. How disgraceful they were. Emma herself knew that.

But since she'd been institutionalized her world had begun to warp, piece by piece. She wasn't sure why. Maybe the air outside the hospital was different.

She made herself up every day like this, lit her room with candles (open flames were banned, but she always found a cunning way to break the rules), and waited there by herself. Why did Sol never come to her?

He'd been unfaithful for a long while.

Emma was angry. And yet, perhaps he didn't know she was in here. Or maybe he wouldn't come if she weren't beautiful anymore. In that case, the chances of him turning up were even slimmer. Her face and body had already lost much of their past beauty (time had sprouted wings and aged only her). He might not even recognize her now.

Or, perhaps, that final discharge had fried his brain. Meaning he might have been put in a hospital like this one, or a prison.

People said that the war was over. Emma noticed Meelians and their mixed-blood kids among the people visiting other patients. But there must be some people still in prison.

Emma hadn't seen his dead body. She didn't believe for a minute that he'd died.

The family had probably got together and decided to feed her that story.

Mari sank into a deep fatigue. She knew now what it meant to come into contact with another's madness. She felt a festering in her mouth, felt as if her body had half melted away.

The sunlight outside had dimmed.

She tried to get up. Green hair spilled over onto her arms and her hairpin caught her brow.

She pulled the pin out and dropped it on the bed (what a messy woman she must seem) and tried to move her body. She squinted, her body still in the same position. She felt numb all over and her muscles didn't work properly.

Both curtains were open. She'd managed to sleep that torturous, not-quite-sleep despite the glaring light. The sun was setting and all she could hear was the sound of the air con.

Luana and Jebba had left the house.

They had things to do.

Those were the people Mari should be with, whose ideas she should emulate, those were the people whose horizons she should slip into. That's how she could become part of the ordinary everyday.

Jebba (or Luana's husband) would make a pass at her, she'd indulge him and learn to feel as they did, with their level of energy, she'd love him and love life.

But she mustn't love too much.

Mari needed to sync with the frequency of this woman locked up in hospital who, with nowhere else to vent her ferocious energy, was building a world of hollow love from the only material available to her—the past.

But how had she managed to transmit herself to Mari? Maybe, in their hollowness, their spiritual frequencies weren't too dissimilar.

Mari gazed down through the window.

A man was walking round and round.

Her heart felt like it might gently float down and cover him from above. It wasn't exactly psychological dissociation, but she felt freed from her body.

Mari suddenly wondered why this man was here, inside the grounds of the residence. Strangers shouldn't be able to get in. Or perhaps he was a member of staff.

He stopped walking. He seemed to be figuring out what to do.

He needs to look upward, Mari thought. He looked upward. She was nineteen and he smiled at her on that street corner.

The man who had got on his bicycle and left her was there, polishing his glasses, then looking at her balefully. Surely you don't hate me that much? No, but I can't be bothered with it. With what? she asked. Coming up here? That's right, he replied. But I'm here for professional reasons, so I gotta be bothered.

With that, he climbed to the upstairs level of the house. What about all those alarm devices?

"They won't sound at the moment," he whispered. Almost seemed like he was still figuring out what to do next.

"Are you here to steal stuff?" Mari asked foolishly.

"I hadn't intended to."

He seemed confused.

"To rape me?"

"I don't feel like doing that right now," he said, looking puzzled, before laughing at Mari.

"You're the new model, right?" he asked, almost too casually.

"Yes."

"Alright, so how about you come along with me?"

"I've got a job to do."

"It'd be helpful if you could put off that job, or cancel it even."

He grinned unabashedly.

"You make it sound like it's not up for debate."

Mari was serious.

"It's not up for debate, in my case."

He sat down on the bed.

"Aren't I so cute anymore?"

Before realizing it, Mari had asked him a question that implicated him in her own past.

"No, you're still very cute."

He hadn't twigged. He reached out his hand and stroked Mari's cheek.

"I can mostly guess what you used to look like . . . Right, first thing once we're out of here, let's go get coffee or something. I'm kinda frazzled."

Jebba would be unsettled. At least, he wouldn't just shrug it off. He's here for professional reasons too, after all.

"Are you married?"

"You're kidding. If I had a wife she'd kill me for chaperoning girls like this."

He was telling the truth, but his manner betrayed a certain vanity.

How was it that she fell in love back then? He would've needed to be pretty proactive to cut through to a shy type like Mari.

"Shall we just get outta here for now? I hate to leave this lovely air conditioning, but . . ."

"What's it like outside?"

"Frigging hot, stuffy and muggy too. Everyone comes out at night. Aren't people crazy here? It's only after midnight that they really brighten up. Then you've got crowds flooding the streets."

"Why do people come out?"

"I guess they're looking for something interesting. Same for everyone. So they go somewhere to listen to music, dance, meet people, drink."

"What about people who don't go to places like that?"

"Guess they've already given up."

There was a strangely deep kindness in his voice.

She was starting to take a real shine to this guy. In movies, it's almost a given that a man and a woman develop feelings for each other as soon as they meet. This feels like a movie, Mari thought. The circumstances were somewhat unromantic, but there was no doubting she liked him.

"We best get going. Hey," he prodded the back of Mari's neck.

"Hmm . . ." she responded wordlessly. I have to go to that mental hospital, she thought. I have to meet the woman putting so much effort into making up such utterly unrewarding love. Because love isn't like a house you can just kick back and live in once it's completed. No, it gets more worn and tattered day by day. So unless you keep on making it up, day by day, it disappears in all but name.

"Do you have any money?" No way could she use the check Jebba gave her.

"Got a little," he said warily.

"Alright, I'll come."

Mari figured that Luana's cosmetics business wouldn't exactly go bust without her, anyway.

"Okay."

They went downstairs. Mari heard something switch on automatically. Then the sound of a film reel running. She thought it was strange to film people only to lose track of them the moment they stepped out of the house.

It was dusk and Mari and the man were in a café.

Didn't seem like anything would happen. Also seemed like anything could happen.

Mari remembered the short, disturbing dream she'd had during the day. All the woman wanted was for that man to be by her side, as compensation for everything until now.

When someone just can't stand things anymore it means their heart has exceeded its capacity. That's when Meelians depart. They kill themselves. Whereas Terran hearts turn into something else. They turn toward a sort of hellish torment.

His hand rested on top of hers. She didn't try to pull away. Mari just sat still and drifted deeper into thought.

～

A selfish telepath was tormenting her.

He was gone. Despite the depth of their love.

The past six years felt like they would be the last ones of her life, these six years without him, and as she looked back on her own life, fervently seeking fulfilment, she found she had never once been satisfied.

Stuck in uncertainty, nothing reaching resolution.

Always tense and strained.

Mari's mind was often blank when she first woke up. Still, he would sometimes try to start a conversation.

"Hey, my love . . ."

After the attempt to jump out of the window of a hele-taxi soaring high in the sky, something finally clicked. She fully realized how much she clung to him.

"Won't a love affair get you into trouble?" Jebba called to her on the street in the drizzling rain. Mari slowly looked up. It was like seeing someone she'd known a hundred years ago.

Mari had gone out to buy milk, bread, and cigarettes, and now she was getting soaked walking in the rain. There weren't so many streets anymore where you could still walk and get wet like that. She didn't know that Jebba would be so familiar with these dilapidated gangways.

She'd posted the check to Luana's address.

The man had introduced himself as an aspiring novelist. He said he'd write about their romance, and sometimes he did indeed sit down at his voicewriter.

The pair would talk for hours on end, piling up ideas and concepts. They considered their relationship worthy of a detailed account.

"Well, make sure you don't start looking like a woman who's finally got her claws into a man."

Jebba flicked away his cigarette and walked behind Mari.

"But no, that's not you. You still got that thirty-'n-flirty face going on. We kept filming, by the way. You know he was on the team before we signed the deal. Once he saw you, he lost interest in the job. Total weirdo, bit of a pompous snob. Right up your alley, I bet, knowing your girlish tastes. We're pretty much finished with the shoot now, so the job's done. All that's left now is the edits. You got a bank account?"

Mari shook her head.

Jebba handed her a plastic card.

Luana had probably planned it this way all along, to give it a more natural feel.

But if Mari hadn't met him after that awful little nightmare, none of it would have happened.

"I'm going to visit her," Mari said one day.

She didn't want him coming. But he tagged along all the same, like there was no question about it.

Mari stood on the lawn outside the clinic, shaking with nerves.

A thin, middle-aged woman came out of the greenhouse, unkempt and dressed in a shapeless shift.

Emma's hair was held back by a wide hairband, a few loose strands dangling from her brow and the sides of her head.

For a moment her wide, keen eyes looked alarmed to see the two visitors.

There was no longer anything beautiful about Emma. Her gaunt face was unpleasant, and in front of other people her lips trembled slightly so the nonsense she talked didn't even come out clearly.

"I've come to meet you. I'm Sol's sister. Well, he died six years ago . . ."

Emma looked puzzled, as though she hadn't expected someone else to ever pronounce his name.

". . . Sol?"

"Yes."

"Sol. I remember him. Not just remember, more than that. But I do wonder who he was. Once I say it I'm not sure. You *are* a pretty girl, aren't you?" Emma said this with envy. Her lips squirmed oddly. "I feel like I saw someone once, yes, long ago. Someone who looked like you."

The doctor had warned Mari to be careful and avoid mentioning Sol, because she'd get fixated and start acting weird.

"Sol . . . I miss him."

Emma frowned like a sulky child.

"It was before the war had even started. We truly belonged to one another. Sol was a terrifying man, you know. He would grow calmer and cooler the more I blew up in his face. He was like a quiet beast. Sometimes I was so unbearably scared of him. He was eerie, creepy, I guess. He'd be silent and just glare, face like a dragonfly. He got skinnier and lankier, grew feverish, and there he was, just glaring with those eyes. Perhaps he was doing drugs . . . No, he was doing drugs for sure. I myself never touched the things."

Here Emma was lying. That slurred speech of hers obviously came from taking tranquilizers for over twenty years. It was also an expression of her low self-confidence, sure, but still. "Honest."

Emma gave a sloppy laugh and started drooling. She wiped her chin with the back of her hand and led Mari to an air-conditioned meeting room.

Her movements were jerky and she seemed as unstable as a puppet doll. Sometimes she'd screw up her face and a net of fine wrinkles would pull in her thin lips, bringing an ugliness to the lower half of her face that made her look even older.

She mumbled and whispered things that made no sense, occasionally darting glances in unexpected directions.

"What sort of a person was he?" Mari chose her words carefully.

Emma seemed troubled and looked up, searching for something to pin her eyes on.

She then looked away and gazed through the glass at the summer grasses outside.

"I am sometimes glad that he's not here. That way he can't see how hideous I've suddenly become."

She sighed and grumbled on.

"Why can't I sleep, why can't I stop smoking? When I wake up in the middle of the night, my skin is so bone dry, I feel like twenty new wrinkles appear each time."

This woman couldn't have been much more than thirty. It made a cruel contrast with Mari's peppy beauty.

"I've grown old and crusty being locked up here, haven't I?"

Emma's pupils slowly sank down until they met the edge of her bottom lids. She remained like that, staring at the ground.

"He had his charm, there were things about him anyone would love. But he himself had very dramatic likes and dislikes. He would always pick out one woman he particularly fancied and draw strength from obsessing over her. Tell the truth, it was only just before he died that I started to positively like him."

Mari wished Emma would stop doing the weird thing with her eyes.

"I got you something," Mari said. She opened the paper bag she'd brought and took out some gifts for Emma: a necklace, a bunch of plastic flowers, a pair of delicate sandals. Emma smiled and tried everything on.

"Might sound a bit strange at my age, but . . . What I really want is a hat with a wide, absolutely massive brim."

"I'll bring you one next time."

But Mari knew she wouldn't be visiting again. This old telepath had no idea that she was tormenting some Meelian woman—her powers were just running, without her realizing. Mari desperately wanted to find ways in which she was different from her, this Terran woman trapped in her own distant memories. Emma was like a malignant growth, a cancer—the mother of some invasive parasite. She was Mari's exasperating mother, no doubt about it. Possessed by an intruder, but all the same.

And she was singing her song of ruin.

The man went to the shops to buy sodas.

"You're going to die soon," Mari told Emma, firmly and spitefully.

"Perhaps. I am suffocating. But people can't live forever. It's what I'm hoping for."

Channeling Sol, Emma saw herself, too, growing weak with age and living.

"But since I've already died once and come back to life . . ." Emma went on. "You'll die in a bed, that's what Sol said to me. Because I didn't die in the war. Not even a nuclear missile finished me off."

"You will die."

If she could pick up telepathic messages, she should also be able to send them. Mari channeled her strength into her eyes, straightened her back, and kept talking.

"You have died."

Emma closed her eyes. "Yes, I know."

"You can't go on suffering forever. You must die. Your love story has ended."

Mari sensed that Emma's telepathy was scrambling the connection between them.

Emma mumbled, her lips wriggling: "It hasn't ended. Some stories never end. But, oh, how I would like to put it to rest. Each day that I love you just wears me out. I lose the strength to keep living. You're not here anymore, for god's sake."

The old woman opened her eyes.

Thick, muddy tears and mucus dirtied her face. She wiped it away with her hands and looked straight at the green face before her.

"Sol, let me ask you one more time. Have you already forgotten me?"

Emma suddenly looked like a little girl.

"I'll never forget," Mari replied without thinking. She regretted it, but it was too late.

An animal-like cry burst out of the aged woman's body. She stood up, writhing, turned around and blundered out. An automatic door in the rear swung open to reveal a long corridor.

Emma fled down the corridor at breakneck speed, screaming and crying.

An opaque door closed and hid the sight of Emma struggling with some orderlies. Her animal cries continued. Mari could hear the footsteps of several nurses behind the door.

Mari stood alone in the meeting room.

"He won't forget. Yes, that's right. We can't help it. We never forget. We can't forget. Some things will never be forgotten, even in death."

The grass outside was limp from the sun.

The man came back carrying some cold drinks. He entered without saying anything, then crinkled his forehead, trying to understand what was going on.

"What happened?"

"I told her."

Mari slumped onto the sofa, all strength drained from her body.

"Told her what?"

"The truth."

"What did she do?"

"It must've triggered a bad seizure."

"Weren't you supposed to avoid subjects like that? What did you say?"

"I told her we never forget. You get it, right? Meelians

die when their hearts reach full capacity. That's because we never forget the things that are important."

"Right."

"That's why we never have changes of heart. Because we never forget, not even in death."

"Let's go," he said. A single gold sandal lay discarded on the rug.

A few weeks later, Emma burned to death in a fire at the mental hospital. The fire started in her room, of all places. She'd lit twenty candles and retreated back inside her memories.

HIT PARADE OF TEARS

"Dinner," his wife called.

He was busy reading *Villains of Japanese Cinema*. Without looking up, he stretched out a hand.

"What's that supposed to mean?"

"I want a ginger beer or something first. A coke would be fine. I'm thirsty."

"You're having a laugh," she reproved dryly. "You really think we have stuff like that at home?"

She was in a very complicated mood. So complicated that it's hard to describe in what way it was complicated.

"Go buy some then, out there somewhere."

"Nowhere around here sells drinks like that."

She spoke softly and a little gloomily this time. She was standing in the doorway, looking into a bare room lit by a single, unshaded forty-watt lightbulb hanging from the ceiling. Her husband sat hunched over on some unmade bedding on the floor. Judging by his appearance, you'd put him in his mid-twenties to mid-thirties, difficult to be any more precise. He was wearing a shiny shirt with a wide collar under a loose, extra-long suit jacket tailored to fit his sloping shoulders. His pants tapered toward the ankles and were bunched up at the hem.

He made his wife use her sewing machine to run up garments in this unique style of his. On the streets, everyone wore jumpsuits. He couldn't stand the lack of individuality. Maybe it was a trivial issue. But he couldn't stand what he couldn't stand.

"What about vending machines?" He closed his book and stood up.

Through the window, the huge, spectacular flames of the steelwork's furnace burned against the dark of the night.

"We do have a bottle of concentrate," she sighed.

"Why didn't you tell me before? Dilute some and bring it to me!"

She gave a wordless response.

When she came back, he had a meek look on his face and was searching under the pillow.

"Have we got any pills? Any ludes or soma? Anything?"

"No."

"Don't waste your words, do you? The pink ones will do. I'd even take some bromisoval."

"It's hard to get hold of that stuff now," she said calmly. "I can always go buy some solvent."

"No way. Puff on a plastic bag of glue? How embarrassing. Solvents actually ruin your brain cells, you know."

"Aren't yours pretty ruined already?" She laughed.

"Look, I'm just not into that loafer hippie shit. Those kids just check out, they're so apathetic. Nothing to salt their wounds. Nothing stimulating."

"So what's stimulating then, pharmaceuticals? They do the opposite for me. Just make me glaze over for a bit. I'm through with them."

"No one's making you take anything, babe. Wasted on you. If we had anything, I'd take it all myself."

"Tight-fisted prick. You know what, it's starting to get boring, seeing you all pilled up. Aren't you bored yet?"

"I don't take them for fun. I take them because I have to. When's the last time you met a smoker who ploughed through the pack just for kicks? Never, right. It's like that."

A vague smile crossed her face.

"But I've got to get my stuff ready in advance. I don't want to end up going to some junkie joint like Fugetsudo, dark, cavernous shitholes with cobwebs everywhere, baroque music playing in the background. Even when that place is full, it still feels empty. So depressing. A woman'll come along with split nails and tatty hair, says she's just off to do a bit of shopping and comes back with a stolen sweater. Just awful. So not my scene."

"A guy used to come into that place packing a pair of nunchucks, you know. Way before Bruce Lee got popular. He had a face like a young Kôji Ishizaka, all keen-eyed, but tighter, more restrained and menacing. He was always dressed in a loose kimono. Our tables were next to each other one time, so we started talking. We both were leaving and straightaway he said, 'Now let's go eat some terrible food,' so off we went. He took me to a place up some stairs a street away. There were papers posted up on the walls, saying 'plate of pickles, fifty yen,' stuff like that, and there was a TV set showing Kenichi Mikawa singing 'Yanagase Blues.' It was late, so he took me to Sasazuka in a taxi and I stayed over in his apartment."

She sat in front of her husband and hugged her knees to her chest.

"That one's news to me," he said, taking a small forty-yen pack of Peace cigarettes from his pocket.

"I've told you it before. Maybe not in this much detail. Anyway, the guy takes me to meet his mom. He's decided we're getting married. On the way he mentions that he's legally incompetent. Well, I had my head in the clouds back then, I didn't know anything. So I didn't understand what he meant. But I found out later about these laws that stopped people with mental issues or whatever from freely accessing their assets. Then I realized he was probably deranged somehow. I mean, he told me he was involved in covert political movements with Okinawan activists. 'Politics is my life,' you know, all that. Even if I give that a free pass, he also did weird things like locking me up indoors and jabbing a sword into the floor to scare me. He was so aggressive. On the other hand, though, he once showed me a flyer for a film by some independent producer and said he'd starred in it with a girl he used to live with. There was a photo of them on the flyer, naked, cuddling each other. It was lovely, they looked like such cute young things."

"You sure talk a lot of garbage, don't you. So that's your 'Yanagase Blues' love story, huh? Alright, let me tell you about my 'Sakariba Blues' or my 'Blue Light Yokohama,' maybe my 'Honmoku Blues' . . ."

He took out a box of Pipe matches and lit a cigarette as she went on:

"Louise Louis from the Cups was amazing! When he played 'Honmoku' on his bass with his head thrown back, all you could see from the audience was the whites of his eyes. And he had such big eyes too, that Mabo did. Something about those goggly psycho eyes really stuck with me."

She smiled again, only now with what seemed like glee. He said:

"Babe, who cares about Honmoku. What were you trying to say?"

"Basically that it isn't hard to guess how politically active they were, the regular crowd at places like Fugetsudo, always smoking weed with their waster pals. The type of kids who'd thread a piece of string through the hole in a five-yen coin to use the jukebox for free at Ki-YO. Once those old jazz cafés started disappearing, they all washed up at Fugetsudo. They'd sit there the whole day. At one time people even used to call them 'Shinjuku residents.'"

"Wait, there was a jukebox at Ki-YO? And it only cost five yen?"

"I dunno. Some drunk critic in Shinjuku told me about it."

"When my jukebox days began, you already needed ten yen to play one track."

"Yeah."

They heard a morose whistle from a passing steam train. First-time visitors to their apartment always figured there was a busy train line running nearby, but in fact the sound was coming from a hi-fi system built into the walls, hidden from sight.

This was how they held their Great Nostalgia Conventions.

They never opened the windows. They couldn't see the steelworks or anything if they did. The scene that got projected on the window during the day was from *West Side Story*, that milquetoast selection being a slip-up on the manufacturer's part. Panes of SceneGlass were usually printed with stills from feature films, and they couldn't find anything about rebellious delinquents from 1960s Japanese cinema that suited both their sensibilities.

He suggested something by Nagisa Ōshima, while she wanted Mako Midori in *Bad Girl Yoko*. She said she saw that film being advertised in her last year of elementary school and just the sight of the poster, showing a girl biting into an apple, had such a strange and deep effect on her.

He knew he'd best just let little lies, like the jukebox one, slide. He didn't believe his wife was the same age he was. She was around thirty. He found that out from the paperwork when he married her. Still, she insisted that she was born "the year before the Korean War."

But he forgave her. When you've lived for nearly 180 years you naturally acquire a level of tolerance, no matter what sort of temper you might have.

She's jealous of me, he thought. She's seething because she couldn't take part in my youth like someone from the same generation could. It was his most glorious period, the place he was always running away to, alone (leaving his wife behind).

When he sank into his daydreams, she always got resentful.

In an oddly high-pitched voice, she'd ask: "What are you thinking about?" His answer was always the same, a terse "Nothing," which put her into a filthy mood. It was like she was making herself upset, assuming he was absorbed in memories of some stunning, special woman she could never compete with. He'd told her this countless times.

He thought his wife was foolish. She was too greedy. She thirsted after everything so much that she couldn't get hold of anything. She was afflicted with illusions about love. She placed excessive expectations and worth on this "love," dreamt of it constantly, and as a result was always terribly unhappy. It was he who'd done this to her. At first she'd believed that their connection was something unique, and deluded herself that she'd found total happiness for the first time in her life.

But when you've been around for 180 years, you discover that lots of women are alike, lots of relationships are alike, and as soon as he told her that it seemed to him like she slipped from a certain psychological plateau and kept on falling.

Her need for affection became a thoroughly neurotic, all-or-nothing pursuit. She knew it was making her more and more miserable, but much like someone dying of thirst who drinks seawater, she began hunting down his past.

She seemed to have done a fair bit of research, too. She'd taken his deepest imprints, the 1960s and early 1970s, and tried to experience them herself from all sorts of angles. Sometimes she'd mention things he had no idea about and make a big show of it. But what was the point in knowing about things he hadn't been through himself?

If she could experience all of his past, completely, she would finally know him in his entirety. And to know him was to own him, mentally.

It was impossible.

She was trying to do something impossible. She was obsessed with recreating the atmosphere of that era.

She'd have no qualms about throwing her life away if it meant she could know him completely. That was the terrifying thing about women.

Another train whistled by.

She was smoking a cigarette, her head drooping. This room of theirs was pretty desolate, save for the piles of old movie magazines in one corner. Two film posters hung on the walls: one for *The Call of the Foghorn*, one for *Leaving Tosa Behind*. He'd wanted some others, too, but they were unobtainable. Material desires couldn't be satisfied just by paying money these days.

"Where did you find these?" He pointed to the posters.

"I went and got copies from the history museum on Sunday. You know I'm a member of the Historical Research Society through my employer. That's why they gave me permission."

He laughed. "Your employer? You mean, the club you set up yourself? To explore the 'Fictions and Realities of Capitalist Society' or whatever it was."

"That's right. I research the fine details of how terrible a world it was, you know, mentioning the trough between the two Anpo protests in 1960 and 1970, that kind of thing. Did I tell you? They approved my report. I don't have to go to the Bureau every day anymore."

"What?"

"They said I was a special case. I'm being appointed to the Propaganda Ministry. They want me to do some more research. The pay's the same, but I can pretty much do what I like, time-wise."

"Wow, babe. So you're gonna spread the news about how great our Dear Leader is? How the world has never known a politician so devoted to the people, right?"

"Yep. My job will be to study just how much the public suffered before the revolution."

A photograph of the Leader hung in every home. The rule was that it must be put up on a bedroom wall. Needless to say, their room had one too. They kept their backs to the wall in question.

You weren't allowed to hide the photo behind a curtain, for instance. If you were arrested for such a thought crime, you'd be sent to one of the camps. And that was as good as the end of your life.

"Man, I'm hungry."

"Oh, I completely forgot about dinner. I even came in here to call you for it."

She went into the kitchen.

"What are we eating?"

"Well, they're stone cold now, but it's fried dumplings."

"Dumplings . . ."

They didn't own a microwave or anything like that, of course.

"Should I throw them out? We don't get our meat supplies till next week. Apparently this will be the last of the bad harvests we've had for three years now."

"How can they know it's the last?"

"There was an announcement about it."

"Oh, whatever. There's rice, right?"

"Yeah, it's gone cold too. I'll steam them both together. What would you call that, rehashed dumplings?"

"Right, it's in the same league as frying liver with leeks or having rice with your ramen. I wanted to pitch pizza, actually, but cold fried dumplings isn't bad either.

"Okay, so he lives in this poxy little room in east Shibuya . . . Of course, the toilet, kitchen and everything like that are all shared. He goes the whole day without seeing sunlight. He writes for magazine columns, buys necessities by teleshopping, pumps iron at the gym, grumbles about his age. He lives off crab croquettes from Kitchen Tiger. He's with a dopey-faced girl he picked up while watching old flicks at the Tokyu Meiga theater. He gets absorbed in figuring how to trick her.

"See, this guy is twenty-one years old. He's yet to wise up so he still tries to get girls into bed by lying to them. When men grow older and wiser, they don't tell lies. They tell the truth, but only when they're really cornered. Even then they answer with the bare minimum."

"Sorry about this."

It was hard to hear his wife's voice from the kitchen.

"It's fine."

He was strangely enjoying himself.

"This guy doesn't have any phone credit, so of course he worries how to invite the girl out. He's also started sharing his tiny room with a pal, a sponger who does underground theater and has zero dough. The girl says she's a virgin.

Unfortunately, she really is a virgin. He loses the will to live. Even though he's known from the start that this is a girl no one but he would think to touch. Then, deprived of other options, they move in together. Nothing suits a tale like that better than a meal of rehashed dumplings and rice."

"Let's eat in here?" She popped her head out of the kitchen.

"Aren't you redecorating there?"

"Oh no, nothing so dramatic. I just ran out of space for my research materials, so I brought some back here. Obviously I did it in secret, I'll get in trouble if they find out. It's okay though, everything's covered up behind a curtain for now."

Come to think of it, he hadn't left that back room for about a week. He'd taken some new drug he'd got from a pharmacist friend, which had given him wild visions and thrown him into hysterics.

He just lay still while his wife was at the office during the day. He never felt bored. He didn't have to work, because he was elderly.

He'd been investigated, twice, because the authorities thought there was a mistake on his records. Once before the revolution, then again afterward.

The techniques used in his dental work dated back to the latter half of the twentieth century. He'd had big holes drilled into his teeth and then filled in with cement and metal. A set of partial dentures was found in a drawer, and though he'd had new teeth implanted since, the dentures fit perfectly into where his old teeth would have been. That proved he already had his adult teeth a whole century and a half ago.

"I lost them when I got into a fight," he'd explained to his wife. She thought he meant a run-in with a gang or some rough kids, but she was wrong.

The real story was that he'd been at home fighting with a girl he was living with when he was nineteen. He left the room in a huff, and what with the darkness and the drugs he lost his footing and fell all the way down a flight of stairs. That's how he smashed his teeth in.

So, along with a few other bits of evidence, like the scar from his appendectomy and the bald patch on the back of his head, he was verified to be the age on his records.

He got the bald patch thanks to an accident that happened seven months after he was born. He was leaning against some furniture, drinking juice from a cup. His mother went into the kitchen, and while she was away he dropped the cup. He lost his balance and toppled over too, and unfortunately the cup was made of very thin glass. The resulting injury was quite severe.

His ripe old age entitled him to a pension, which wasn't the worst position to be in. If he wanted he could go to the library or the film archive in the middle of the day.

But lately he'd just been sleeping all the time. He hardly ate. His wife would grumble when she came home in the evening to find he hadn't touched the food she'd left for him in the morning.

"Just let me be a grouchy old codger!"

It was hard not to laugh when those words were coming from a man dressed in baggy school uniform like the class bully. He was very proud of how he dressed, and it took balls to go out on the streets looking like that.

He wouldn't use the toilet, either. He pissed in a flower vase and emptied it out the window. Right below them, just before the steelworks, was the Dear Leader's Memorial Theater. It wasn't exactly clear what the memorial was commemorating. The building was magnificent, and it had its back turned to him. He therefore found it imperative to sprinkle his urine on it. Since he was barely eating, it was mostly water anyway.

He began picking at his dumplings and rice in the kitchen.

"Hold on."

She dove behind the curtain briefly, and reappeared.

"What?"

He could hear someone singing, a calm and mellow voice—was it Peggy Hayama?

"I was in Yokosuka when this song came out," she said. "There was even a movie about it. Akira Kobayashi is in jail at the start, and when he hears this song it really moves him. It's at a recital for prisoners or something. Those parachute-style skirts and dresses were in fashion at the time, I remember. We wore petticoats under our skirts. I've forgotten the storyline after that, but I think Kobayashi goes blind. When he goes into a phone booth to make a call, he dials the number by feeling the holes in the dial."

"Sure are clued-up, aren't you?"

"Keiichirō Akagi was in *The Gun like Lightning,* wasn't he? I was still in primary school then, so I didn't hear the title right. I thought it was *Guy like a Lighter.*'

"A guy like a lighter? What kinda guy would that be?"

"A show-off. The kind who whips out his fancy high-end lighter and lights everyone's smokes. And he does it at the speed of light."

"We're talking about different eras now, but there was once this hero character called Golgo 13. He had a face you couldn't really call human. He'd bring his lighter up to that face and when the flint wheel struck and lit the wick it always made such a sumptuous sound. It was custom-made, he had a microscopic speaker, this tiny sound device, embedded inside it. And then—"

He burst out laughing and couldn't speak for a moment.

"Then Golgo sneaks into the secret base of some organization that was targeting him and he purposely flicks the lighter to make that sound. It was a way of showing he was there. But it was scary to think he'd get caught, too. What a thrill."

"Flowers Blooming in the Rain" came on. He listened attentively.

He also liked "Louisiana Mama." He tried to remember where the mole was on Hisahiko Iida's face, but couldn't.

Was it Hiroshi Kubo who sang "Girl in the Mist" and Tokyo Romantica who did "You, from Otaru"? He wasn't so sure about those.

He stopped eating and a hollow look came into his eyes.

"What's wrong?"

She frowned anxiously.

He put his elbows on the table and propped up his chin.

When Kazuko Matsuo's "Reunion" started, he slumped face-down on the table.

"What is it? I'll turn the music off."

"Don't turn it off!"

"But—"

"Don't!"

He was shouting at the top of his voice. It was bad enough already, but when he heard Sachiko Nishida on top of everything else, he was helpless, he was already gone from the trumpet intro.

When it got to the first line, "Caught in the acacia rain," he began sobbing loudly.

Even after he'd calmed down, the tears kept coming for a bit.

"What's wrong?" his wife asked him firmly.

"Just that one line, 'I'd gladly die like this,' it's so direct and powerful . . . You can see why this song became an anthem for the student protesters in the sixties. But, you know, there's no such thing as shared experiences. All people have are their own totally individual experiences. Although, sure, those can happen simultaneously, they can be universal."

"I don't think I want to hear this."

"No, listen, I don't need any more of your analysis. Don't you have a scrap of feeling in you?"

"You've been acting pretty strange lately."

"That's what happens when you've lived for one hundred and eighty years."

"You blame everything on your age!"

She was still standing with her arms folded. Then, this time more softly, she repeated the same words. Like she was saying them to herself.

"And maybe that's the case. But . . ."

"Quiet!" He shut her down. "I've made up my mind."

With renewed determination, he headed out into the city. As if he'd ever put on that stupid jumpsuit they'd issued him. Those things were what babies wore.

What he was determined to do was make the coastal industrial region spanning Kawasaki, Yokohama, and Yokosuka into an independent political state. Nothing as petty as some dumb, cheery historical reenactment village, no sir. It would encapsulate Japan from 1960 to 1970, so it would be violent and reckless and cruel.

He wondered whether he had it in him to become a dictator. The Leader strayed into some mischief with an actress the other day. Well, seemed like they still had some energy, even aged sixty-odd. The rumors were thoroughly suppressed but a select few did know about it. He'd heard the story from his wife.

The Leader's (fourth) wife, an ex-model, threw a can of paint over the leading lady during a curtain call at the theater. Scarce though they were, actresses, singers, models, and suchlike did exist in this country. There were nightclubs, too. Even hostess bars. The cream of the crop were employed there to service high-ranking government officials and their spouses.

To appease the first lady's anger, the Leader decided to go bald and had everything shaved off, eyebrows included. All the same, he thought, the Leader did look a bit unnatural on TV now. Like the hair was a wig, the eyebrows stuck on.

The person who really held the power in this country now was the Leader's wife. The Leader had lived it up when young, which had accelerated the aging process.

(And this wife was a hysterical sort, so if you were to provoke her cleverly enough, she'd probably do what you wanted. First, take the legitimate approach: try to persuade her. If that doesn't work, no choice but to threaten her. But you'd need some real juicy material for that to work . . .)

He was marching along the street, hunched forward with his brows furrowed.

People stopped and turned to look at him.

He paid no mind and walked on. Music played in his head. "Bus Stop" by Koji Taira was popular in his second year at high school, Procol Harum's "A Whiter Shade of Pale" in his last.

Not that he ever diligently attended school. He couldn't remember whether he got his graduation certificate or not. He definitely didn't go to any ceremony.

(What was he doing back then? Selling battered octopus chunks in Osaka? Screwing a geisha-house landlady and smuggling out a bunch of kimonos or something while she was in hospital with endometritis? Or was he selling cash registers? He'd have to ask his wife. He'd told her almost everything.)

More and more people were watching him.

"Hello there," a patrol officer called softly.

He shot a sullen look at the officer and shoved his hands into his pockets.

"Are you an actor?"

Instead of answering, he swayed to and fro, then spat on the ground.

"Got a troublemaker here!"

The officer grabbed him by the collar.

"Never could stand you cop bastards!"

"What did you say?!"

He knocked down his opponent with a straight right hook. The crowd surrounded him.

"Did your husband really get arrested?"

She nodded in response to the sculptor's question.

The two were meeting in the sculptor's studio. He was recognized as a top artist, which meant that he was working on a figure of the Leader.

"How did that happen? I thought he was weird from the moment we met, but I figured it was because of his age. It's odd calling him 'elderly' or an 'old man' when he looks so young physically."

"I do think it was his age as well. When people live too long, it seems like they return to the experiences and environments of their formative years."

She smiled faintly and opened up a pack of Peace cigarettes.

"Really? Kinda like when ordinary old folks become childish, maybe."

"It's not quite the same."

"When we first met three years ago he said he had a feeling we'd get along. He told me all sorts of stories. Stuff from over a century ago. What was strange was how he wouldn't tell me anything about what he did from his thirties on. So I had my doubts, you know. I thought, he could just be the same age he looks. It would be odd otherwise. And he's married to you, someone who's been researching the nineteen-sixties for a long time. Perhaps he used to do that too. Put his heart and soul into the research and then ended up like he did."

"You're wrong," she said softly.

"Isn't it just a mistake on his records?" The sculptor narrowed his eyes.

"It's not a mistake. I know that better than anyone. I mean, it's already a hundred and twenty years or so ago now, but I met him back then."

She seemed shy.

"Seriously?" The sculptor sounded skeptical.

"Maybe it's more accurate to say we *saw* each other. Just for three months. We broke up because we were both married. He was in his forties then, had a face like a seventeen-year-old."

The sculptor lost his patience and shouted, "You're having me on again!"

"No, what's wrong is this idea that he was a useless layabout. From what I heard at the time, he was at the best schools from kindergarten to university and he graduated with top grades. To use a term from the time, he was one of the 'elite.'"

"But what about family, relatives . . .?"

"I know what you're after. You want me to prove I'm a long-lifer, like him. Well, parents die, siblings and their offspring gradually grow distant. So there's no need to let anyone know we're long-lifers."

"I mean what about your kids, your grandkids?" He seemed confused.

"We can't have children. It's the same for all of us."

"All of you?" His mouth hung half-open.

"Look, there must be others who've lived as long as a hundred and fifty-something years. They really do exist. And a world like this just isn't the place for them."

273

"What are you talking about?"

"The Leader's wife is a friend of mine from high school. That's why I can say these things so freely. My husband got arrested because it'd become common knowledge that he'd lived for such a long time. He wasn't in good physical shape and he kept having to go to hospital. We grew apart, lost touch. And then the longer people live, the less they want to believe reality."

"So did he lose his memory? Like about a hundred years' worth of memories, from the start of the twenty-first century right up until recently?"

"He was in an accident. Not like a hundred years ago but more, in fact. Some government offices got good and torched in that rebellion."

"You'll get taken away for calling it a rebellion. You've got to say 'revolution,'" said the sculptor.

"Amid all the chaos I went in and changed the data in the official records of every long-lifer I knew, to make things smoother for us. He and the others were totally forgotten. Then when I ran into him, I thought it was over . . . There are three other people aged over one hundred and sixty in this country. People that are known publicly, I mean."

She fell silent.

Maybe it wasn't worth talking about this stuff. She'd been haunted by visions of death for years now. There was no denying it anymore: not only her looks but her body, too, had started failing her.

"How d'you all get to be like this?"

The sculptor asked the question with his eyes cast down.

"I reckon it was a small-scale military experiment involving a new type of gas in the late twentieth century. I don't know the details, though."

No doubt about it, we all have regrets about our youth. Anyone who doesn't is looking at the past from a completely skewed perspective thanks to some powerful biases. But maybe if you live long enough (and go through a range of experiences in between), you're able to see the past as something glorious without having to do those sorts of mental gymnastics.

"What do you guys want?" the sculptor asked, after a brief silence.

"To live in peace. We don't want to suffer any harm for thinking or saying things. I mean, it's lonely, living for this long."

He was shut inside a triangular, white room. The ceiling, walls, and floor were all a dazzling white. The room was intended for psychological torture.

He sang softly to try and cheer himself up.

When the acacia rain stops . . .

During the investigation he declared his intention to instigate a coup and establish an independent state. He just wanted a little bit of this country.

Ten days had passed since he'd been labeled a thought criminal and put in solitary.

That time and its gorgeous summer setting began to spread inside him with ebullient life.

Even though he was mortally tired it would be a waste to even close his eyes, because there was still something to do, there was still something interesting out there. He thought sleeping would be a shame.

Sure, he found some things scary. But those things were simply stimulating, and he wasn't really afraid at all.

Vast flames burned with a ferocious beauty in the darkness.